OCEAN BLUFF

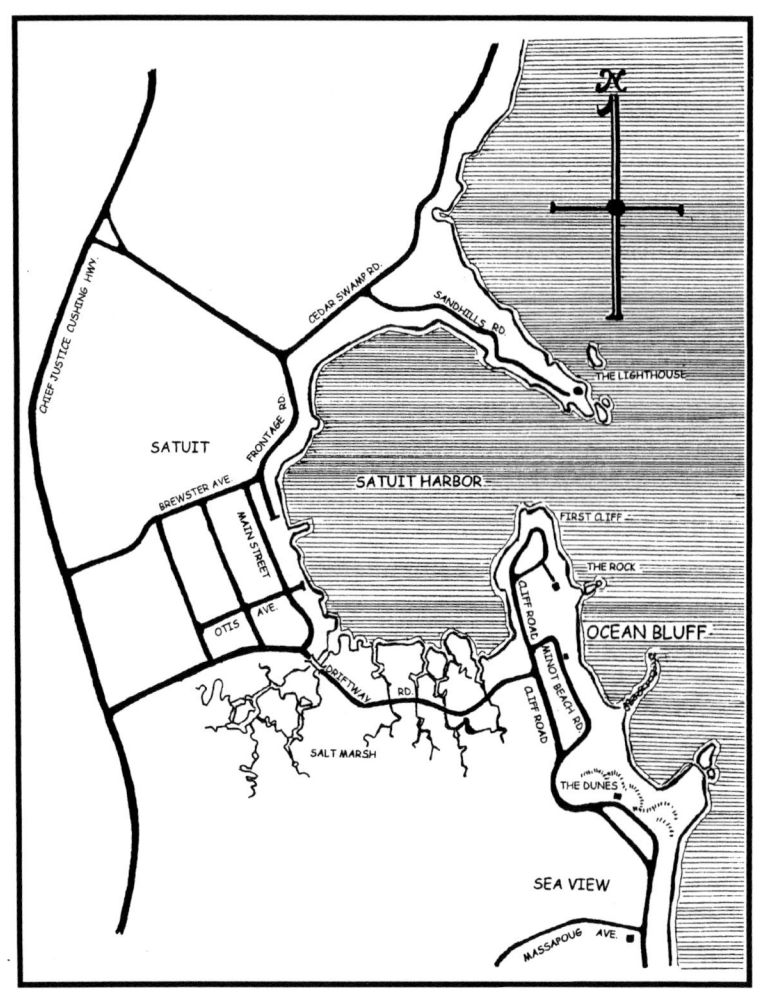

A GIFT ONCE GIVEN

The cottage at Ocean Bluff 1957

Robert O. Barclay

Copyright © 1999 by Robert O. Barclay.

Library of Congress Number: 99-91446

ISBN #:   Hardcover   0-7388-0766-4

Softcover   0-7388-0767-2

All rights reserved. No part of this book may be reproduced or transmitted in any form or by any means, electronic or mechanical, including photocopying, recording, or by any information storage and retrieval system, without permission in writing from the copyright owner.

This is a work of fiction. Names, characters, places and incidents either are the product of the author's imagination or are used fictitiously, and any resemblance to any actual persons, living or dead, events, or locales is entirely coincidental.

This book was printed in the United States of America.

Cover art by Erik Barclay
Map & title page art by the author

To order additional copies of this book, contact:
Beaver's Pond Press, Inc.
1-952-829-8818
www.BeaversPondPress.com

This book is dedicated to all those who were so supportive. My friends and associates, instructors, the members of a very special writers group, and especially my first editor Paul Simmons, whose honesty made me re-examine and revise every aspect of my novel.

Poetry quoted in Chapter 7:

Intimations of Immortality
    William Wordsworth

Thanatopsis
    William Cullen Bryant

A Psalm of Life
    Henry Wadsworth Longfellow

Concord Hymn
    Ralpoh Waldo Emerson

TO BEGIN WITH...

... this is not the story of my life, but it is a very significant part of it; a part of my misty–eyed youth, a delicate time of change and growth, a transition from childhood to something else.

My determination to write this memoir is based on a desire to preserve certain recollections concerning the events that characterized my first love in 1957 when I was only sixteen. Now, more than forty years later, it occurs to me that a great deal has changed since that fanciful summer on the beach. In that far away place, and that far away time, I met a remarkable young girl and fell hopelessly in love. Everything was so simple then; life seemed uncomplicated and choosing between right and wrong looked so easy. It was a special time of innocence, when young people were not under the same moral persuasion as they are today. It was all black and white, or so I believed.

My family was staying in Ocean Bluff, a small town on the Massachusetts coast. It was a quiet seaside community filled with grand old homes hinting at a glorious Victorian past, a wonderful era that had long since faded away. We had come here like many others to rent a home for the summer. We couldn't afford any of the posh mansions that sat behind the dunes; ours was just a simple cottage. Still, the fact that we could escape from the hot city to the breezy shore for a couple of months was a great luxury.

I can't remember any place that I have ever lived that fills me with a greater sense of nostalgia. As I reflect back to that summer, my mind is flooded with images of that outrageous little shack on the beach. Yet I am hard pressed to describe it to you, so that you can see it as I used to. Even my own recollections are clouded by time. I want to visualize it as a cozy comfortable place full of pleasant memories. In reality, it was small and crowded and lacking in every convenience and comfort. The stove worked when it felt like it, the wiring was inadequate, the screens needed constant patching, and there was no foundation. My mother could tell you that other than shelter from a summer storm, it was a place that she tried to escape from as often as possible. I must admit, I spent little time there myself. There was always plenty to do on the beach, and I often stayed with my friends, who had much larger homes.

The house was a narrow provincial structure, unsophisticated, with no discernible style. The roof was unusually steep, and the high pointed gables at either end faced the sea and the shore respectively. The pudgy windows set deeply under the end of each gable were all out of proportion and gave the impression of an enormous eye looking out from beneath the darkly shaded overhang. Somehow they had managed to tuck two small bedrooms neatly under the rafters, but the stairs were an atrocity. With no room for a proper run the builder installed something called a 'ship's ladder'. Built into a boxy closet in the middle of the north wall, you had to open a makeshift door to get at it. The tread was too narrow and the risers abnormally high, and they were awful to climb, but they did the job of getting us from the kitchen to the bedrooms above.

Because it was larger and faced the sea, my room was the better of the two. But I had it by default; because it was bigger I had to share it with my little brother. My older sister Margie had the second room, which was separated from ours by a crowded landing at the top of the stairs. There were no doors. The only privacy came from thick scratchy curtains that hung off wooden rings. The partition dividing the two rooms, and the short knee–walls under the eaves, were covered with wide pine boards. The rafters, ugly and bare, were exposed all the way to the ridgepole. It was like being in the belly of a whale and looking up at its bowed ribs. Everything was painted a flat white, with some of the grain and all of the knots bleeding through, giving it a mottled look that added noticeably to its rustic appearance. In my room there were two small metal–framed cots with narrow mattresses, one set against each knee–wall. At the end of my bed was a battered steamer trunk with a broken hasp, that held my clothes, which were few in the summertime. Timmy had a similar box, but his was slightly larger, because he needed room for his toys. An assortment of clippings from various magazines decorated the walls: a couple of advertisements for cars, one for a 55' T–Bird and another for a British MG TD in racing green. A drawing of a B–17 bomber hung at the head of my bed. On my brother's side of the room were some Disney characters, that were his favorites, and a cutout of Superman from one of his comic books. These were all taped or tacked in place. The only picture that was properly framed was an old clipper ship hanging above the doorway, and it wasn't ours; it had come with the cottage and belonged to the owner.

Downstairs, in the southwest corner, was my parent's bedroom. The rest of the first floor was an area that we called the 'great room', although it wasn't very big. This served as our kitchen, dining room and living room combined. The kitchen had a gas stove fueled by a silver tank that was mounted just outside the kitchen wall. A colorful chintz curtain hid the pipes under the soapstone sink, and a few cabinets were crowded above and to the right. There was also a GE refrigerator; one of those goofy looking things with the tin can compressor mounted on top. All of this was on the west wall, squeezed between a tall skinny broom closet and the door to the bathroom. In the middle was a round table with five chairs, which were never quite in order. One or more always seemed to be out of place, either by the kitchen door or next to the refrigerator where my mother could climb up and rap the compressor with the heel of her shoe to stop it from growling.

In the front, in the area that served as our living room, the landlord had provided a couch, an overstuffed chair, and a lopsided floor lamp. The couch faced the double windows, which looked out on to the porch and the beach. It was lumpy and uncomfortable and I remember that the upholstery was made of some awful scratchy material that made my legs itch whenever I sat on it in my swim–trunks or shorts.

I'm sure that the cottage was old enough to have once been served by an outhouse, but I could never figure out where they had put it. The present bathroom was an add–on. It hung off the back of the house; a cubical shaped room with a little doghouse roof that was so low–pitched that it was almost flat. The fixtures crowded in so close that there wasn't room to bend over, so we never tried to dress or undress in there—we always wore a towel or a robe if we needed to shower. Which presented another problem, the stall was barely wide enough to turn around in and had only a single cold water faucet, with a black 'C' in the middle that reminded me constantly that only one kind of water would come out of it. Whenever I stepped in and closed the pink plastic curtain behind me, I had to cozy up to the handle and pray for the courage to turn it on. And when the icy spray hit my face and chest, I would dance a crazy jig until I couldn't stand it anymore—then rush out to bundle up in a big warm towel.

I don't know how old this place was, but when we first took it over it was in bad shape. The summer sun and spring rains, the cold winds and winter storms had definitely taken their toll. The cedar shingles had turned gray, bleached by salt–air and sun. The trim around the windows and doors was split and weathered, the grain raised and rough to the touch, with only traces of the original paint left here and there. The owner did just enough repair to keep it serviceable, and Dad volunteered on weekends to make other improvements, which is why Mr. Collingsworth never charged a higher rent.

There was no basement. Instead a number of long cedar pylons had been driven deep into the ground. And these silvered posts, along with the drainpipes and soil stack, dropping from the floor to the sand below, gave the impression of an old tree stump with its roots exposed by the long erosion of the tides.

I had spent three previous seasons here at Ocean Bluff. Carefree summers passed in the company of good friends, and consumed by lying in the sun, flying kites over the marsh, and swimming in the cold Atlantic. But this summer, the summer of '57, would be different. This was the summer when she came, Linda Richards, someone who would turn this lazy uncomplicated time, into a frenzied confusing world full of passion and delight. And the pain and conflict that this created was both marvelous and frightening.

CHAPTER 2

IT WAS late in the afternoon on a hot, sultry day near the end of June when this tall, slender girl first appeared on the beach. It's not that she was incredibly beautiful. At least not the sort of girl that other guys would fight over, but there was something about her that commanded my attention, a dauntless air of self-assurance that set her apart from the other girls I knew.

My friend Earl would probably have described her as skinny. Of course everyone was skinny to him. Earl was fat. Not obese fat, but he did have a roll of flesh that hung over the edge of his swim trunks, the sort of thing that is affectionately called love handles. That wasn't really so bad, it was the weight he carried a little higher that was disturbing—he had breasts. Not like a woman mind you, but they were kind of pointy and they stuck out enough so that they jiggled when he walked. That's why he covered his body with a T-shirt, even when he went swimming.

This shafty girl wore a one-piece suit that stretched tightly over her boney frame and showed a budding figure that I found intriguing. Her hair was cut short, well above the shoulder. It was parted in the middle and perfectly rounded in back where it dropped away sharply to the nape of her neck. The golden color of honey, it was starting to bleach out with exposure to the summer sun.

There was something wonderfully brash and buoyant in her manner, as she sauntered down the beach parallel to the water. She had a quick natural smile and a sassy way of cocking her head to one side and swinging it back to flip the hair out of her eyes whenever the ocean breeze pushed it across her face. Maybe I wasn't being very objective, but I saw everything about her including her long straight figure as pretty. No, more than that—the beauty that I saw was enchanting—magical—spellbinding!

Earl and I were sitting on a large flat rock that was usually under water, but now, at low tide, the rock was fully exposed. We were looking for sea life; periwinkles and starfish that had attached themselves to the sides when the rock was submerged. Sometimes we could find baby crabs that would get caught in the tidal pools.

I looked up at the sound of a gull flying close above our heads. Following the bird as it moved away toward the beach, skimming the wet stones, I watched it land in the seaweed that formed a line at the high-water mark, and saw her heading in our direction. I observed her approach, with her easy gait, and I found myself studying her with an unusual fascination.

I had a normal healthy interest in girls, a natural curiosity about what made them different. But I knew very little about sex or the actual dry-bones mechanics of how it was done. What little knowledge I did have came through casual encounters with friends, when certain forbidden material fell into our hands.

****

Back in May, a few weeks before we got off for summer vacation, one of the guys smuggled in a girlie magazine and was passing it around in the boys' room. I had just as much desire as the next fellow to see what was hidden inside. But when it finally came to me, fear, or maybe a touch of conscience, caused me to flip through the pages hurriedly and I only caught a furtive glimpse of pink flesh and bare breasts.

A few days later my friend Dennis got hold of a nudist magazine; something called "Sunshine & Health". Hidden under his jacket we smuggled it up to my room and with a flashlight we sat down on the floor of my closet to study the contents. The pictures here were much more explicit and depicted whole families without clothes. Men and women, young and old, fat and skinny, some sagging, some wrinkled, with everything exposed, even their private parts. The pictures weren't provocative; they showed people reading, mowing the lawn, listening to the radio, playing tennis or volleyball; there was one of a man grilling steaks while the kids were waiting at a picnic table. Just ordinary everyday events, only they had no clothes on. Still, provocative or not, these pictures were disturbing.

In those days phys–ed. was mandatory, and though I wasn't comfortable about it, I showered and changed in the locker room with the others. Not that any of the guys were happy about stripping down and going into an open room with a row of showerheads hanging off the wall. It wasn't just the fact that we had no privacy or that we were forced to compare each other's dangling manhood; it was having to stand there in the altogether while the coach checked us out through a little window in the corner. Somehow it seemed perverted.

Whatever my limited experience with anatomy, my own or other boys my age, I hadn't been around *men*. I had never before seen so much pubic hair or a penis so large (except for Anthony Baldassario, who was so well endowed it was scary). And now the fleshy corpulence I saw in these grainy black and white pictures looked crude and deformed.

When it came to girls, I knew even less. I had never seen a girl naked, young or old, at least not completely. The pictures that I did occasionally get hold of showed bare breasts, but from the waist down the model was always covered. She wore some sort of costume or underclothes and even what was shown was usually touched up with an artist's brush. The sort of stuff that appears so commonly in magazines today was against the law then.

Looking through this particular issue of "Sunshine & Health", I saw several people, both men and women, who had classic figures, and I admit they were somewhat attractive, but it seemed that all of them had one fault or another. In these amateur photos, no effort had been made to enhance or improve upon what nature had provided. Every blemish and imperfection was revealed. Certainly, I was aware that primitive tribes who lived in tropical climates went around naked, but after this experience I was glad that we didn't have to. Other than the fact that it would have been embarrassing, I expect that some of the people I knew would have looked pretty awful, myself included.

When it came to dating I was just as unenlightened as I was about nudity and sex. Oh, I did some dating, group dates, where a bunch of girls and guys went to a movie and then paired off. Since we generally didn't know each other very well there wasn't much intimacy involved. Holding hands, or successfully getting your arm around the girl's shoulder was considered to be pretty daring. And something like that was only done inside a dark theater, never outside where someone might be able to see you.

In the eighth grade there was Patsy Bauer, who was my first real crush; the first girl I looked at and didn't want to gag. We had two dates, chaperoned by my mother. And then there was the time that I kissed her at a party, because one of her girlfriends dared me to. It was done quickly and I barely hit the target. She must have thought it was something special though, because she did a lot of giggling about it afterwards, while she was sharing the details with her friends in the corner.

Even with these brief forays into the realm of human sexuality, I wasn't obsessed with the opposite sex or with sex generally. I didn't feel I was ready for such things. I guess I was just too busy being a kid. Girls and sex seemed very much a part of the adult world, and I wasn't quite ready yet to be that grown up. Besides, just because I had seen the equipment didn't mean that I had any real idea how it worked. And, my lack of experience made the whole notion of kissing or hugging, or any type of physical intimacy seem very scary.

****

Once I saw Linda all that changed. It didn't seem to matter anymore what I did or didn't know about love or sex.

From the very beginning I was attracted to her, and I studied her unashamedly as she walked along the beach. Turning to face us, she changed her course and began to follow a path that would lead her straight to the rock where I stood watching. Winding her way through the stones and debris that the falling tide had left exposed, she stayed on the sandy path between, until she stopped a few feet away from me.

"Heyyy-o" she called, "You guys mind if I come up?"

Earl jumped like a startled kitten; he had been so engrossed in his work that he hadn't noticed Linda's approach.

As he turned to see who was calling out to us, I answered her. "No, not at all. Here, let me help you up."

I kneeled and reached out for her extended hands and when she placed her bare foot on the rough outcropping, just below, I pulled her toward me. As she moved upward I brought myself to my feet, and when she had come to her full height she was at least two inches taller. Standing eye to eye (or eye to nose), I was so close to her that the slightest movement might have turned into an embrace. Looking upward, I could feel her soft breath gently disturb my lashes and brush against my hot cheeks and the unexpected odor of mint filled my nostrils. The clean fresh smell of her breath was such an agreeable sensation, but a sudden weakness in my knees took me by surprise and I thought, this is silly. She's only a girl!

I could detect tingly little currents traveling the length of my arms, and I quickly let go of her hands hoping to stop that electric charge before it reached my brain and turn it into a basket of worms. Shaken, I tried to speak. After a single noise that crackled like cellophane, this cool calm collected voice, which was my own, but that sounded distant and unconnected, took over. "This is my friend, Earl." I said pointing to his crouching figure. Other than a quick glance to see who was talking about him, Earl didn't react, he just moved deeper into the narrow crevice he was exploring. "We're here scouting for periwinkles and crabs and whatever else may have been trapped by the falling tide. If you'd like, you can help."

Standing much too close, my head cocked back at an uncomfortable angle, she looked directly at me—her eyes staring straight into mine. Those tiny electric currents suddenly began to move again. Starting at my tail-bone and coursing upward, they played dreadful games with the feathery hairs along my spine. Her eyes were the most incredible blue, with a touch of violet that moved delicately along the edge of the iris. As I stared deeply into her dark pupils, I was conscious of their fluid movement as they adjusted to the changing light reflected off the water. My view of her gradually expanded, until I saw that those eyes were set below full dark eyebrows, too dark for such light hair. The contrast was startling, but it was not unattractive. Her nose was long and graceful, with a tiny flat spot at the tip. Her lips were full and inviting, without makeup, but having a warm natural coloring that made me think they would be delicious to kiss. Kiss? This was too much; how could I even imagine such a thing? I barely knew this girl. My face was already hot and I could feel a new warmth rising to my cheeks, which had little to do with the afternoon sun. If it hadn't been for the fact that my tan was already well advanced, I'm sure my face would have been bright red. Thank heaven, it wasn't necessary for me to say anything just then, because whatever might have come out would certainly have been unintelligible and embarrassing.

"My name is Linda. "My family has rented a house up there behind those dunes," she said stepping back and pointing toward the southern end of the beach. "We got here last night and things are pretty frantic—I mean what with moving in and all. Mom told me I was in the way and to find something to do. Anything. So, I skipped out and headed down here. That's when I spotted you guys." She fell silent, and when I didn't say anything, she went on. "I'd like to help, but I haven't got the foggiest idea what—winklers are."

"Periwinkles," I said, correcting her, then bit my lip for being so presumptuous.

"Peri-wink-les," she said, looking at me for approval. Then in a sudden flip-flop, "by the way, you told me your friend's name, but you didn't tell me yours."

This had been going so well. After all she was doing most of the talking and now she was asking me such a simple question. Only my name. But having her this close was too unsettling, and now that it was my turn to speak I had this horrible fear that I would open my mouth and nothing would come out. For some odd reason I couldn't remember my name. It was idiotic. A long minute passed before it came back to me and another long minute before I could find my voice—but it wasn't what I had hoped for. What came out was a painful croak, that made me sound like an adolescent bullfrog. "Uh, uuughh," I gargled as I tried to clear my throat. "Um! Mi-Michael!" I nearly shouted as I pushed the name out. But, once I got started, it wasn't just my name, a whole bunch of stuff spilled out of me and I began to ramble, jumping from one inane subject to another.

"My name is Michael Jablonski. I live in that cottage almost straight up from here. See, that one over there," I said pointing. "The gray one with most of the paint worn off . . .the one sitting on pilings," I added, realizing that several of the houses were worn and gray. "My mother and Margie, my older sister, are there now. Dad's only here on weekends. He stays with my grandmother in Dorchester, so that he doesn't have to commute every night. He's an accountant for a company that sells gears—not those little things that you find in watches, but the big stuff that they put into machinery. The foundry is in North Quincy, but my dad's office is in Boston. I went there once—to spend a day with him. We took the train into South Station and walked over to Franklin Street. I'm not crazy about the city. I guess some people think it's great, but I thought it was dirty." At this point I paused, but only long enough to suck in my breath, and then I plowed on without leaving any space for Linda to jump in.

"It can be scary too. There's all these big buildings smack up against the sidewalk, and with the streets running helter-skelter, it made me think of a giant maze. I couldn't help worrying about how easy it would be to get lost—how awful it would be to have to ask someone for help. Course I was pretty small at the time. That sort of thing doesn't' bother me now.

"After all, last fall I took the Subway all the way from Columbia Station to the Museum of Fine Arts. And that meant changing from the train to the trolleys when I got off at Park Street. It was kinda fun going through the tunnels and climbing up and down stairs in order to make my connections.

"Margie—my sister, is older than me—five years in October. She can be an awful drag and sometimes we have big fights, but she's also been a good friend when I needed one. Whenever I'm in trouble or want some answers, I can always go to her for help.

"Timmy, my brother, is only eight; he's the baby—well—not really a baby. I'm afraid I can't say much good about him; he's forever under foot and constantly getting into my things. He's a pest and it's even worse here, because we have to share the same room. Can you imagine? I have no privacy. One night he got up to tell me he was sick and threw up all over me. Another time, I found him walking in his sleep. He was standing over my good shoes, peeing on them. The smell was gross. Mom tried everything to get rid of the odor until finally she just put them out on the front porch and left them there.

"Boy! Is my tongue in gear or what? I don't know *why* I'm telling you all this stuff. Earl doesn't know half—I mean..." Somehow things seemed out of control, I couldn't imagine what was happening. Since I first saw Linda walking along the beach, my mind had turned to muck. No one had ever had such an immediate effect upon me before. She must be wondering—who *is* this jabberwocky?

Linda was looking at me and it seemed that I was being held captive by those incredible blue eyes. I wondered: could she really see me—see inside of me? Did she know what she was doing to me? Then with an easy smile and a promising gleam in her eye she said, "Michael, you surprise me. The boys I know don't say much. Most of the time I end up doing all the talking."

"Pretty awful, huh? I don't usually wig out like this."

"No, actually it was kind of neat," she said, tossing her hair back with that same provocative flip that I had seen as she walked along the beach.

While I was filling Linda's ear with all this nonsense we had gradually made our way to the seaward side of the rock and were sitting with our feet hanging over the edge. When Linda arrived, the water had only been a few inches deep. Now the rock was surrounded and the tide was coming in rapidly. If we didn't leave soon the rock would be completely covered and getting back to the beach could get a little hairy.

"Hey!" she said, with a half serious expression. "Weren't we going to find some of those—what were they again?"

"Periwinkles," I answered.

"Yeah, that's it. Sorry if I'm kind of a bonehead when it comes to this fishy stuff. I guess you'd call me an *inlander.*"

"A what?"

"An *inlander;* you know, one of those people who doesn't know about the water."

"You mean a *landlubber.*"

"Right," she said looking down at her hands which were folded in her lap.

"That's okay, you'll figure it out. But right now we have to get off this thing. The tide's coming in and if we don't head for shore the water will soon be up to our necks."

Standing, I took hold of her hands and pulled her back to her feet. It was then that I remembered Earl. For the entire time that Linda and I had been talking he was simply forgotten. It wasn't intentional, but I felt badly. I don't know what he thought of all this, but whatever was going on in his mind he had been gracious enough to move to the far side of the rock and leave us to ourselves. He had kept himself busy in a tidal pool that was at the bottom of a wide chasm where he was mostly hidden from view. I was sure that he would have lots of questions once we were alone again, but for now I turned my attention back to Linda.

Pulling Linda along I suddenly became aware of feelings that were disturbing. A whole host of wonderful new sensations were attacking my nervous system and though the effect of this sweet turmoil was agreeable, it was making me feel a little wobbly on my feet.

As I turned to Earl, I wanted to apologize for ignoring him, but instead I called out a warning.

"Earl, we better move it! Tide's comin' in!"

He looked at me with a curious grin on his face, but he made no comment. He just took a few steps across the surface of the rock and slipped into the water. By then it was almost to the top of his swim trunks.

I took Linda by the hand, led her to the edge of the stone face, and showed her how to gain her footing so that she could ease herself down into the water. It was cold as usual, and frothy, as the breaking waves swept around the rock and converged before heading toward the shore. She let out a squeal, as the sea circled her waist and sent a jet of salty spume up into her face. As she swung away from me and headed toward the beach, she moved with measured step, faltering at hidden obstacles.

Her feet were still tender. They were not yet callused from going without shoes. And now that the churning sea was hiding the bottom it wasn't easy to avoid the sharp stones and find the soft sand in between. Instead of joining her, I crouched on the edge of the rock where I could watch her skittish movements. As she hopped back and forth in a kind of slow dance, I wanted to laugh, but I couldn't do it.

When I had seen enough I followed her into the frigid water, and plowing through the roiling surf I raced towards the beach.

As I reached the shore and fell gasping on the sand, I looked up at Linda and shrieked. "HOLY COW, that water's cold!" Rolling back and forth I started laughing. I couldn't help it; I felt incredibly silly and I must have looked a sight with sand stuck to my palms and plastered all over my arms and legs.

Then, as if infected by some whimsical genie, she picked up more sand and started to douse my wet hair with it. Without waiting for my reaction she turned immediately and ran away.

finger pointing at the horizon. The rhythmic cadence of the waves; the sough and purl of the surf breaking on the shore and washing toward the line of debris deposited at the high-water mark; the sucking sounds of the water pulling at the sand and stone as it deserted the land and hurried back to become part of the next wave; the gulls surging upward and descending, skimming the shallow sea, dodging each other as they searched for a place to land among their brothers; these and a dozen other images combined to create a gentle pageant of sight and sound that distilled upon my soul and worked a powerful magic. Nothing Linda might have said – nothing she might have done could have helped to seal this new friendship more surely than this quiet contemplative time spent watching and listening to the sea.

Linda turned to face me and briefly gazed into my eyes. Then looking upward at the top of my head, she extended her hand and brushed the dry sand from my hair. It was a sweet unconscious act, a simple courtesy that caught me totally off guard. I felt a fluttery stirring in my stomach. Only a tiny tremor that quickly passed, but it was replaced by an urgent desire to kiss her. Kiss her? This was the second time since we'd met that that crazy idea had sprung to mind

Fortunately there wasn't time to act on that impulse. As Linda turned to look behind us at the setting sun I saw her soft expression turn to alarm. "Oh my gawwd I had no idea it was so late!" She exclaimed. "My Mother will kill me! I was supposed to be back by five. If I don't go right now, I'll be on ice for a month."

"It's okay. I have to go too!" I said. "Can we meet?" I asked, desperate to see her again. "Will you meet me tomorrow? At the end of the jetty? That is if we don't both end up being grounded."

I felt like I was rambling again. I wasn't leaving any opening for her to reply. Now that I had paused for a moment Linda asked: "When?" Then with a questioning look on her face she waited for my response.

"When what?"

"What *time* tomorrow?" She asked, sounding annoyed.

"Oh! I don't know–nine–ten o'clock? Whatever's good for you?"

"Ten is better. I like to sleep late." She confessed with a smile.

After making our way down from the seawall, we said our hurried goodbyes and separated, heading in opposite directions along the shore. As I walked around the end of the wall and up into the sharp grass at the top of the dunes, I thought over the events of the last few hours and suddenly remembered Earl. I had no idea what had become of him and I must say I was a little ashamed of myself for being so callous. Earl was my best friend, so was Tooey.

If Earl was fat, Tooey was skinny–painfully so. He would have been the perfect model for the Charles Atlas ads; the one where the muscle–bound bully kicks sand in your face and then walks off with your pretty girlfriend. Except that he didn't' have a girlfriend, pretty or otherwise. The two of them together were like Mutt and Jeff or Laurel and Hardy and they could be just as funny. Up until now, all my summer adventures had been shared with them. The three of us were nearly inseparable.

I wondered, had Earl been watching while Linda and I were so full of whimsy on the beach? Does he think I've lost it?

"What about this girl?" I said aloud. "I mean it's like a dream." I thought, do I even dare to imagine that she is as mixed up as I am? Could she at this very moment be troubled by the same doubts and could she be just as lost for answers? "Naw, she's too classy, too with it," I said, looking around to see if anyone heard me talking to myself.

Today had started the same as any other that I could remember, but this chance meeting had grossly altered the outcome. I wasn't a seer or prophet, but I didn't have to be to predict that this tall, skinny girl would somehow change my life.

CHAPTER 3

IT WAS after six when I walked into the house and Mom was in a hostile mood. She didn't scream at me. But there were cutting remarks about being responsible, about how much she trusted that I would follow the rules, and why she didn't think that she was asking too much. Then there were comments about how worried she was—how frightened she had been; not knowing whether or not I had fallen victim to some terrible disaster. This was all designed to make me feel guilty, and it worked. Then came the ultimate threat, "Wait till your father gets home."

This wasn't something that I wanted to hear. Dad was great and I loved him dearly, but I was also afraid of him, especially when I was guilty of some misdemeanor. Fortunately he wouldn't be back until Friday evening, so this final pronouncement left me free presently from other restrictions. For the moment I would not be confined to the house or kept from seeing my friends, which meant that tomorrow's meeting with Linda was still possible. Of course I had no way of knowing what horrible scene might be transpiring in *her* home right now. I could only hope that her parents would be generous. I mean, she had met someone new, and had gotten a little forgetful; that wasn't exactly a crime. Maybe they would allow for the confusion of the move, the excitement of the sea, the hope of fresh adventure and see that as an excuse to forgive her.

It was an awful night! Even under the best of circumstances sleep would have been difficult. The upstairs bedrooms in the cottage were always uncomfortably warm. Ocean breezes tended to make it more tolerable, but it was still necessary to sleep without even the lightest of covers, and I wore nothing but my cotton undershorts. Pristine thoughts of Linda occupied my mind and filled my fitful dreams. There were images of her slender figure walking along the shore, her hair floating gently upward as she led me by the hand, her agile form gracefully stepping along the narrow edge of the seawall, her wonderful blue eyes staring back at me. Awake or asleep, I worried whether or not she would appear as we had agreed. Would she face some awful punishment, or would she be able to keep our rendezvous?

In the early morning hours as the sun began to rise over the sea, sending beams of light creeping through the multi-paned window, I awoke lying in the middle of my bed staring up at the naked rafters. Though worn out from an exhausting night, I couldn't struggle any longer with the pretense of sleep. Leaving my furrowed bed, I crossed to the window and gazed out onto the beach and the ocean beyond. Before me was a fresh vision of the newly rising sun. Its warmth reflecting off the low moving clouds created a legion of colors, which alluded to celestial realms and a bright day of promise, maybe even a chance to pledge my love. Of course it wasn't love, not yet. I didn't know her well enough. First I would have to see if my feelings for Linda were genuine, and if they were, then I would have to find out if she felt the same way. Whatever I discovered, about her, or about me, this was bound to be a new experience; one loaded with promise—the promise of sweet joy or the harbinger of a desperate heartbreak.

But good or bad, nothing was going to happen while I stood in front of my window daydreaming. Turning back to my room I could see Timmy asleep on the other cot. He was on his stomach with his arms and legs splayed loosely across the bed. Asleep he was an angel, in another hour that would end. I wanted to be out of here before he woke up. Otherwise he would follow me as he always did, and I didn't want him around when I met Linda.

I wrestled myself into a pair of cut off dungarees, pulled a faded red T-shirt over my head and padded down the steep stairs and into the kitchen. As I leaned into the open refrigerator searching for the orange juice, there was a knock at the back door. Looking out the window above the sink, I could see Earl standing there waiting for someone to let him in. The inside door was already open. Closing the refrigerator and coming around, I reached up and lifted the hook on the screen. I heard the twang of the spring as he pulled the door toward him and stepped past it to get in.

"What's up?" I offered agreeably.

"That's what I should be asking you," he said, sounding offended.

"Okay, okay. I suppose you're right. So go ahead, bawl me out, I deserve it."

"No, I'm not gonna' say anything. If you wanna' get all goggly–eyed and mushy over some girl, that's your business."

"I was not!" I protested. "Besides, how can you say that unless you were watching us?"

"No way!" he insisted.

"Look, I like this girl. Is there something wrong with that?" I asked.

"It depends."

"On what?"

"On when you're gonna' see her again?"

"What makes you think I'm going to see her again?"

"Oh come on!" Earl objected.

"All right! We're supposed to meet around ten this morning."

"See! That's what I'm talkin' about," he said, putting his hands on his hips and giving me his 'what for' look. "Well, that burns it. I guess we won't be hangin' out together, not *this* summer anyway."

"Jeeze Earl, you're my best friend. I'm not going to throw all that away. So I've made a new friend and she happens to be a girl. It doesn't mean we won't do things together." I reasoned.

"You may think I'm a little dumb and I admit I don't know a lot about this *lovey–dovey* stuff, but I understand one thing. My brother made a new FRIEND last fall and suddenly everything changed. He spent all his time with her, and somehow anything I wanted to do was too bor—ing! That new *friend* is gone now, but he's already replaced her with another one. And I'm still out in the cold."

That was a long speech for Earl, and strangely enough it made a lot of sense. I was half prepared to submit to the logic of his argument when we were interrupted. Looking past Earl out the kitchen window, I saw Tooey coming toward the house. Earl turned to see what I was looking at and saw him too.

"Well here's someone I can still count on," he pronounced bitterly. "Tooey and I are taking our bikes and heading into Satuit to see what's up at the town pier." The screen door slammed loudly, as Earl left to intercept Tooey before he could reach the house.

I stood there watching Earl and Tooey walk their bikes down the dirt drive to the road, leaving me there alone to ponder my future. I was forced to consider that I had likely lost two good friends.

"Damn!" I said aloud, as I turned from the door and directed my attention back to the job of finding some breakfast.

CHAPTER 4

THE TIME passed slowly, but the hour finally arrived for our meeting. As I sat at the top of the dune just above the rocks that formed the barrier separating the cove from the angry sea beyond, I saw her coming toward me along the outer shore. She was wearing tan shorts made of a thin cotton that fit tightly around her hips, then flared out loosely about her upper legs. Swinging freely when she walked, it gave the impression of a very short skirt. Her blouse was a dazzling white in the bright sun and had an open neck with puffy sleeves that were pushed down off her shoulders. A stiff linen, it was gathered in billowy folds that ended abruptly just below her breasts, leaving her midriff bare. On top of her head was a straw hat with a high crown and a narrow brim, which was set low upon her brow. The effect was both charming and sexy. The shorts emphasized her long legs, the hat framed her lovely face; and her bare midriff and shoulders, and the fluid movement of her body presented just the right hint of sensuality. Approaching from the south with the sun high enough now to be at her back, her face was partially hidden in shadow – softening her features and lending an air of mystery, while she was yet far away. Altogether I was impressed.

As I joined her on the beach she took my hand and we picked our way carefully over the enormous granite blocks till we reached the end of the jetty. We chose to sit down on the flat chiseled surface of a stone slab that allowed us to face the shore. Looking back along the broad curve of sand, which was hedged in by the broken sea–wall, we were able to see a row of white and gray cottages. Partially hidden by the coarse beach grass, they were crowded together along Minot Beach Road. The houses wandered down this route in an unbroken line, until they came to a sharp bend where the road was forced to turn westward along a low rock facing. This was the beginning of what was known locally as "First Cliff". From here the ground rose rapidly until it was well over a hundred feet high. Above these lowly beach houses, at the top of the cliff, were the bright green lawns that surrounded the Lawson mansion. The mansion itself, with its white, fluted columns and wide veranda, stood at the edge of a rocky precipice that plunged dramatically to the beach below. It was a magnificent view, but I had seen it all before. I was much more interested in studying the young girl who was snuggled so contentedly at my side.

"I had a bad night," I said. "I was worried about you. What did your parents have to say?"

"Nothing—nothing happened." She assured me. "My parents were too busy with the move to even realize that I had been missing. When I came in they didn't say anything. They didn't ask—and I didn't offer."

"All that time, and they didn't wonder where you were?"

"Well, Mom mentioned it this morning. I just told her I had found a new friend and she let it go."

"My parents would never let me get away with that." I explained.

"Mine either, ordinarily."

"My mother had lots to say. But nothing happens until Friday when my father comes home."

"Will he go into orbit?" she asked.

"Maybe. Still, it's a couple of days away. Sometimes Mom decides that waiting has been punishment enough and doesn't tell my Dad."

Then she put her long delicate fingers around my neck, pulled me gently toward her, and gave me a quick kiss on the cheek. As she withdrew, her hand dropped down my back and wrapped itself comfortably about my waist.

"That's for worrying about me," she said.

The kiss came and went with such speed that I wasn't sure it was real. Her lips were wet and felt cool against my fuzzy cheek. It wasn't passion, or blood rushing hot, but my heart did an unexpected tip–tap against the bone in my breast and the sweet smile on her face sent me straight to heaven.

Speaking softly and with some gentle coaxing, I encouraged her to tell me about herself. Then I listened attentively as she chatted about her family, her home in Stoughton, her friends in High School. The information itself was meaningless, since I knew none of these people. Yet she expressed all this with such enthusiasm and animation that it told me volumes about the kind of person she was. She spoke with such loyalty concerning her friends, with such pure devotion toward her little brother and such genuine praise for her parents, that I was convinced she loved them all unconditionally. Surely that kind of dedication and constancy would make her a wonderful friend.

She spoke of her hopes and dreams and she had such a positive vision of her future. Definitely she would go on to college; maybe nursing or teaching; certainly something where her sense of compassion would have some real meaning. I saw nothing shallow or vain, nothing at all pretentious concerning her nature. Joy seemed to be a fundamental part of who she was; yet she was not silly or light-minded like so many other girls I had met.

After a time she looked up. I had been listening intently to every word, concentrating on her facial expressions and watching her lively gestures with warm–hearted delight. Realizing that she had captured my full attention, she became suddenly self–conscious. A warm rosy flush spread over her lovely face and she seemed distracted and momentarily ill at ease. I could tell that she was flattered. But she didn't seem prepared for the intimacy that was implied by such blatant devotion, and I could see that she was struggling to regain control.

"Let me show you where I live," she suggested, as an obvious diversion. She stood, and taking charge, led me back along the jetty.

Once we had returned to the beach, we headed off in a southerly direction retracing the route that she had taken earlier. As we moved along, there was a marked transition from Spartan cottages to more substantial homes. These were turn-of-the-century Victorians, with gables and turrets and lots of *gingerbread*. Passing through a rift in the dunes we marched along a narrow channel that brought us out in front of her house. It was a large two–story home that looked like something out of a novel. It was everything that my home was not. It had a high-pitched hip roof, punctuated by several small dormers that faced the sea. The porch was wide and airy, extending around three sides of the house, and in the northeast corner there was a charming circular gazebo.

On the second level at the very center, jutting out into the porch roof, I could see a large bay window. Linda pointed toward this and said: "You get an incredible ocean view from up there."

"Really? Is that your room?"

"Don't be a goose, that's the end of the hallway," she explained. "Here, let me show you!" Grabbing my arm, she propelled me toward the broad steps that rose up to the porch; and when we finished climbing she continued to lead me on through the front entrance.

Walking into the expansive foyer, I could see that the rooms on either side were sunny and spacious. There were still packing boxes in the middle of the living room, but the house was quiet. I couldn't hear anyone else moving about or working as they might have been with the unpacking still in progress. While she directed me toward the stairs Linda explained that her mother had left earlier to stock up on supplies in Satuit. As we came to the top of the main staircase and turned about, we were indeed in a large hallway, at the end of which was the bay window I had observed from the beach below.

Except in pictures, I had never seen a hallway as impressive as this. There were bright hardwood floors covered with plush oriental rugs. Resting my hand on the top of an elaborate post, my attention was directed along an oak balustrade, which led back toward the front of the house. Then turning sharply, the railing wrapped itself around in a giant 'U' and returned to another post on the other side of the landing, which perfectly matched the one that I was holding. The two stood like ancient sentinels, guarding the head of the stairs. The distance from the walls to the railing was great enough to accommodate several pieces of furniture. High-backed chairs with needlepoint upholstery, narrow tables polished to a glossy finish and fat potted plants filled the spaces between the doors, which likely led into the bedrooms. As we followed the length of the hallway towards the window, I could see that all the sashes had been thrown open and a fresh breeze was tossing the white–laced curtains in flouncy billows. A wooden seat had been built into the window bay. Covered with soft cushions it beckoned for someone to sit and enjoy the salt air, and we accepted the invitation.

We were seated for only a moment when Linda announced that she had something she wanted to show me. She left me at the window and went through the door to our right. In a flash she returned with her yearbook tucked under her arm. When she dropped it in my lap I could see *Stoughton High* printed on the cover. Inside were a number of photos taken with various student groups of which she was a part; and she was third row, second from the right in a picture of her sophomore class. A couple of candid shots of the school showed her in Chemistry class and Home Economics. These were taken from a distance and included several other students, so it took a little searching to pick her out.

"Here's our drama group, and here's one of me with the Glee Club," she said, pointing to the back row of a black–and–white picture. "This is Larry." I looked to see a young man whose good looks were spoiled by big ears. "You'd like him, he's really a kick, he keeps us all in stitches."

I could tell by the way she spoke of him that he was a good friend, but not a boyfriend. "You seem to be active in everything!" I said.

"Mom tells me I'm a gadabout, and I suppose she's right. I like being with my friends and that usually means joining the things that they're involved in."

It was obvious that she was a popular girl, but then that was no surprise. Outgoing and gregarious, she was an amazingly easy person to get to know. But that was intimidating too. She could obviously pick anyone to be her new friend; how had she come to choose me? Alone in this big house with Linda sitting beside me, was the kind of thing that made me want to pinch myself. But if this wasn't real, I was certainly having a wonderful time imagining it.

Her shoulder brushed mine as she pointed to another picture in the book, which now lay stretched across my lap. Ignoring the photo under her finger, I studied her profile and for the third time since we'd met, I thought of kissing her, but I was too far gone to do anything about it. This was scary. Just the lightest pressure of her body next to mine, the smell of her hair, the thickness of her lashes as she cast her eyes down toward the page, taunted my senses, stirred up an angry flutter of butterflies in my gut and turned my mind to mush. Worst of all, why did I have this compulsion to kiss her, and what would happen if I ever found the courage to do it?

****

Over the next several days before the Fourth, we spent oodles of time together, swimming, scavenging along the beach for shells or playing at card games. They were games, like Go Fish and SlapJack and War, and mostly I lost. It was hard to concentrate or follow even a simple strategy when I was playing against Linda.

One afternoon, when it was raining, Linda called me on her phone. In those days the telephone was big and black and ugly, and most people only had one. At our winter home in Wakefield, ours was on a small table in the front hall, but here at the cottage it sat on a ten-inch shelf in the kitchen. Which meant that whenever Linda called there was no privacy. That hadn't been a problem before. If Tooey or Earl got on the phone it was only a word or two, and I didn't care who heard my end of the conversation. Now it was different. Linda couldn't just say what she wanted and get off, she always had to include something intimate for which she expected a response, and I would be forced to shield the mouthpiece and whisper.

Linda invited me over for a game of Monopoly. Later, she asked me to stay for dinner and then we watched Milton Berle on TV. When that ended we ate popcorn and played checkers till after eleven. Earl was right, there didn't seem to be any time for old friends.

Whenever I was not with her, I was thinking about her. The way she looked when we were together last. The silly things she would do sometimes to distract me when I was trying to concentrate, or when she thought I was being too serious. The way she looked one afternoon bending over a sandcastle that we had built near the water, scooping furiously at the sand on the seaward side as she tried to establish a dam to protect it against the rising tide. When that failed, and the castle began to collapse, she plopped down in the wet sand and laughed uproariously at her own folly.

I wondered constantly about what Linda was doing—what she was thinking. Was it possible that she was as preoccupied as I was, with similar thoughts about me?

Although I had little experience in matters of romance, I knew that I was hopelessly in love with her; and though she hadn't said so, I felt there was reason to imagine that she had similar feelings towards me. I wanted desperately to believe that what she felt was love, but somehow it seemed strange to think of any girl being in love with me. Whenever I stared into the looking-glass and saw the image reflected back, I was not impressed. Not that I was ugly, but I could hardly find anything that would stir someone's heart to passion.

****

The Fourth of July was to be a family affair and we were required to spend the day with relatives. Occasionally an exception was made for a friend, but not often. Linda's mother and father felt the same way about family and holidays. Since our two families had not been introduced, and my parents knew very little about Linda, she was not invited. So we were resigned to spending the day apart.

It was a holiday filled with traditions. The local parade in Satuit was made up of veterans, the school band, Boy Scouts and Girl Scouts, along with a few local merchants and of course, the politicians. There were speeches and music on the Common in front of the War Memorial. Later there were picnics and cookouts, and games that included croquet and badminton and softball. Finally, in the evening, we would gather to watch the fireworks display, which was set off from a wooden staging set up below the lighthouse on the other side of Satuit harbor. Normally, I looked forward to these events with great anticipation. It was this holiday that marked the real beginning of summer and the easy, lazy days that lay ahead. This year I found it rather depressing. If it meant a day away from Linda, it hardly seemed worth celebrating.

So, I was pleasantly surprised, when in the middle of the afternoon, Linda stole away from her family and came to the cottage to find me. She was just as discouraged as I was by this forced separation, and she had come in secret to plot against this obvious injustice. We agreed that both our families were being unfair, and she suggested we rebel and meet somewhere later on.

"Can't we find a spot where we can be alone? Someplace where we can watch the fireworks together?" she asked.

I was thrilled by the idea. For the first time that day, I found myself looking forward to one of those traditional activities that a moment before had seemed so meaningless. I told her to meet me at the stairs in front of the sea–wall just before nine.

CHAPTER 5

THE REST of the day was filled with anticipation, as I looked forward to our secret meeting on the beach. Convinced that our parents' determination to keep us apart was unjust Linda and I decided to defy their authority. This simple act of rebellion made our little adventure seem dangerous. It wasn't really, but it was a lot more exciting to think of it that way.

As the hour approached for us to carry out our plan, I began to wonder what excuse I could use to get away. Finally, I decided not to say anything, but to just sneak off when an opportunity presented itself. In a moment of confusion, while my relatives fussed over running out of ice for the soda and complained that the hamburgers were under-cooked, I saw my chance and hurried down the stairs to the beach. Ducking behind some tall grass in the half-light of the dying sun, I crouched down and scurried along until I reached the sea-wall. Once behind the wall, I was able to straighten up.

I felt strange creeping off in the dark, but it was oddly exhilarating too. Normally I didn't do bad things, at least not on purpose. Not that I wasn't tempted, it was just that I always got caught and had to suffer the consequences. So, I generally stayed away from anything that was likely to get me into trouble. But when it came to Linda, I was prepared to take any risk. Well, that's what I wanted to believe anyway; and this was hardly life–threatening. I mean—even if we did get caught, what could happen?

From a distance I saw Linda standing barefoot at the bottom of the stairs, wearing fitted jeans and a pretty printed blouse. As I came up to her, she was looking away and didn't see me at first. When she finally turned and realized that I was nearly upon her, she started pacing back and forth. My guess was that she didn't feel all that comfortable about defying her parents.

"Were you waiting long?" I asked.

"No, not long. Where shall we go?" she asked, pulling anxiously at the pointed end of her shirt collar.

"At the northern end of the beach there's a rock." I said. Then I took her arm, to stop her neurotic pacing and pointed down the beach. "Right over there–below the Lawson Mansion, at the bottom of the cliff." I glanced her way, checking to see if she was looking at the right spot, "There's a break, and then that big rock." The craggy formation that I was describing stuck out at least a hundred feet and rose thirty to forty feet above the water

"It's humongous!" she said, with a tinge of doubt in her voice.

"Yeah, but once you're up there you can see forever," I promised. "The land end of the rock, where that channel is, is never more than a couple of feet deep, even at high tide, and the tide won't be full for at least another hour."

"Am I going to have a hard time climbing that thing?" she asked, tossing her head to get the hair out of her face.

"Not really. Look, I know you've only seen this thing from a distance, but I've been up there lots of times. It's not that hard, and once you're at the top it's way neat! There's even a place on the other side where the rocks come together to make a cave. Believe me, it's worth the effort."

"Sounds super!" she said, showing her enthusiasm by clamping her hands together under her chin as if she were about to applaud. But there was no slap or explosion, only a soft thump. "So—what do they call this place?" she asked.

"The 'Rock'," I said, taking her hand.

"That's it?"

"That's it,"

"The 'Rock'," she repeated, as if she were hoping for something more impressive. "Well, what are we waiting for? Let's do it!"

We started at a slow easy jog, following a straight course along the water's edge. When a spent wave raced up and surrounded our ankles with a couple of inches of swash, we laughed and tried to skip clear. Then as we progressed along the beach we began to zigzag up and down chasing the edge of the waves. It was a childish diversion that quickly ate up the time and brought us to our goal sooner than we expected.

Linda bent down and rolled her jeans above her knees, so that she could negotiate the water at the base of the Rock. I waded in ahead and showed her a hole in the rock where she could get a foothold. Then grabbing her by the waist, I gave her a boost. Reaching up, she began to search for something to grab on to. Struggling to prop her up while she tried to hoist herself onto a kind of shelf protruding from the rough facing, I soon found my fingers pressing into her soft buttocks. Not that I didn't appreciate the situation, but I wasn't comfortable with the idea of having my hands spread over her behind. Still, if I let go the way I had the other day on the beach, she would have gotten awfully wet.

The narrow shelf that she was trying to get to was only a few inches above the surface of the water. But, I was standing in a rising and falling surf that sometimes came well above my knees, and the shifting sand under my feet was making it difficult for me to keep my balance. At last she pulled herself free from my grip and finding some convenient holes where she could get her footing, she moved vertically for a few feet to another ledge. Here she sat down and extended her hand to help me up.

From this point on, though rough and irregular, the path rose more gradually, and Linda continued cautiously upward. I stayed close behind, watching her struggle over terrain that presented no real challenge to me. Of course I had made this climb often, and this was her first attempt. I never heard any complaints, and except for boosting her onto that first ledge she didn't ask for any help. She seemed determined to find her own way to the top; and she did. Mostly she followed a well–worn route, but she found a couple of detours that truthfully made the climb a little easier. Coming to the top, we stepped out onto a relatively flat plain. The surface here was split into a maze of cracks and crevices, and in some places a scrubby growth had broken through. Stunted bushes competed with patches of coarse grass, both fighting to hold onto the same thin layer of soil. We came to several spots where we could sit comfortably, but decided on a place on the far side, that allowed us to face in the direction of the harbor.

Sitting down we discovered that the stone was still warm from the sun, which had only recently disappeared behind the trees on the far horizon. In front of us the mica speckled ledge dropped off sharply, and below large slabs of granite had broken away creating a multitude of hiding places that now cast ominous shadows and echoed with the sounds of the waves striking the windward side of the rock.

We had hardly settled in when the fireworks began. Because of the distance, we couldn't see the displays, which were being set off, close to the ground. The trees on the far shore blocked all but some tiny flickering lights, which showed here and there between the branches. Even though some parts of the display were barely visible, those rockets, which shot high into the blackened sky, still left us with a startling exhibition of color and noise. Linda's head rested casually on my shoulder, and along with the smell of gunpowder and smoke that drifted across the bay, my nostrils were filled by the pleasant aroma of strawberries, which came from her freshly washed hair. When she moved excitedly and lifted her hand to point up at the sky, a few strands swept delicately across my cheek and tickled my ear. It was terribly distracting, but distracting or not, I refused to push them aside. I was afraid if I did, she would get the wrong idea and pull away—and I *didn't* want that.

Feeling the fuzzy warmth of her face, conscious of the slightest movement of her body; the gentle touch of her long fingers as they rubbed my waist—these marvelous sensations, combined with salt and perfume and the sticky odor of nervous perspiration, became immensely important, and I tried hard to concentrate on each one. This was all so different, so foreign to anything I had ever experienced before I was afraid if I didn't focus on every detail I might miss something. And everything—everything seemed so blissfully exciting.

Suddenly I heard the *whoosh,–whoosh,–whoosh* of the rockets, as one after another, they were sent soaring toward the stars. Crackling and popping, the noise rose to a marvelous crescendo. The explosions reached an almost deafening level and then fell silent. Both of us stared in amazement, directing our attention upward at the darkening sky, as the last few sparkles of light descended toward the sea. It was a stunning show and all the more enjoyable because I had shared it with Linda.

After the piercing boom of the exploding rockets that had so rudely hammered our ears, the contrasting silence had an almost tangible power of its own and we sat for a long moment wrapped in its embrace. The air was electric, charged with some special energy that was peculiar to that moment and those particular circumstances. For some reason I had been holding my breath and when I was finally forced to let it go, I felt a sudden chill—not because I was cold, not at all. The tiny tremor that crawled up from somewhere deep inside had nothing to do with the temperature. But whatever the source or reason, it was oddly exhilarating.

When I thought I had a grip on my emotions, I stood, and reaching down—palms open, fingers curled—I invited Linda to take hold. Willingly she hooked her fingers over mine, and giving a tug, I swung her upwards in an easy arc that brought us face to face—nose to chin. She looked down and gazed unflinchingly into my eyes. I returned that look with equal intensity and the effect was almost libidinous; looking into those blackened depths, sparked a kind of primitive arousal, which swept over me with a tingling energy that was so fresh and essential it left me feeling woozy. Struggling to regain my equilibrium, a new sort of dysfunction swept over me: a hot ripple of excitement burst instantly upward to stab at my heart. I hardly knew what to think. Was this sweet agony part of the business of falling in love? And if it was, was there more to come?

It was dark now that the glow from the fireworks had faded.

Only the light from the newly risen moon reflected off Linda's face, flattering her delicate features and giving off a soft pale glow that was so enticing it was painful. I wanted desperately to establish some physical connection, to bond in a way that was far more intimate than just touching. There was a genuine unseen force driving me toward her, filling me with an undeniable desire to kiss her. This kissing stuff was new to me. I had no real experience and I felt awkward and unsure of myself—afraid that if I tried, I would botch it, or worse that she would give me a well-deserved slap across the face. But Linda knew what needed to be done, even if I didn't. The soft breeze wafted upward off the cooling sea and along with the sweetness of her words swept away my indecision.

"Kiss me," she whispered. Somehow she sensed that I wasn't quite brave enough to act on my own, and I could detect an urgency in her voice, which told me I had better do *something*. Still, even with her generous invitation, it wasn't me but Linda who finally got things moving.

She released her hands from mine and brought them upward, letting them skip lightly across my breast. Progressing swiftly, her hands moved higher, resting briefly on my shoulders, then sliding easily around my neck. Her movements were smooth, but her touch was unfamiliar. It was more deliberate and sensuous than it had been before, and I felt the tiniest quiver as her fingers brushed across the back of my neck and pushed upward separating the thick tangle of wind-dried hair above. My own hands reached out and went clumsily around her waist. Our lips moved experimentally towards each other. We bumped noses awkwardly, until we finally discovered a way to avoid this by turning our heads in opposite directions. Standing on my toes, to match her height, my lips tickled hers tentatively, testing their delicious softness. The effect was intoxicating, and my hand moved shakily along her spine stopping between her shoulder blades. Pulling her toward me, I pressed more firmly, and felt her moist lips part slightly. With a tiny twist, her mouth opened a little more and her fingers pressing the back of my head pushed me deeper until my lips were crushed against her front teeth. I held her briefly, then a sudden peculiar stirring of my blood, made me release her.

"WHOooa!" I said with a gasp, as I struggled to get my breath. "Heyyy-ey-ey! She sang with a long quavering sigh, that showed her clear satisfaction. It was a delightful reward, especially since I felt that my part had been so amateurishly done.

The ensuing stillness was almost overpowering. Everything seemed to have stopped; the wind, the sound of the ocean playing upon the rocks below, even our breathing was subdued. I worked hard to try and come to terms with the powerful emotions that Linda's persuasive kiss had unleashed. That kiss was such sweet joy, but my body ached for something more, something that would relieve the terrible tension that tightened around my shoulders and neck and then shot downward through my loins and beyond. The desire to continue this experiment, and kiss again, was incredible, but I didn't dare act upon it. Nothing I'd done before had ever been so exciting or so frightening and I had the sense that Linda was frightened too. Without a word I let go and took a step back—Linda did the same. Then with her fingers spread wide she combed her hair up and away from her face—continuing, until it slipped through and swirled back into place. "Brrrrr!" she said. Lifting her hands in the air, her whole body shook in one quick convulsion.

I couldn't imagine what that meant and though it was alarming I didn't dare ask. Reaching out absently, I tugged at the edge of her blouse, which somehow had come undone and was half in, half out. Before I could pull away her hands shot downward and surrounded mine. Trapped, she lifted it slowly to her face and lovingly kissed the end of each finger. It was such an endearing performance and it was so unexpected that I came wholly undone. My heart felt as if it had leapt into my throat and the sudden constriction brought me close to tears. But before I could do or say anything, she took that same hand and began pulling me slowly towards the path that would lead us back down off of the rock.

As we began our descent, no word passed between us. Partly

because I didn't know what to say (and I don't think she did either); and partly because I didn't want to do anything which might alter the present mood. This was my first kiss and I knew somehow that there would never be another quite like it.

With nothing more than a touch or a gesture we clambered over the side and went from one foothold to another. Sliding off the bottom ledge into the water, I reached back and helped Linda to swing clear.

Splashing through the swirling troughs and crests of the gentle breakers we made our way to the shore. Then walked high along the beach heading toward the sea-wall. Returning to the weathered stairs from which our wonderful adventure had begun, we were reluctant to bring this affair to an end. Linda seemed to understand before I did that it was time to part, and she began to pull away. Holding her back and breaking our self–imposed silence, I said: "Call you in the morning?" It was really part statement—part question.

There was no reply, just a knowing smile and as she withdrew slowly, my grip gradually loosened. We kept moving further and further apart until, with our arms stretched to the limit, only the tips of our fingers touched. At last Linda broke the tenuous connection and quickly ran off. With her arms extended to form make-believe wings, she twirled and leaped, soaring to fanciful heights and dancing to some silent rhapsody. I watched in quiet fascination as she glided along the outer shore and faded into the long shadows behind the dunes.

CHAPTER 6

OUR ESCAPE had not gone unnoticed. According to Linda, when she got home at about 10:30 the big house was crowded with guests. Her mother spotted her from across the room came to ask where she had been. *"Outside with a friend"* she had told her, which was at least half true, and that was the end of the matter.

I wasn't so lucky. The cottage was too small, and with only Gramma Rose, Aunt Vera and Uncle Fred, and my two cousins, I was missed ten minutes after I slipped away. By the time I got in, the house was dark and my relatives had already left. When I eased open the screen door, and stepped into the darkened kitchen, Mom and Dad were sitting at the table waiting for me. *"And where have you been, young man?"* they said, together, while I nearly jumped out of my skin. Hoping for clemency, I told all. Well not about the kiss—that was too private. There was a long silence before dad pronounced his sentence: *"When you get up tomorrow you're restricted to the house."*

The next morning with dad back in the city, mom amended that to include the front porch. She even allowed me to go to the bottom of the stairs and stick my feet in the sand, but that was it. No friends, and no Linda for twenty-four hours. One monitored phone call was allowed to warn Linda. Everyone else who came by, was chased away by my mother. It was embarrassing. I was too grown up for this sort of treatment, but I wasn't sorry.

****

For good or bad (and I could hardly see anything bad in it) that one kiss had somehow changed everything. What that meant to me or what it might have meant to Linda was uncertain.

For the next two days after my *restriction*, little was said about what had happened on the Rock. There was something rather magical and mysterious about the whole business and it didn't seem necessary for us to share those feelings with each other—or anyone else. That might not have been wise. Perhaps it would have been better to touch upon those feelings, at least discuss some of the details to see if we could make any sense of our distorted emotions. But whether from youthful uncertainty or our combined inexperience, we avoided the subject. For the moment we seemed to be content to bask in the soft afterglow

****

Thursday morning, we went to a predetermined spot in the dunes on the outer shore. The day was surprisingly cool, almost chilly, with a sharp breeze coming in off the ocean. It was about ten o'clock and there were few people on the beach; only a couple of mothers, who were relaxing, while their youngsters dug holes in the sand. Passing these beach-goers, we continued on to a secluded setting in a shallow depression hidden in the dunes. The natural barrier formed by the sand and rough grass on either side, helped to reduce the cooling effect of the wind, and added to a cozy feeling of privacy. Once settled in, no one could tell that we were there unless they happened to be standing on the crest of one of the hills surrounding us.

Loaded down with gear, we descended to the bottom of this sandy hollow and began to set up camp. Spreading the blanket and taking advantage of the sloping sides, we positioned it so that it would face the westward moving sun as it rose towards its southerly zenith. I pulled out a portable radio, tuned it to a local station and began to get comfortable. Laying belly down on the blanket and supporting my head on my folded arms, I glanced over at Linda who was kneeling beside me rummaging through a white canvas bag. Along with a sandwich and a thermos, she unpacked a couple of magazines and some baby oil. She picked up the baby oil and began applying it generously to her arms and legs.

"Here," she said, "let me put some of this stuff on your back."

My first thought was that it wasn't necessary. Why would I want Linda to cover me with oil? But then I reconsidered, and the idea of her massaging my back with that slippery stuff seemed very enticing.

"Aw right—pour it on!" I said agreeably. "But, I get to do you next."

I don't know if she had ever done this sort of thing before, but she was *good* at it. When she first poured some oil on my warm back, it was cold and I shivered slightly and let out a tiny squeal. Laughing, Linda accused me of not being very brave. Slowly and rhythmically, she moved her hands along my lower back starting just above the waistband of my swim trunks and then progressing gradually upwards along my spine. Occasionally she would slide her hands to either side of my rib cage and at last she moved to my shoulders and applied the same treatment. Her long fingers worked skillfully, her touch sometimes gentle, sometimes brisk. The combination of subtle friction and soft pressure, as first her palms and then her shifting fingers tenderly manipulated the underlying muscle, made me feel as though I had been transported to some heavenly paradise. Relaxing was the first word that came to mind, except that I had never felt this relaxed. Stimulating also came to mind and it was, but not in any way that I had ever experienced before. Pleasant, pleasurable, exotic—there simply were no words that could accurately describe what was happening to my body or how exquisitely the delicate motion of her hands was affecting my sentient spirit.

This certainly was ecstasy, but it ended all too quickly and now it was my turn. I brought my knees up under me and then sat back on my heels, trying to put myself into a comfortable position beside her. As I fumbled with the cap on the bottle of lotion, Linda lay down and turned over on her stomach. Today she was wearing a two piece bathing suit, a bikini, but not like the miniature suits that became popular later on. The top was reasonably modest and the bottom cut across her hips just below her natural waistline, which left her navel well exposed. It was amazing how sexy that small dark cavity could be. Maybe it was because in the past, even when the girls wore two pieces, the bottoms always came high enough to cover that little hole. And now, the newer swimsuits let them show it off. But only on the beach, you still couldn't see it on TV or in the movies.

All of a sudden the idea of rubbing her down seemed far too personal. I would have to put *my* bare hands on *her* bare back. And supposing I could do that, I had to wonder if I would be half as skillful as Linda had been when I was the patient. Hesitant, my uncertainty was turning me into a coward.

As if the situation wasn't already bad enough, Linda reached around to untie the knot at the back of her neck; then she unhooked the band holding her top in place and let the ends fall loosely to either side of her body. It's not as if she had suddenly taken all her clothes off. But even if she had, the effect couldn't have been any more alarming. As she lay with her head resting on her arms, her eyes closed waiting for me to begin; I looked down the length of her long straight figure and except where the ruffled bottom of her suit cut across her hips, she was uncovered from head to foot. Which to me made her practically naked.

Looking back at the straps draped loosely over top of her shoulders and running across the blanket under her arms, I could see that the slightest rise or turn might reveal more of Linda than I was ready to see. I'd hardly touched a girl before except to hold her hand, and this—well—this was panicsville. Still, I'd promised Linda a rub down and if I couldn't pluck up the courage to do it I'd look like a fool.

My hands trembled and I felt thankful that she couldn't see how nervous I was. Tipping the bottle I started to pour some oil on her back, and like Linda before, I misjudged and more than I had intended fell upon her—a lot more. The oil ran down her spine and formed a puddle in the hollow just above the waist to her bikini bottoms. It was cold on her heated body and she jumped. And when I saw her hands snap back and she started to push herself up off the blanket, I nearly lost it. I reached out instinctively and pushed her back down. The action wasn't rough, and Linda didn't offer much resistance, but as she slumped into the folds of the blanket, she did complain.

"Not so much! That stuff is cold." She cried.

This incident swept away my indecision, and with my hands planted firmly on her back, it seemed prudent to push that puddle of oil around and rub it in. I started awkwardly at first, and then as I became more comfortable with the idea, my confidence grew and along with it my expertise as a masseur. As my hands moved gently down her back I could tell by the agreeable murmuring sounds that she made that my oily fingers were pushing her towards a lovely, listless, state of euphoria. I kept this up for as long as I dared. Then, tracing her spine with the tip of my index finger, she accused me of tickling her. So I moved my hands quickly to her sides and playfully poked at her waist, testing for vulnerable spots and tickling her in earnest. Twisting and laughing, she wanted to pull away, but she couldn't escape.

"Stop! That's not fair!" She shouted.

And it really wasn't fair. Without her top she couldn't get away and so I abandoned my attack. Quickly she gathered up the straps, fastened the catch, and with a new knot around her neck, she became the aggressor. She pushed herself up off the blanket, sprang to her knees and when I tried to escape she made a flying leap for my legs. Before I could rise to my feet, she got hold of me and sent me flopping down on the sand. With my bottom half still on the blanket, I rolled onto my back and she climbed on top of me. Straddling my waist, she began probing for sensitive places that she could use to torture me.

"Okay! Okay!" I giggled. "UNCLE!" I shouted in surrender, hoping she would stop, but she didn't.

Struggling to keep my dignity, I got hold of her wrists, restricting her ability to provoke me. Straining to be free, Linda sat down, pressing her weight heavily on my lower abdomen.

"I give!" I gasped as her clumsy attack knocked the wind out of me. "You win!"

She relaxed and stopped straining against my hands. Looking tenderly into my eyes and with an abundant and knowing smile, she announced: "Michael, *I—love—you.*" The words were soft, and slow, and deliberate, and she said them with such wonderful intensity.

Before I had a chance to consider what she had just said, or to react to it, she descended upon me and willfully pressed her lips against mine. Her kiss was not harsh or forceful, but it was sudden, and her eagerness was stimulating. Stretching her legs and extending them, she brought them down next to mine. Then, relaxing her arms, she let her full weight fall upon me. Tall as she was, she wasn't particularly heavy. Long and thin, she couldn't have weighed much more than a hundred pounds, so I wasn't concerned about her crushing me, but I was surprised to find the length of her body pressed so closely against my own. There wasn't time to think about what was happening or to oppose this tender assault. My reaction was impulsive. My arms encircled her and I brought her closer, drawing her tightly to me. When our lips parted briefly, I whispered to her with equal conviction.

"*I love you too!*"

I never thought that I could possibly say that to a girl. Well, maybe sometime in my life, but not now, and especially not to Linda. Not because I didn't feel that way about her. I did, which was the very reason that I thought I couldn't tell her. It wasn't that I was ashamed of those feelings, I just didn't know what to do with them. Nothing in my short life had prepared me for such stuff, and I didn't want to make a fool of myself. But now that she had brought it up, I could hardly keep my feelings a secret—though I suspect she already knew that she'd won my heart. Whether she knew or not, she seemed wonderfully pleased to hear the words.

Lying on the ground with her weight pressing down upon me,

her lips repeatedly engaging mine, I was hopelessly within her power, and her warm enthusiasm tested my resolve. My body wasn't ready for such an intimate assault and it was running away from me. Worse still, Linda was crushing a part of me which strained to extend itself in another direction, but instead was trapped and grievously distorted.

Pinned down I couldn't easily move and I didn't want to physically push her off. But I needed to get some kind of relief. So with a painful groan I simply let go of Linda and tossed my arms back over my head in surrender. She looked at me quizzically at first, but I gave no further clues. Then suddenly she slid her legs onto the blanket, drew them up under her, extended her hands and in a single quick movement brought herself back to her original position. Half sitting, half kneeling, she was again straddling my waist.

Slipping one hand behind her, I gave what I hoped was an inconspicuous tug at the crotch of my swim–trunks, which literally straightened out my problem. Then plunked that same hand into the small of her back hoping she would think that was my intention all along.

Placing her palms lightly against my chest for support, her long fingers accidentally brushed my nipples, which were erect, and I flinched under her touch. A quick smile appeared and disappeared as her hands moved slightly downward and came to rest lightly against my ribs. Hot stabs of embarrassment freckled my face as I realized that she must have had some understanding of what she had done.

She sat staring down at me, and once again I was trapped by those incredible blue eyes. Her lips parted and behind their soft moistness I saw an even row of white teeth. Slowly a sweet smile spread across her face, and after a long pause she spoke. "Did you really mean it?" She asked earnestly. "Did you really mean what you said?"

"You mean do I love you? Yes." I replied, bearing testimony to the fact, because I knew it was true.

"Did you?" I asked.

"Michael!" she said with a sharp wrinkle in her brow. "Do you suppose that I would say something like that if I *didn't* mean it?"

I didn't answer. Instead I asked, "What do we do now?"

"What do you mean?" she asked with another frown.

"Are we a couple? Is this like being engaged—should we make some kind of pact, like cutting our fingers and sharing each other's blood?"

"I have no idea!" Linda said.

"Me either!"

"I'm not in the habit of kissing boys, or falling in love with them."

"Me either," I repeated. "Well, I kissed a girl at a party—on a dare."

Why did I say that? Was it a confession? That's silly—it happened long before I met Linda and it happened so fast I couldn't even remember if my lips actually landed on hers. For crying out loud, I wasn't there long enough to tell if she had bad breath! All these thoughts were crashing around in my head and I felt so mixed up. But instead of keeping those ideas locked up inside as I normally would, I began to share some of them with Linda.

"How can this be happening? *You*—love—*me! ME*—Michael Jablonski—gawwd, how can you love someone with a name like that? It's so—uncool! But you *said* you loved me. And I believe it, I really do. Up here," I said, tapping my forehead, "I'm a little unsure. But down here," I added, pressing my fingers into the hollow of my chest, "I know it's true.

"I mean, my mother loves me and my family. But they sort of *have* to—don't they? No one has ever loved me just because I was *ME!*"

Linda didn't respond; she just sat there staring down at me with a brightness in her eyes that made me think she was going to cry. And I did see the moisture build along her lower lid, swelling until it escaped and a fat round droplet splashed down into the notch at the base of my throat. I asked her if I had made her sad.

"I'm not *sad,* silly—I've never been happier."

That wasn't logical. But it seemed pointless to try and get her to explain why she was crying when she said she was happy, so I changed the subject.

"A moment ago, I asked you what we should do about this, and you said you didn't know . . ."

"And?" She asked when I didn't continue.

"And I think we ought to do more kissing," I said, raising my eyebrows.

"Me too." Linda replied, with the same wide-eyed expression.

"And maybe we should make a pact," I said. "Something to make it more official."

"That's fine as long as there's no blood involved," she said, making a cross with her fingers and holding them in front of her face as if she were trying to fend of a vampire.

"Just the same," I said, "this kissing stuff is kind of scary."

"How's that?" she asked.

"It's kind of a boy thing, I don't think you'd understand."

"I don't know—I'll bet it's not all that different for a girl

"Tell me about it?" I said.

"Well—I mean—you know. It's, it's exciting—but it's kinda weird too. There's this electricity—you know the sort of thing that makes the hair on my arms tickle and stand on end. And then there's this odd stirring at the pit of my stomach, as if something were alive down there. It seems almost wicked—but—but I like it—you know what I mean?"

"Yeah—I guess so," I said, not willing to admit that I had no idea what she was talking about.

"It's hard to explain, and it's happening to *me*. So I guess I can't expect you to understand it. Whatever causes these feelings," she said, looking down and covering her stomach with her hands, "I certainly don't want them to go away."

"Then it's settled," I said happily. "Kissing is in. We get to lock lips, smooch, lay on a wet one . . ."

"Hey!"

"Pucker up, suck face, mug . . ." I continued.

"Stop already! Is that all you're going to do is talk about it?"

Whereupon she leaned over and gave me a long lingering kiss, which renewed all the strange stirrings that we had just complained about. When our lips parted again we looked at each other and decided that it might be safer if we took a long swim in the icy Atlantic.

Afterwards, shivering from our dip in the ocean, we ran up the beach to our hideaway in the dunes and grabbed some warm towels. Briskly we began to rub ourselves down. Then wrapped up in the damp towels we paced back and forth and waited for the sun to warm our frozen bodies. Later, we discarded the towels and lay side by side on the blanket. For the next several minutes we baked in the heat of the midday sun. On my back, I closed my eyes and saw the orange brightness of the sun, which somehow penetrated my lids. As my eyes moved, I found myself chasing black spots, floating around the edges of my vision. Relaxing, the heat making me feel sleepy and listless, I thought, right now I am exactly where I want to be. With Linda lying quietly next to me, I felt such an amazing sense of belonging.

CHAPTER 7

EVERYTHING NOW was done together. We met at the beginning of each day as soon as we could escape from our parents and stayed together as late as possible. So that we wouldn't have to separate for meals, we frequently finagled invitations to one household or the other. Mostly we went to her house, because there was more room. I got to know Linda's mother pretty well, but I only saw her little brother occasionally and for the whole summer I only met her father twice. Her brother was constantly asking to stay overnight with his friends; and her father was some kind of an executive with Fidelity Investments in Boston; and there was always a meeting or appointment that came up suddenly and kept him away.

Of course who was, or wasn't there, didn't really matter. We were so wrapped up in each other that we weren't particularly conscious of anyone else. I suppose this was rather awful, but we didn't do it on purpose. We were just too involved to see that we were shutting ourselves off from the rest of the world.

All this did not go unobserved. We weren't particularly secretive and anyone who saw us knew that we were getting pretty serious. Still, whenever we could, we looked for privacy. That was hard to find with Earl and Tooey spying on us. Just as I predicted, they had formed an alliance. They viewed us from a distance and what they saw apparently didn't impress them. I'm sure, that to their minds at least, this was just a lot of mush and gush.

They could see that we were vulnerable and they continually looked for ways to bug us. If they happened to meet us walking to the store they would fall in behind and talk loudly. Saying disgusting things that we were obviously meant to overhear. If we were on the beach they would sit nearby whispering, then make goofy faces and point at us. I'm not sure what they were saying. It could have been all gobbledygook, but whatever they were up to they were certainly having a lot of fun at our expense. We did our best to avoid them, but it wasn't easy to escape. Sometimes if we could keep our cool and ignore them, they got bored and went away.

Usually when the sun started to drop and the long shadows of evening began to spread across the sand, people would pick up their gear and go home. Occasionally, one of the cottage dwellers would take a walk, or a father just home from work would come down for a late swim, but other than that the place was pretty empty. Tonight Earl and Tooey had gone off to Satuit with their parents, so at least for a few hours we would be free from their constant badgering.

Descending the slope of the shore, Linda and I plunked ourselves down a few feet away from the ripple of the backwash. Half recumbent, I laid on my stomach with my chin propped in my hands and watched the fetch and curl of the soft breakers. Linda, sitting beside me, scrounged through her canvas bag and removed a pocket-sized book. The cover was black with a red binding and the pages were gilt-edged. On the face, in large gold letters, was the title: "Famous Poetry" and below in smaller print: "An Anthology of American and English Poets". The book looked well-worn and was obviously a favorite, so I wasn't about to tell her that I thought poetry was boring. Linda extended her hand and offered me the book.

"Michael," she said matter-of-factly, "if you're anything like most of the boys I know, you'll think that poetry's pretty boring. But, boring or not, I love it. There's something about the way it sounds, something in the ebb and flow that rubs gently against the spirit and as the English say: 'warms the cockles of your heart.' I don't know what *cockles* are, but it has a neat sound to it."

"I don't know what cockles are either," I said with a self-conscious grin. "I think they're some kind of shellfish.

"Anyway there are some awesome ideas in here about life and

death, love—and war. Neat, heart–kicking stuff that . . ." She stopped suddenly, and pushed the book towards me. "At first the words may sound a little hokey, but if you pull at them a little—draw out their meaning—you'll begin to see things in a way that you never thought possible."

I had never heard Linda speak with such eloquence and it would have been foolish for me to try and argue against her obvious passion.

She continued to hold the book in her hand, gently cradling it as if it were a special offering. And as I reached out and took it from her I rolled over and sat up. I saw that the binding had broken in several places from having been opened and read often. The book fell open now to one of those places. Holding the book high, to catch the fading light, I saw that the page was dog–eared and the corner smudged. The title of the poem was "The Chambered Nautilus" by Oliver Wendell Holmes. *Born 1809, Died 1894.* I started to read.

"No!" Linda said. "Don't read it to yourself, read it aloud," she insisted. "You can't get a real sense—you won't be able to feel the power of the words, unless they're spoken."

I wasn't prepared for this, but I knew intuitively that it was really important to Linda, so I took a deep breath and began.

"This is the ship of pearl which, poets feign . . ."

I continued, trying hard to watch punctuation and to put some feeling into the words, which to me seemed meaningless and dull. But when I came to the end something clicked.

"Build thee more stately mansions, O my soul,
As the swift seasons roll!
Leave thy low vaulted past!
Let each new temple, nobler than the last,
Shut thee from heaven with a dome more vast,
Till thou at length art free,
Leaving thine outgrown shell by life's unresting sea!"

The words pricked at my heart and made my spirit swell—I don't know why—I couldn't quite get hold of it, but somehow it was like remembering an old dream. One of those foggy things full of mystery that are so clear while your in the midst of them and so fractured when you wake up. Except that this time the fractured pieces came together and I understood—at least in part. I looked at Linda and smiled. "I like this!" I said with some surprise.

I read through those last verses again, this time more slowly. Then I went back to the beginning. All of it still wasn't clear to me, but again there was something in those last few words—a familiarity. There was no way I could explain it to Linda, but I think she already knew.

I suppose I had no real reason to hate poetry, I'd just never given it a chance before. The problem was that I'd always assumed that it would turn out to be nonsense. But here, tonight, with Linda's help I found out I was wrong.

"What should I read next?" I asked, giving her back the book.

"Here's one I think you'll like," she said, flipping through the pages, *"Once upon a midnight dreary—while I pondered weak and weary..."*

"Where have I heard that?"

"Quoth the raven nevermore..." she said, laughing merrily.

She put the black volume back into my hands and I read a frightening, melancholy poem by Edgar Allen Poe. Then I read another, and so it continued into the soft summer's eve.

There were poems full of hope: *"Our birth is but a sleep and a forgetting; the soul that rises with us, our life's star, hath had elsewhere its setting and cometh from afar."*

Others were morbid and spoke of death and the moldy grave that awaits us all: *"yet not to thine eternal resting place shall thou retire alone, . . . Thou shalt lie down with patriarchs of the infant world, . . . with kings, the powerful of the earth, . . . the wise, the good,. . . they are but the solemn decorations all, of the great tomb of man."*

They also spoke of courage: *"In the world's broad field of battle, in the bivouac of life, be not like dumb cattle! Be a hero in the strife!"*

And again they bore record of great deeds which changed the

course of history: *"By the rude bridge that arched the flood, their flag to April's breeze unfurled, here once the embattled farmers stood and fired the shot heard round the world"*

Marvelous words expressing noble deeds and high ideals, stories of humble men and kings. It was wonderful! No, I didn't understand it all, and it was necessary to return and read some parts over again. Certain verses seemed obscure, and Linda sometimes had to interpret. After all, to her these poems were old friends, and that long familiarity made it easier for her to explain things that were a little too deep for a beginner.

In the years that followed, especially when I went off to college, I was required to read some lengthy pieces, filled with the kind of verses that were terribly dull and boring. My professor tried to tell me that these poetic soliloquies were full of profound meaning, but I couldn't find any; maybe it was because Linda wasn't there to interpret for me. The poems that Linda had chosen to share with me that evening weren't like that, and though I never became a great lover of poetry, I did gain an appreciation for *some* of it.

Best of all, I found out something about Linda. I had a better understanding of who she was and what was important to her. These weren't just words to her, she obviously believed in these ideals. And I discovered that I believed in them too.

My parents had always taught me correct principles. They insisted on things like hard work, honesty and self–reliance, but I understood them differently now that I had seen them written down in a book. I realized that heroes are not always people who are larger than life; sometimes they're just ordinary people who are struggling against extraordinary forces.

We had to stop. The light was gone and darkness covered the pages making it impossible to continue. I fell back on the cool sand, physically and emotionally exhausted.

After a time Linda and I began to talk. In the darkness, she explained, with wonderful reason and passion, her love for books and poetry. We talked late into the night about what might have inspired these authors. We wondered aloud about the effort and devotion that went into their work. What does it take to write, a book, a poem, or even a single line that has the kind of enduring power to touch someone else's life; not just when it was written, but a hundred years later, after the author has long since turned to dust?

As Linda spoke, her eyes reflected a zeal and enthusiasm for her subject that was hard to ignore; and it wasn't very difficult to feed off that intensity. Particularly now that the book had been put aside and we were huddled together against the coolness of the night. Still, after hours of reading and discussion, we were both too tired to do anything more than hold on to each other.

At last I walked Linda home and under the porch light I kissed her goodnight. My eyes were heavy and a lazy contentment filled my spirit. I took Linda's hands in mine, looked into her soft eyes and saw that same sleepy contentment.

CHAPTER 8

WITH ALL the days and weeks that we had been together and the first rate experiences that we had shared, we still had not gone on an official date. That is I hadn't actually asked Linda to go someplace special and then spent some of my hard-earned money on her. I hadn't demonstrated my good manners by treating her to whatever her heart desired, or lavished upon her all the splendid things that she deserved. Realistically, none of that was necessary. She didn't ask for it and I knew that she didn't expect it. That doesn't mean that I didn't want to give her all those things anyway; I just couldn't do it. Most of the time I was broke. Well, not entirely broke. I did have some money stashed in the corner of my footlocker, but that was supposed to be for an emergency—or so I had determined when I put it there.

This summer I had chosen to be unemployed. Since meeting Linda, I scarcely wanted to do anything that might keep me away from her. I did have one lawn to mow for $2, a leftover from the previous summer when I had built up a small lawn–mowing business. Dad gave me a dollar and a half each week for an allowance and between the two it seemed to be enough. Enough for one, but now there were two of us.

Most of our time was spent on the beach. Mom had a car, but I couldn't use it. I didn't have my license yet and even if I *could* drive, there really wasn't any place for us to go. The nearest town was Satuit, and that was deadsville. The only thing that we could get to, that was of any interest to us, was a Mom & Pop variety store a couple of blocks from the beach on Egypt Road. And we did walk there occasionally for penny candy or an ice cream sandwich or a soda from the cooler. Penny candy was obviously a penny, and we could buy ice cream or soda for five and ten cents respectively. I did treat Linda to those things whenever we went to the store together, but that was just nickels and dimes. I wanted to do more, and besides none of that seemed like a date.

For all of the lack of affordable entertainment there was one place that would fit my budget, and that was the Playhouse in Satuit. In 1957 a ticket for a movie only cost a quarter.

Checking the listings in the evening paper, I found the perfect picture; it was called: "Love in the Afternoon". A Billy Wilder production, starring Gary Cooper and Audrey Hepburn. It was a romantic comedy about an innocent young girl in Paris who falls in love with an American playboy.

As simple as going to a movie sounds, it still took a considerable amount of planning. For one thing, I didn't want to ask my parents, or hers, to drive us there. Which was a problem at first, because I had no friends who could drive and it was a long walk. Then a simple solution came to mind. If we went to the matinee, we could ride into Satuit on bicycles. And the afternoon matinee wouldn't be very crowded, so we could find a dark corner and create a few romantic moments of our own. Of course, neither Linda nor I *had* a bicycle, at least we didn't have one here in Ocean Bluff; but Tooey and Earl *did*.

Of course I hadn't been much of a friend lately, so asking for their help could be awkward. But I had known these two for a long time, and I couldn't believe that if I made an honest appeal, they would say no.

I went to Earl first because I knew if I could win him over that he would be able to convince Tooey to go along. Reminding him of our old friendship, I promised him that I would do the same for him, if the situation were reversed. That wasn't very persuasive. Earl wasn't in love, and he didn't expect to be, at least not very soon, so he wasn't terribly sympathetic. In desperation I started to beg, and when I got down on my knees and started tugging on the front of his T-shirt he caved in.

"Alright, alright," he said, "you can have the damn bike! Just let go of my shirt, you're stretching it out of shape." As if it were possible to make it look any more distorted than it already was.

"What about Tooey?" I asked, with a hopeful grimace.

"I'll get him to go along. Don't worry, if I tell him to do it, he'll do it." It seems that Earl knew a few things about Tooey, and he wasn't opposed to the idea of a little blackmail if he thought it was necessary.

Now that Earl had sworn to help, the question was, would Linda be willing to ride a *boy's* bike? At first she said no, but once she understood that it was the only way that we could get to the theater unchaperoned, she was more than agreeable. She said that she would ride a *tricycle* if she had to. Besides, if she wore slacks, riding a boy's bike wouldn't be a problem.

****

When we started out on a gorgeous, sunny Tuesday afternoon, the day was full of promise. There had been thunderstorms the night before, and the air felt fresh and clean. It was a perfect day for biking; the temperature was a moderate seventy-four degrees, there was a light steady breeze and not a cloud in the sky.

We started our journey on Cliff Road, in front of Linda's house, and followed it to Driftway. The road here was fairly level, and wandered back and forth between the cottages and marshland until we crossed the Strawberry Point Bridge. About a half-mile past the bridge, we began climbing to the top of Prospect Hill. This was the first real obstacle that we had encountered. It was a steep grade and it was necessary to stand on our pedals and pump hard to make it to the summit. By then we were hot and winded, so it was a relief when we started our descent and headed toward Main Street.

Magnificent old elm trees lined both sides of the street, forming a luxurious green canopy that covered the pavement and shut out the sun. After riding the five miles into Satuit on barren roads, where the only trees were scrub pine, the cooling shade was refreshing. Beyond the high curbing edging both sides of the street was a ribbon of well-trimmed grass, then came the sidewalk and the storefronts. With wrought-iron benches placed here and there beneath the trees, Main Street took on a park-like quality that was both charming and inviting. Continuing along this enchanted thoroughfare, we glanced up occasionally at the sun flickering through the thick leaves, and watched the people coming and going from the vintage buildings. Some carrying packages hurried to their cars, while others hustled along the crowded sidewalk. At one point a busy mother pushed her screaming kid away from the doorway of a toy store, and further on two beefy women bumped into each other in front of Millecente's Dress Shoppe.

On the corner of Otis Ave we spotted the theater marquee and knew that we had reached our goal. Dismounting from our bikes, we pushed them into a wooden rack next to several others and walked around the building to the theater. The two of us got in line with half a dozen people and waited for the box office to open. We passed the time with excited chitchat, full of anticipation, looking forward to the movie and the promise of romance, both on and off the screen.

Once inside we stocked up on popcorn and candy in the lobby, then pushed against the swinging doors and entered the cool darkness of the movie–house. By the time the lights faded and the curtains rolled aside to reveal the image of Bugs Bunny on a bright red background, we had found a spot at the back of the theater next to the north wall, where even the rosy gleam from the shaded lamps along the center aisle couldn't penetrate. It was so dark, in fact, that if it weren't for the dancing glow of the picture on the screen, we wouldn't have been able to see each other at all.

Linda, who was normally a little taller then me, lost that advantage when she sat down. Apparently the extra height was in her long legs. Scrunching down in the plush seats, I put my arm around her and she rested her head on my shoulder with her soft hair crushed against my cheek. The show started with the usual cartoon, followed by a newsreel and coming attractions, but we were too absorbed in each other to pay much attention to what was happening on the screen, or to worry too much about the people who might be sitting nearby. Some whimsical attempts were made to feed each other popcorn. Since it was so difficult for us to locate the other's mouth, we mostly fumbled and missed. Amused by these silly antics, we got a little carried away, and when our giggling got out of hand the other moviegoers let us know it.

"Shhhhh!" They whispered in our general direction. "Shhhhhhh!" They hissed more forcefully when it appeared that we were ignoring them. These queer noises had the opposite effect; the shushing sounds struck us as outrageously funny and our giggles quickly turned into a chirpy sort of belly laugh. Now we were definitely too loud and we made a real effort to shut down, but that only produced a kind of sniggering that threw us into silly fits of coughing and cooing. At last we ran out of steam and wheezed out our last sigh. By that time the final credits had rolled off the screen and we could see Maurice Chevalier standing at the top of some kind of monument. He was snapping pictures with a telephoto lens—pictures of a rendezvous between a man and a woman in a hotel suite below him. We straightened up in our seats, brushed away the loose popcorn that littered the front of us, and took a more serious interest in the movie.

"Don't you think that Audrey Hepburn is beautiful?" I whispered, as the star of the movie walked into her father's office. "I never noticed before, but both of you have the same dark eyebrows. And her nose—long and straight," I said softly, as I traced my finger along the ridge of Linda's nose. I stopped briefly at the tip and then dropped neatly to the small cleft just above her upper lip. Holding my finger to that reference point, I leaned over in the dark and gave her a quick kiss.

"Michael, you're incorrigible," She gasped. "Are you trying to tell me that I look like Audrey Hepburn?"

"Nooo. You don't *look* like her—not exactly. But you are long and thin, and your skin *was* just as white, before the sun got to it," I said, thinking back to the day we met. "Audrey Hepburn has always been one of my favorite actresses. Maybe that's why I thought you were so attractive when I first saw you."

We had tried to keep this conversation to a chummy murmur, but there was another harsh "Shushhh" from the couple three rows ahead of us. The theater was practically empty, so it didn't take very much for the sound to carry. This time feeling properly chastened, we fell silent, but Linda didn't remain quiet for very long. Apparently my last comment was just too disturbing and she couldn't settle down without asking.

"Did you really find me that attractive?" She whispered anxiously in my ear.

Pressing in closer and speaking in hushed tones, I could feel my hot breath sweep over her cheek, while my lips teased the lobe of her ear. "Couldn't you tell?" I said. "When I pulled you up onto the rock that afternoon, couldn't you see that I was a wreck?"

Her response was delightful. I could hear a deep husky laugh, which she tried to suppress by clamping her hand over her mouth. Nothing else could have done more to convey her satisfaction at the thought of my being so shaken by her. All because she happened to be standing too close. It probably hadn't occurred to her before that she could have that kind of effect on a boy.

As much as we had hoped to keep this private, and as subdued as our voices had been, it was enough to attract the attention of the usher standing under the exit sign at the end of our row. We had been snuggling together in the dark, enjoying an intimate embrace, when the beam of her flashlight suddenly engulfed us. In fact we were so closely entwined that we might just as easily have taken up a single seat; and when the usher's light hit us we twisted and turned in an embarrassing effort to get ourselves untangled. The young girl, whose gold braid glistened in the backlight from the movie projector, warned us we would have to leave if we couldn't clean up our act. This scolding had a very dramatic effect. Much the same as dousing someone with cold water, it completely destroyed the mood.

Directing our attention back to the screen, we looked up to

see Audrey Hepburn as she eased herself precariously along a ledge and climbed onto the balcony outside of Gary Cooper's hotel suite. She had come to warn him that John McGiver, the angry husband of the woman Gary was presently entertaining, was outside in the hall waiting for an opportunity to burst through the door and shoot him. By now she and Gary were in a flurry of conversation trying to determine how to handle this dangerous situation. They decide to let McGiver's wife leave by the balcony and Gary dismisses the gypsy band that he has hired. This turns out to be the cue for John McGiver to make his dramatic entrance. But instead of his lovely wife, he encounters Audrey Hepburn hiding under the veil of his wife's hat. Embarrassed and confused, he apologizes for his mistake, but still insists on searching the closets and under the bed before he will agree to leave.

Audrey and Gary are alone now in his suite, which is hardly an appropriate place for an innocent and impressionable young girl to be. Following a brief round of questions Gary kisses her. It is an unexpected and passionate kiss, which hails the beginning of their romance. Gary still wants to know who she is, and after more questions he invites her to come back the next evening. But she's not easily convinced and he soon discovers that the only time that she can possibly see him is in the afternoon.

Audrey is obviously infatuated with Gary, but he is a notorious playboy. He has had a long history of scandalous affairs, all with married women. All of these affairs involved frivolous romps, which were very romantic, but devoid of any form of commitment.

Now the movie becomes both funny and frustrating as Audrey begins an elaborate charade. She pretends to be a woman of the world, who has had many lovers. In fact she is an inexperienced young girl who has never been in love before.

Linda and I are now fully engaged in the plot and have briefly forgotten each other. But as the film progresses and the actors fall more and more in love, we are carried away by the mood of the film and begin to copy some of the romantic action we see on the screen.

When Frank (Gary) covers Arlane's (Audrey's) hand, I impetuously slip my own over Linda's as it rests in her lap. In the next scene, when Frank put his arm around Arlane, I move my own, placing it casually over Linda's shoulder; and she responds by freeing her hand from under mine and reaches across to rest it on my stomach. Several minutes later, with Arlane lying across Frank's lap, I unconsciously pull Linda to me, and she responds by laying her head against my breast. Sliding her fingers around my waist she crushes her cheek anxiously against my collarbone in a quick painful hug that makes me groan softly. And Linda, not knowing that I am in pain, murmurs in agreement.

And so we progressed, each action on the screen followed by a similar one off-screen. By the time the movie rolls to its dramatic conclusion, Linda and I are completely caught up in the gentle pathos of this bittersweet love story. And tied together in an affectionate knot of heads, and arms, and legs, we are fairly boiling over with pent-up emotion.

Now we can see Audrey running down the platform alongside of the slowly moving train, tears streaming down her face, as Gary, filled with indecision, stands on the steps of the coach. Suddenly he reaches down and pulls Audrey off the platform and onto the train. Dragging her inside the coach, he kisses her roughly and with sudden comprehension she throws herself at him with equal passion.

Then, Linda and I, with our adolescent hormones raging, pour all our energy into a fiery kiss of our own. When our lips finally part, we are overheated and breathless. Audrey and Gary were wonderful, but after all—our kiss was the real thing.

The house lights come up and we rise quickly from our seats, brushing away bits of popcorn and adjusting our clothes, which are in shameful disarray. Thank goodness the rest of the people are still directing their attention at the screen and not at us.

Outside the theater the weather has deteriorated badly, and we find ourselves staring out from under the marquee at the pouring rain. Our original plan was to get something to eat after the show; so hand in hand we rushed out into the storm and across the street to Call's Drugstore. Pushing wildly through the front door, we stopped momentarily to shake the rain loose, before looking for a place to sit. Locating an empty booth, we sat down. I pulled a couple of menus from the wire rack that held the condiments and handed one to Linda.

"What do you think, do you want a shake, or would you like something to eat?"

"I don't know, we had candy in the theater. I'm not interested in something sweet. Actually, a burger and fries sounds awfully good," she replied.

"Yeah, me too! I've really got the hungries."

Looking at my watch, I saw that it is only five o'clock, but the dark slate-gray storm clouds make it seem much later. The store lights were already on, the bright fluorescence chasing away some of the gloominess. Waiting for someone to come and take our order, we sat staring out the big plate-glass window next to our booth. The rain was coming down hard. The water gushing from the downspout on the corner poured out onto the sidewalk and ran off into the street. Surging and foaming, it combined with other rivulets of water and created a small flood, which swept down the street past us. Sitting comfortably on the high-backed red-cushioned benches that bracketed the table, we were grateful to be inside. Other than a little residual dampness from scurrying across the road, we were comparatively dry. The waitress comes over and takes our order and we spend the time while we're waiting for our food discussing the movie that we have just seen.

"I like Gary Cooper, but don't you think he's getting kind of old?" Linda argued.

"No, why do you say that?"

"Well, wasn't there some flak about having him play opposite Audrey Hepburn, because of the age thing?" she asked.

"What age thing?"

"Oh, give me a break," she moaned. "Gary Cooper is about a hundred years old!"

"Yeah, but still, when they were on the screen together I wasn't thinking about their age. I mean people fall in love at all ages, don't they?"

"I guess." She agreed, then changed the subject. "Weren't you worried at the end, Michael—that Frank would leave Arlane at the train station?"

"Nah. They couldn't have ended the film that way. It was a comedy. Can you imagine if he had left her? It would have been gloomsville."

"True, I would have hated it if Frank hadn't realized that he was in love with Arlane. Don't you think that's a pretty name?"

"More like pretty weird. But it's probably French," I said.

"So, what's that got to do with it?"

"Nothing, just that her name sounds foreign."

By this time our food has arrived, and we eat and talk. We had been in the drugstore for nearly an hour when I looked up to see that the rain had stopped. It was already beginning to clear, and the sky was starting to brighten in the west where the sun had dropped closer to the horizon. Watching from the window, I could see the wind pushing the clouds along. They were cold and dark, swirling about in billowy vapors as they broke up and scattered to the east.

I paid our bill and left a small tip. We went in search of our bikes; anxious to see what condition they were in after the rain. They were pretty soaked, particularly the seats, and there was nothing we could use to dry them off. We swept the excess water away from the upholstered surface, using the edge of our hand and climbed on, knowing that by the time we got back to the house, it would probably look as though we had peed our pants. Pedaling briskly down Main Street, we enjoyed the fresh coolness of the air and the strong smell of wet grass that had apparently been cut while we were inside the movie-house. The sharp smell of the grass and the steam rising from the warm pavement, the long rays of the setting sun reaching beneath the scattering clouds and glistening off the puddles, all worked their special magic. It seemed the perfect end to a perfect afternoon.

We are well along Driftway Road when the skies begin to darken again. A curtain of rain streaked with faded sunlight is forming directly in front of us and we are heading straight into it. My house is the nearest and we can only hope to reach it before this second storm breaks. Big black thunderheads are moving over us and it is obvious from the distant flashes and the forbidding rumble of thunder that these clouds will bring more than just rain. We still have almost two miles to cover before we can get off Driftway onto Minot Beach Road and make a beeline for the cottage. I wasn't very fond of lightning, especially the kind that comes down in ragged streaks and crashes into objects on the ground, but Linda was positively petrified.

We probably weren't in any great danger. It wasn't likely that we would be hit, but likely or not, our fears were driving us to the point of panic. Leaning over the handlebars and standing on the pedals, the adrenaline started to flow, and we began to surge ahead. We made it as far as the signpost for Minot Beach Road before the rain came. That wouldn't have been so bad, but the rain didn't start gently. It was like rushing into a wall of water. One minute we were dry and the next we were soaked to the skin. Our hair hung in wet masses, sometimes falling into our eyes, and water trickled along our bare arms. The clothes we had on became heavy, clinging to our bodies and dragging against our legs, sapping our energy and making it extremely difficult to continue pumping.

Dropping our bikes at the end of the drive, we sprinted along the walkway, threw open the screen door and fled into the kitchen. As we burst through the doorway, my mother brought us to a sudden halt.

"STOP!" she shouted. "Stay right where you are until I can get some towels."

When she returned, in addition to the towels, she had some dry clothes for me, and shorts and a top, borrowed from my sister Margie, for Linda. The problem was how to get us out of our wet clothes and into the dry ones without letting us out of the kitchen. My mother considered this for a moment, and then without saying anything she grabbed an old beach blanket that was neatly folded beside the back door. With Margie at one end and Mom at the other, they held it up between us forming a makeshift wall. They didn't have to explain what was expected. For modesty's sake they both looked away as I stripped off my wet clothing on one side and Linda shed hers on the other. First my shirt came off, then I peeled away my trousers and finally I struggled with my undershorts, which clung heavily to my skin. Linda worked her way through a similar process, as piles of soggy clothing built up on the worn linoleum floor between us. In a few moments we were both standing there naked, our wet skin feeling the chill of the cool wind blowing in from the screen door at our backs. Using the clean towels that had been waiting on the floor nearby, we rubbed ourselves down, and then picked up the dry clothes Mom had provided.

Looking at what she brought, I realized she hadn't given me any underwear, and when I thought about it I hadn't noticed her giving any to Linda either. It felt odd, but I was anxious to cover myself, so I didn't make an issue out of it. Since I didn't hear any complaints coming from Linda's side of the blanket, I gathered that she wasn't bothered by it. Or maybe she just saw the impossibility of the situation. She couldn't continue to stand there naked while Margie or my mom went to get her some underclothes. Besides, my mother was a large woman, and my sister's undergarments wouldn't have fit her much better. Margie's briefs would have been baggy and loose in the waist, and the bra would be way too big. I didn't know a lot about size, but I could tell that Linda was just starting to develop and that my sister was already there. But then none of this really mattered, because if either Margie or my mother were to leave, the wall would come down. And Linda, at least, would have been caught without a stitch on.

The fact is that this whole thing made me nervous. The blanket between us didn't offer much protection, and Mom and my sister were getting tired, which caused the wall to droop a bit. If I had a mind to, I could easily have looked over the top, and actually, I didn't even have to do that. This old blanket had several holes in it. Nothing very large, but when I bent over briefly to pull on my trousers I did catch a flash of white as Linda struggled on the other side. Quite honestly, I *was* tempted to lift my head and take a quick look. But even that quick flash of white had been enough to make me feel guilty. Besides, if Linda wanted to, she could have peeked over the top as well. And since she was taller, she would have had a better view. Nevertheless, in an age when common decency prevailed, I don't believe that either one of us would have dared to look. It just wasn't done.

When the job was finished and Linda emerged from the other side, I could see that her clothes were obviously too big. She had tucked the shirt into the shorts and was holding onto the waist to keep them from falling off. It was an amusing sight. The baggy clothes made her look vulnerable, and in some illogical fashion she looked kind of sexy too. Maybe it was the idea of what might happen if her fingers accidentally slipped out of the loops that she was using to keep her shorts from dropping down around her ankles.

Mom took care of her problem by giving her a large safety pin, which Linda used to crimp the edges together.

Now, warm and dry, we went to the window at the front of the house and sitting on the scratchy old sofa we watched the storm outside. The wind whipped the rain in sheets against the thin cottage walls and water ran in upside-down waves along the edge of the porch roof.

We had known each other for only a few weeks, yet I felt safe and comfortable sitting here beside Linda. How was it that I could be so at ease with this girl? And she *was* a girl; someone who until recently was supposed to be the enemy.

CHAPTER 9

THE NEXT several days were plagued by foul weather. Rain and thunderstorms, along with high winds, struck along the shore from Cape Cod to Gloucester. All this was just the edge of a much larger system that was moving up the East Coast towards Maine. Most of the really serious storms were farther out in the Atlantic. This brooding, melancholy weather kept Linda and me confined to the house, either hers or mine, and we soon ran out of things to do. So, it was a marvelous relief when the skies finally cleared. By midday on Friday, the sun returned and the temperature soared into the eighties.

Pulling my swim trunks from the footlocker and tossing them onto the bed, I began to change for the beach. Having been away from the water for so long, it was exciting to slip them on again. Most of the time I practically lived in my bathing suit and was never more than a few hours from a swim in the ocean. My suit hadn't been this dry, for this long, all summer.

Linda met me at the top of the dunes and we took off at an easy lope down to the water's edge. In the aftermath of these ocean storms the sea looked cold and forbidding and seemed to be in constant turmoil. Far offshore gray crested waves were colliding in cross–seas and enormous combers were rolling in and crashing against the beach in a spectacular display of foamy scud and spindrift. It was exciting just to watch, but we hadn't come down here to be spectators. We rushed into the frigid waters, screaming from the cold shock, and exhilarated by the surf crashing against our bodies. There was a real sense of danger as we felt the awesome power of the sea surging around us; one minute pushing us toward the shore, the next minute dragging us away. Truly it *was* dangerous, but we were gifted with a magical feeling of invincibility, and we worked the combers fearlessly trying to catch a wave and ride it back in. Linda and I were completely caught up in this wonderful game, pitting our puny strength against the white mass of sea that curled, and plunged, and came smashing down on top of us. It was great fun, but that didn't mean that it wasn't a little scary too—at least for me.

I remember during my first summer at the cottage, on a day very much like this one, when the ocean was choppy and the waves were running high. Again I was trying to jump the waves and ride them in when I found myself being pulled down by the frightening power of the undertow. With incredible energy it was dragging at my feet, and churning up sand and stone along the bottom, so that a new wave could rise. As it grew, the water built higher and higher, until it crested and broke, falling from the mass of its own weight. Then I started to roll and spin as it swept me along the bottom. Finally it spit me out onto the rocky shingle, and I scrambled and fell on the slippery stones, gasping for breath, as I tried to climb the steep shore. Even at eleven I knew that I had been held under for too long. I knew too, that the sea had taken hold of me, had threatened to take my life, and then for some unknown reason had tossed me back. Now older, and taller, and stronger, I still couldn't forget how easy it had been to get into trouble. And though Linda may have thought I was being overly protective, I kept warning her—telling her to stay close to me and to follow my lead.

The icy water forced us to stop now and then to warm our frozen bodies. Drying ourselves off, with quick invigorating movements, using a rough scratchy towel, feeling the hot sand under our feet and the warm breeze thawing our numbed flesh—all this was stimulating and self-indulgent, and just as delightful as our gambol in the sea.

Still, we didn't stay long on the beach; as soon as we had recovered, as soon as our circulation was restored, we rushed back into the water. Diving headlong into the cold blackness, we fell victim once again to the wonderful onslaught of the pounding waves.

This time we decided to slog back into the shallows. We stood on our knees, waist deep, in the swirling froth of a newly spent wave. The water suddenly dropped away, and we could feel the force of the undertow sucking at the sand and pebbles around our lower legs and feet, drawing the gritty mixture back towards the depths of the sea. Ahead of us the curl of a new wave crested and broke. Rushing forward, the water rose again above our waist and a soapy scud rippled around us as we interrupted its progress toward the beach. This wasn't as inspiring or as dangerous, but it was still great fun. As if we weren't getting wet enough, we added to the game by cupping our hands and pounding the surface, sweeping the water high into the air. Aiming at each other, we screamed and laughed with delight if we hit our target, and laughed just as heartily if we missed.

When we grew tired of this, we scrambled to our feet and began chasing each other along the beach, moving in and out of the spume and backwash at the edge of the waves. Finding some seaweed, I scooped it up and started after Linda, threatening to cover her with it.

"Michael!" She screamed, "Don't you dare!"

Laughing, I caught up with her and boldly decorated her hair and shoulders with the long slimy strands. Pulling away and shaking the seaweed loose, she turned back upon me with a terrible vengeance.

"Michael, I'll get you for that." She promised.

I turned into the surf to avoid her, and she overtook me. Coming from behind and throwing her arms around my neck, she climbed upon my back and wrapped her legs around my hips. Her sudden attack put me off balance and we both went plunging into the water. Unwinding myself from her long legs, I made another attempt to escape, this time heading out of the water and up the beach.

Linda followed in hot pursuit, and extending her arm, she

took hold of the only thing that was within her reach. She tucked her fingers into the waist of my swim–trunks and once she'd gotten hold of the band, she tried to halt my advance. Fortunately they were soaked, and plastered to my body; otherwise she would have had them down around my ankles. She wasn't really trying to strip my suit off. Her intention was only to slow me down. It's just that stretching to reach my waist had caused her to overstep, and when she realized that she had lost her footing and could tell that she was about to fall, she tried to use the handy grip she had on my waist to save herself.

It didn't work. Instead of righting herself she brought me down with her. We both landed rather unceremoniously on the wet sand just beyond the wrack and flotsam left by the receding waves. As I got to my feet, I was facing away from Linda who had fallen in an awkward heap on the ground behind me. Suddenly she started to giggle and turning my head I saw her sitting up on a ripple of sand pointing at my rear end.

To begin with I couldn't imagine what she thought was so funny. Then bringing my head front–to and glancing downward, I could see that my swimsuit had dropped and a wide ribbon of white skin showed between the waistband and my tan line. Thankfully Linda was behind me and couldn't see, because a pubescent patch of wet hair had escaped, and was clearly visible hanging over the edge. It wasn't any more than a dozen wispy curls, but I was still mortified. Other than a little lip fuzz, and some whiskers on my chin, it was the only other place I had grown any body hair. And although that was important to me (important to my sense of becoming a man), I hardly wanted to show it off, especially to Linda. In quick panic I brought my hand around to my backside where I could feel soft flesh, and a deep cleft, and knew that I was at least half uncovered. Immediately I hauled my drooping drawers up to a more respectable level. But it was too late, by now Linda had lost all control. When I swung around to look at her again, she was holding her sides and rolling in the sand, which was sticking to her arms and legs and plastered to her soggy hair. Finally she stopped laughing long enough to offer a suitable judgment.

"It serves you right! Although that's not quite what I had in mind when I came after you." Then breaking into a squeaky laugh, she said. "Don't feel so bad, we all have one you know." Then she concluded. "Of course yours looks awfully pale."

There seemed to be no end to the delight she was getting from the sight of my bare butt. Considering how embarrassed I was, I really couldn't find any humor in it—not at first anyway. But when I stopped to reflect upon it, you might say that I began to see it from her point of view. I suppose that if the situation had been reversed I might have been laughing too. Although I think I would have been a little more sympathetic. Still, it was such an improbable accident it was hard not to forgive her.

Moving to a spot in front of me, Linda stepped into a shallow depression. A retreating wave had left a pool here, and squiggling her feet from side to side, she sank down into the mushy sand at the bottom. This, and the hole she was standing in took four or five inches off her height and for once she was forced to look up at me. Reaching upwards and laying her forearms casually behind my neck, she suddenly dropped her smile and replaced it with a clownish frown.

"I'm sorry Michael. I suppose that I should have been more sensitive, but I couldn't help myself. Give me a kiss and tell me that you forgive me," she begged, as she dropped her chin in an act of humility. Then lifting her head slightly and peeking at me from beneath her thick wet lashes, she said, "Please!" She looked so woebegone and her sweet expression of sorrow sounded so genuine. It was enough to melt the coldest heart, and with her standing so close, what was I going to do? It was useless to try and pretend that I was still mad. Besides, though I hadn't told her so, I had already forgiven her. So I kissed her and told her that I loved her.

"Linda, you're too much. It's impossible for me to stay mad at you." I said generously. "Besides, I have to take some of the blame. If I hadn't dumped that seaweed in your hair. . ."

"It *was* awfully cute," she whispered, and then she kissed me again with girlish impetuosity.

"What?" I asked as soon as her lips left mine.

"Your tiny heiny!" she said with a grin.

"Cut it out!"

"Done," she said, swinging her hands up in mock surrender. "Shouldn't we call it quits?" she asked.

Taking note of the sky and the position of the sun, I realized that it had to be early evening. "Jeeze yes!" I said in alarm. "It's gotta' be at least five."

We walked back to our towels and Linda pulled a wristwatch from her tote bag. "You're right;" she said, showing me the time. "It's almost twenty past.

"Mom's going to need me tonight—at least for awhile. But she and Dad will be leaving for the city later. Can you come over, Michael? Maybe around seven? I have something neat to show you."

"I'll be there, but I probably won't make it before seven-thirty." I said. "Dad comes back from the city tonight. He'll be with us for the weekend and he usually wants to check up on me. Well, not really check up on me, but he likes to hear about what I've been doing. So generally after supper we sit down and talk for awhile."

Linda pulled on a man's white dress shirt that she was using for a beach robe, and stooping to pick up towels, sandals, and sunglasses, we headed in different directions, confident that our separation was only temporary. In a couple of hours, we would be reunited. My whole perception of time had changed. Now, only the hours we were together counted. Those periods spent apart were only a necessary inconvenience. And even then, every free moment was consumed with thoughts of her.

What was she doing now? When I saw her again, what would I say to her? (It ought to be something brilliant and wonderfully romantic). *What did she really think of me? How could she honestly be in love with me? Was her mind as cluttered as mine with silly lovesick ideas? Did she spend all her waking hours, when we weren't actually together, thinking about me?* Somehow, that didn't seem likely. Just because Linda had become the center of my universe, it was hard for me to believe that she was preoccupied with the same thoughts and emotions that were currently ruining my concentration and keeping me awake at night.

"Isn't love grand!" I said aloud as I went through the screen door into the kitchen.

"What did you say, Michael?" Mom asked as I passed her on the way to my room.

"Nothing, Mom. Just thinking out loud, that's all."

CHAPTER 10

A LITTLE past seven-thirty, I was at Linda's house ringing her bell. She came to the door wearing a deliciously sexy halter-top and well-worn cut-off jeans, the ragged edges just above the knee. Since they fit so tightly, I suspected that she had done the same thing my sister did with her jeans; when they were brand-new she put them on wet and let them shrink to her form. However she accomplished it, I certainly approved whole-heartedly of the effect. Letting me in with an affectionate kiss, she led me to the living room.

Her mother and father had gone shopping in Cohasset and had plans to see a movie later. No one else was at home; her little brother was visiting a friend over on Driftway Road and wouldn't be back till morning. So we had the house to ourselves for awhile. She brought me over to a brand-new portable record player. Reaching in, she pushed a lever, which dropped a shiny new record down onto the turntable. Suddenly the room was filled with the romantic sounds of "Fascination" from the movie *Love in the Afternoon*. Linda's father, no doubt following her request, had purchased the soundtrack album. During the next several minutes we listened to these simple melodies and remembered the innocence of a pretty young girl as she tried to pretend to be a woman of the world. It also reminded me of the rain, and the drugstore, and the drenching we got coming home. I pictured the two of us stripping off our wet clothes, as we shivered in the wind that swept through the back door. And I saw Linda, sitting beside me with a giant pin holding her shorts together, as we looked out the front window at the storm raging outside.

As the light began to fade and the evening settled in, we decided that we wanted to dance. Well, Linda wanted to dance; I wasn't so sure.

The breezy porch seemed a lot more inviting than the warm sticky living room, so Linda removed the album that had been playing and propped the portable phonograph next to the open window. Selecting some *45's* from the top of the bookcase and loading a stack of them onto a fat black cylinder; she pushed the lever and started the machine.

Taking me by the hand, she led me through the foyer and out onto the large, open front porch. We pushed aside some of the wicker furniture, and cleared a space where we could dance. My training was limited, which is why I was somewhat reluctant to do this. Margie had taught me the Lindy and a few simple steps, which allowed me to do a passable Fox-trot. Other than that, I was a pretty hopeless dance partner. If I had been with anyone else, I might have felt terribly self-conscious, but I knew that Linda didn't care how well-practiced I was on the dance floor. The record-changer clicked and a new *45* fell onto the turntable. The husky voice of Nat King Cole drifted through the window. And when we heard the plaintive lyrics to a slow, sorrowful ballad, we embraced, and began to rock back and forth to the easy tempo.

As I listened to the opening lines, I couldn't escape their sweet logic. They were words about being too young—too young to really be in love. Then as the song continued we both saw how perfectly the lyrics fit our situation. And when the song concluded—And yet we're not too young too know, this love will last though years may go, we both understood, even though we didn't want to think about it, that when the summer ended our romance would likely end with it. Not that we would stop loving each other, just that circumstances and distance would prevent us from doing much about it. And as the song said, our age was against us; we were way too young to be this much in love.

Wrapped in each other's arms, swaying gently to the music; I felt the breeze blowing her fresh smelling hair across my face, her sharp chin pressed against my shoulder, and a sweet sadness swept over me. A tender ache constricted my throat and I thought: if this song lasts much longer. . .

Linda whispered in my ear. "I love Nat King Cole, and this ballad is the best, but it makes me feel kind of gooey, like I'm going to cry. Not because I'm unhappy," she quickly amended. "I mean—this makes me sad, but . . ."

"I know, I feel the same way," I said, with some appreciation for the pain this was bringing to both of us.

The record ended and we stood there waiting. Next came the Latin sounds of a Mambo. This was a dance that I knew nothing about, so Linda decided to teach me. And she showed superhuman patience when I awkwardly tried to follow her directions. It wasn't a hopeless effort, but it wasn't without mishap. First I stepped on her feet and she muttered something unintelligible. Then she had to suppress her laughter when I caught my heel on the leg of the wicker chair behind me and tumbled into it. Once, when I attempted to lead her into a turn she came round too quickly and fell against me. She wasn't very heavy but when she lost her footing she pitched me onto the hard porch floor and then came down on top of me.

But, as I repeated the steps again and again, my feet started to fall into the right places and my body began to pick up the rhythm of the music. Finally I was able to bring some smoothness to the stiff jerky movements that I had started with.

As the evening grew old and the witching hour approached, her endurance and mine began to falter. Dancing for so long was tiring, and learning to dance proved to be exhausting. When we finally decided to stop we moved into the circular gazebo that was built into the southern end of the porch. There, we stood leaning against the railing and I could see ample evidence that our effort had been hard work.

The front of Linda's halter-top was soaked with a circle of perspiration and the back of my shirt felt just as wet—not to mention the sticky dampness under my arms. I was sweating profusely and when the breeze came up I could tell that my body was giving off a pungent odor. I couldn't imagine anything very desirable about the smell of old jock straps and dirty socks. Still, Linda didn't seem to be offended, and she didn't try to put any distance between us.

She had proven to be a good teacher. With her help, I had mastered several new steps, including the Mambo and a little bit of the Rhumba, whose movements turned out to be very sexy. I had discovered that dancing, real dancing, was not only good exercise, but also good fun.

This evening taught me something else, too. I had come to appreciate that Linda wasn't just the girl that I had fallen in love with, she was also my best friend. I suppose that Linda had been my friend from the beginning, but for some reason I hadn't seen it that way before. Up till now, romance and friendship didn't seem at all connected. It was rather neat to find out that I could have both all wrapped up in the same package.

CHAPTER 11

MRS RICHARDS reminded me a lot of Mrs. Cleaver on *Leave it to Beaver*. Her hair was straight out of the box, with tight little curls as if she had just come from the hairdresser; her makeup was done to perfection, her clothes sleek and tailored, her dresses and suits fashionable. Whenever I saw her, she was dressed to kill. She didn't wear high heels; well, not tall pointy ones anyway, but otherwise she always looked like she was ready for church or some high-flown social event. And oftentimes that's just what she did. Linda told me that her mother was connected with several important charitable organizations in Boston. Which was why most of the time when I came by to pick up Linda, the rest of her family was missing.

During a casual conversation with Mrs. Richards one afternoon, while I was waiting for Linda to change, her mother let it slip that she was working on plans for a surprise party. Linda's birthday was August 10th. When her mother brought up the idea of a party I asked how old she would be. Her answer wasn't what I expected. She told me proudly that her daughter was about to turn sixteen.

In the beginning when Linda had shown me her yearbook, I had the distinct impression that she was already sixteen. I'm not sure how I had gotten that idea, and I suppose it wasn't all that important. But at sixteen, when you're constantly trying to convince yourself that you're grown up, every year is important. Not that it would have made any difference. Even if I had known from the start that she was only fifteen, it wouldn't have changed anything, I was too quickly smitten.

My real concern now was how to find the perfect gift in less than two weeks.

This was not a problem that I thought I could solve by myself, and I wasn't too proud to admit that I needed help. My sister Margie would probably have some good ideas and it might even be necessary to get my dad to help.

Money—where would I find the money I needed to buy this thing? If I wanted to get a nice gift, something posh and elegant, it was going to take a lot more than my weekly allowance. There was always my stash—my emergency fund—twenty-four well-worn dollar bills rolled up in a rubber band, plus three more in quarters and eighty-nine cents in smaller change. All stuffed in a tobacco tin and buried in the corner of my footlocker. I suppose today that doesn't seem like much, but in 1957 it wasn't too shabby. It wouldn't buy a diamond tiara, but if I were careful about my choice I could buy something pretty nifty.

I know, the money was supposed to be for an emergency, but this *was* an emergency! I mean I couldn't let a special occasion like this pass without giving Linda a present. And if I intended to give her something extraordinary, just dipping into the fund wasn't good enough. I wanted to be able to use it all, and more, even if that meant talking my dad into a loan.

The next day I had an opportunity to speak to Margie. She knew that Linda and I were an item, and after I explained what I was looking for, she said she would give it some thought and get back to me. She kept her word and the following afternoon she came to me with a small list of things that she thought Linda might approve of. Margie suggested that short of giving her an engagement ring, the gift should be romantic and personal. She made it clear that jewelry was always appropriate. So the first item on her list appealed to me immediately. It was a little gold charm in the shape of a heart. She advised me to have it mounted on a gold chain, so that Linda could wear it around her neck. She also suggested that having it engraved would give it just the right personal touch.

When I expressed my opinion and told Margie how much I liked the idea, I also asked her advice about where to get something like that. She proceeded to pull a folded newspaper ad. from her pocket. Opening it and handing it to me, I recognized an advertisement for a jewelry store on Newbury Street in Boston. They were having a sale on gold charms. The illustration at the head of the page included several items, one of which was a small cutout in the shape of a heart. All were fourteen-karat gold and included free engraving. With ten percent off, the heart was only $12.95, well within my budget. But I couldn't be sure how much more the gold chain would add to the cost. Margie couldn't help me with the chain, but since the store was offering free engraving, she suggested that I have L & M cut into the face of the heart, to represent Linda and Michael. Honestly, sometimes having an older sister had its advantages. Without her help, I don't think I would have come up with anything half so good. It was all the things that Margie said it should be: romantic, personal, and with the added engraving it seemed wonderfully intimate. I was already filled with anticipation, wondering what Linda's reaction would be.

But, I was getting ahead of myself. I knew what I wanted; I just hadn't figured out yet how I was going to get it. Should I go in by train, take a bus, locate a friend with a car? What do I do? There *was* no bus, the train was in North Scituate, too far away even on a bike, and I didn't have a friend who owned a car. In the beginning it all seemed rather hopeless, but after some painful consideration a simple and obvious solution presented itself. Dad worked in Boston. He was there all week, from Monday through Friday. It would be relatively easy for him to get over to Newbury Street. He could take the subway if needed, and then when he came back on the train Friday evening . . .

Of course it would be close, the party was scheduled for Sunday afternoon, but it was definitely a workable plan. There was only one obstacle in the way: would my father go along with the idea? Would he sacrifice his lunch hour for the sake of his lovesick son?

****

Friday, when Mom left to pick up Dad at the train station in North Scituate, I wanted desperately to go along. Instead, I waited impatiently at home. With Mom in the car, I knew I wouldn't really have an opportunity to talk to him. I had every reason to expect that she would listen to our conversation and I felt awkward enough about explaining this to Dad, without risking comments or questions from my mother. Besides, I understood that the ride home from the station was their catch-up time.

Mom didn't like him being away in the city all week, but both had agreed that commuting was too tiring. For that reason they lived with the five-day separations, so the rest of the family could enjoy the summer here at Ocean Bluff. On weekends they did their best to make up for his absence. Personally, I thought for 'old folks' they were much too affectionate. Certainly much more cozy and cuddly than any of the other parents I knew. All that kissing and hugging was embarrassing. It seemed to me that there could have been a lot less smooching around us kids, especially when we had our friends over.

At the time Mom seemed old. But I suppose, when I look back, she was still quite attractive. Her hair, which was very black, came from my grandmother, who was half Cherokee. If I had taken the time to look I might have seen that she had a decent figure. On those occasions when she dressed up she looked pretty sharp, but mostly when I saw her she wore a shapeless house dress that buttoned up the front and that always seemed to be decorated with faded flowers.

There *was* something exceptional in the relationship between her and my father and it wasn't just the way they kissed. Sometimes I noticed how she put her hand over his while they sat next to each other at the supper table. It was only for a moment as she spoke with him, but I sensed some special meaning in it. And whenever my father came into the room, she always presented an enigmatic smile. My father's reaction made me wonder what secret signal was being passed between them. Otherwise her expression was sober and her soft gray eyes sometimes were filled with a terrible sadness—probably from the loss of Elizabeth.

She never talked about her, even when I asked. Most of what I knew came from Margie. She told me that Beth was Mom's first child, born three years ahead of her. But Beth had died just a few days before her second birthday. There were no pictures; at least there were none on display. It was a subject that was carefully avoided and Margie had very little information; only that Elizabeth was blue-eyed and chubby, and perfectly healthy until the fever. What fever and what brought it on she didn't say, only that it was sudden and that it was over in a couple of days. Margie said that mom could never quite hang it up—that she just couldn't understand why Beth had been taken that way. One morning, walking into her bedroom unexpectedly, Margie'd found Mom crying. And even I had caught her occasionally wiping away tears for no apparent reason. Somewhere in Quincy there was a small grave. Mom and Dad would visit every year around the end of May; but except for Margie, who went with them once when she was twelve, none of us were ever invited to go along.

****

My time with Dad was generally after supper. He liked to discuss his week, but most of all, he said that he wanted to hear about what I had been doing. Lately those talks were a lot shorter than usual, because I wasn't comfortable sharing all the details, now that Linda had become such a large part of my weekly experiences. Not that he didn't know about Linda, I just didn't tell him everything.

It was hard to wait until after supper. I was in an awful hurry to explain my plan to him, and hopefully win his quick approval. My inclination was to jump on him the moment he came through the back door; but I knew the rules: no personal stuff before supper. Only light conversation was allowed at the table. Dad wanted a chance to relax, to sit and eat, before he had to take on the more pressing problems of home and family. Car troubles or broken plumbing or the time Timmy climbed out Margie's bedroom window and jumped off the bathroom roof, or the day I shot the neighbor's cat with Tooey's BB gun—these and a host of other disruptions could best be dealt with later, after the meal and after he had read the evening paper.

When Dad left the train and slid into the front seat to come home with Mom, he set aside the part he played as breadwinner and became a caring husband. That was a title that he carried easily, because he loved my mom so much. But here at home, having to fix the dull stuff connected with running the household and trying to resolve some of the headaches that we created, just by being kids, wasn't always pleasant. He loved us too, but handling our problems wasn't nearly as exciting as being a lover and companion to my mother. Besides, she had come into his life first, and she would be with him for many years after we had gone out on our own. I understood that, and I respected the basic soundness of these rules, but tonight it was terribly hard to follow them. I suppose the situation wasn't a matter of life and death, but in my mind it certainly possessed that kind of urgency.

When we finished eating and the dishes were cleared away, Dad finally gave the signal that it was time for our weekly interview. This was the *children's hour*, an hour or more as needed, dedicated exclusively to the essential requirements of each child, starting with the oldest son, then Margie, and lastly my little brother Timmy. It was a time when we had our father's undivided attention. For that hour or so, each of us knew that he or she was the most important person in his life. Actually, it was rather neat and it made us feel special.

We went out onto the front porch alone and Dad settled into a wooden rocker that had become his favorite. I sat across from him on a metal and canvas campstool, and before he could begin, I jumped in with youthful exuberance and made my appeal.

"Dad, I need your help. In fact, you're my only hope," I pleaded.

"Michael, you make this sound pretty grim. What's your problem, and what can I do to help?"

"You know Linda Richards," I said. "She and I—well—I mean, we've been seeing a lot of each other this summer and—you know—that is, we're more than just friends." The canvas complained a little as I twisted and rocked the stool.

"Look Mike, I understand that you're uncomfortable about this, but you shouldn't be. I've met Linda a few times, I don't know her very well, but she seems to be a nice girl. She's attractive enough and I'm aware that you've spent a lot of time together this summer. You haven't told me very much, but I still get reports from your mother and sometimes Margie tells me things."

Somehow hearing this wasn't particularly reassuring. Not that I had anything to hide, but this was pretty personal stuff, and who knew what his mother and Margie were telling him?

"You know, you're not the first person to fall in love. I've been there myself. You may have noticed that your mother and I have some feelings for each other."

"Daaad!" I said sharply, thinking that I didn't need to hear this.

"Of course kids don't want to imagine that their parents are—shall we say—romantic."

"Daaad!" I said again getting more and more uncomfortable with the direction this was taking.

"Or that there was ever a time that they used to be—romantic. I met your mother when I was eighteen. Did you know that?"

"No."

"So you see, I know about these things—about your feelings for Linda that is. In fact I think it's—what do they call it these days?"

"Cool!" I suggested, fidgeting again on my stool and nearly knocking it off its legs.

"Right. Now, what's so important and what does this have to do with Linda?"

"Her birthday is coming up on the tenth and I want to buy her a gift." There it was, straightforward and to the point.

"I don't see any problem with that. What is it that you need from me?"

"Let me show you. Margie dug this out of the newspaper," I said, as I handed him the clipping. "It's for a jewelry store on Newbury Street and they have just the kind of thing that I'm looking for. See this heart-shaped charm here?" I continued, as I pointed at the artist's rendition. "I want it mounted on a gold chain for her to wear around her neck. And since the engraving is a freebee, I want that too."

"That looks kind of expensive, Michael. Where is the money coming from?"

"It's my money, Dad! I have some put aside."

"If it's your money, you can do whatever you like. But you still haven't told me how I figure into all this."

"I haven't been able to come up with any way for me to get into Boston—to Leavett's, so that I can buy this thing. And I thought—you're in the city all week anyway. Maybe you could pick it up for me. I mean, I'll give you the money—and then you can bring the necklace back with you on Friday," I added, straining to see if I could read the answer in his troubled expression.

"It sounds simple enough, but there's a major flaw in your plan, Michael. I'm at work in my office during the same hours that Leavitt's is open. That means the only hope I have of doing this is on my lunch break, and that's cutting it pretty close. Even if I use the subway, I might not be able to finish your errand and get back to the office without being late."

"Does that mean you can't help me?" I asked, beginning to feel panicky.

"No, Michael. I'll still do whatever I can. But you need to realize that it's not as easy as you thought. Look, let me take this ad, and if I can't get out of the office, perhaps one of the secretaries can. They sometimes leave the office on other errands and one of them might have a chance to swing over to Newbury Street. I'm sure that they would be more than happy to help Cupid plant his arrow deep into Linda's heart," Dad said, with an impish grin.

"Dad, you wouldn't!"

"You bet I would!" he chuckled. "After all, if the girls in the office are going to make the effort, there ought to be some kind of reward," he added.

In spite of these minor threats to embarrass me in front of the office staff, I was relieved, knowing that my father would make every effort to fulfill his promise. He understood that this was a matter of the heart, and that it would be hurtful to me if he failed. He could be a stern disciplinarian when necessary and not the type to show much affection, physical or otherwise. To his wife perhaps, but not towards his children or others. Yet there was no one kinder, or more caring, if you were honestly in need.

There is a special place, which cannot be described in words. It is an undeclared province in the hidden recesses of the heart, where we seal up the treasured memories of life's experiences shared. Exclusive events spent with those we love: parents, siblings, spouses, or maybe a special friend. Nothing earth-shattering, just the day-to-day things that are often so common that they seem relatively meaningless. And yet we hold them so dear, because they were acted out against a background of love and self-sacrifice.

Through dozens of small indulgences my father had earned the right to a large portion of that space. A candy bar divided between us on a rainy Sunday afternoon. A short drive, just he and I, to the news stand to pick up the evening paper, a hike through the bright fall woods. A few quiet hours fishing out at Speckled Lake, a simple word of praise spoken at an opportune moment. He and I standing outside on a cold winter's night staring up at the stars, not a word passing between us. The cumulative effect of all this and dozens of other like experiences was the sure knowledge that he loved me and that I was a person whose companionship he valued. I never heard him say those special words, but he didn't have to.

****

Even with all my confidence in Dad, it was a long slow week waiting impatiently for his return from the city. As further proof of his enduring kindness toward me, and knowing that he had left a troubled son at home, he called from his mother's apartment in Dorchester on Wednesday evening.

"Put your mind at rest," he said. "The deed is done, the present is in my hands. They even put it in a little velvet box. It's a pretty sight to behold all polished up and sparkling in the light here by the phone. Linda will certainly appreciate it. Debbie, my secretary, went to the jewelers' for me and loved doing it. You owe her a thank-you note, and I'll expect you to have one ready when I get back on Friday."

"Thanks Dad, I knew I could count on you."

****

Linda still had no knowledge of the party coming up on Sunday. I had to watch what I said so as not to give any hint of what her mother had planned. There were a few secretive exchanges with Mrs. Richards; words that passed between us in a whisper during my comings and goings to pick up Linda.

Things got really awkward on Thursday evening, when Linda brought up the subject herself. "Are you aware that Sunday is my birthday?" she asked. I wasn't sure whether to answer or not, so I didn't say anything. "Well it is," she said emphatically, "and I think we ought to find something to do together to celebrate."

"I—I can't. I have other plans for Sunday afternoon."

"Did I say anything about the afternoon?" she asked.

"No. But—but, I'm busy in the evening too," I stuttered, trying to cover my tracks

"Something with the family?"

"Actually, it's probably more important than just family." I answered truthfully.

"What do you mean? What's more important than family?"

Now I'd done it. I didn't know how to answer that. "Well, you know," I stumbled.

"No, I don't."

"I've got to go—to—Dorchester—to my grandmother's," I lied.
"But that's family, isn't it?"

"Yes, I suppose." I was in deep poop now. I never could lie, even when I thought I had a good reason. "Linda, I—I can't explain this—at least not now. I'll tell you all about it later. Okay?"

"Grrrrrrr," she growled. "I won't forget this, Michael. And when the time comes, you'd better have a good story."

Linda's mother had invited me to her party, but because Linda and I had been so exclusive all summer, she didn't have any other friends in Ocean Bluff. So I knew that the rest of the guests would be strangers to me. Her friends from Stoughton and her cousins and grandparents would be coming. All people I had never met and it made me feel uneasy. Going to parties, birthday or otherwise, was not something that I did very often. Social affairs, even among friends, made me very uncomfortable, and here I would definitely be an outsider. Nevertheless, this was an important event in Linda's life. A ritual celebration designed to mark the passage from pigtails and pimples to young lady, and I was determined to make the best of it.

I knew that she would want me to be there, but obviously for my own selfish reasons, I didn't want to have to share her with anyone else. I had to convince myself that this was all being done for a noble cause and that I could overcome my fear, face a roomful of strangers, and not commit some ridiculous faux pas that would turn me into a social outcast. Again, I was being overly dramatic, but somehow it was helpful.

When Dad handed me Linda's present on Friday evening, I was surprised to find that he had included some embossed white wrapping paper and a small card. He told me that he knew I would want to see the necklace first so he had left it unwrapped. I gave him a quick hug and thanked him profusely. Judging by the look on his face, I think the hug caught him off guard. Then I hurried off to my room to look at what all this effort and sacrifice had bought.

Sliding the box out of the bag, I opened the top slowly, and lifted the necklace out. The late evening sun coming through the window from across the hall struck the polished gold and I watched the bright reflections flash against the walls as the heart spun freely from the end of the chain. The gift was a costly one, more than twenty-two dollars including the chain, the wrapping and the tax, but it represented much more than money. It might just as well have been my real heart, all polished up ready for Linda to cherish or cast aside as the spirit moved her. I suppose that I was being too sensitive, but at that particular moment I felt incredibly vulnerable. Giving Linda my heart, my real one or a golden one, somehow seemed fraught with risk. Not that I wasn't sure of my love for her, nor that I hadn't had splendid assurances of her love for me, but what if she didn't want this; what if she thought it was too personal? I suppose it was all just a part of the insanity of being young and in love, but suddenly I was full of uncertainty.

"P-shaaaw!" I said, aloud, disgusted with myself for being so weak-minded. Carefully wrapping the gift, I signed the card and put them both safely away in my footlocker.

****

Early Sunday morning as soon as I was out of bed I removed the package from its hiding place. Later, I took a cold shower and dressed in my best clothes, which were not notable, but they were clean and well-pressed. Leaving with my family for church, I knew that I would have a terrible hour trying to concentrate on the sermon. In fact I didn't hear a word, and was more than a little embarrassed about it afterwards when I shook hands with the minister and he asked for my opinion. I knew that Linda was in church too, though she was Catholic and had gone to a late Mass at St. Mary's in Satuit. Maybe I would have done better if I had gone with her and her family instead. But with her sitting beside me I probably wouldn't have heard the priest any better than I had the minister.

I arrived a little late to the party, at least by the clock, but Linda was late too. Her father had taken her out just after dinner to keep her busy while the others set up and decorated. When she finally came in I participated in the shouting and excited exchanges, as they all yelled *Surprise!* and *Happy Birthday!* Linda certainly acted the part of being surprised and she did it well, but I had my doubts.

Walking into the dining room, I saw that a card table had been set up, and all the gifts were piled on top. Heading toward the table, I stopped to reconsider. I decided I couldn't put this miniature package with the others. Quickly, I slid it back into my baggy trouser pocket. I hadn't thought this through, but suddenly I knew that my gift was symbolic of something far too private to share with all these strangers. When the presents were handed out, Linda no doubt would wonder. But whatever her thoughts might be, surely she would repent of them later when she realized why I had waited. There had to be a quiet time when we would be alone long enough for me to make a proper presentation.

The party progressed from greetings to introductions, to ice cream and cake; then on to opening gifts and some simple party games. When the games started, the adults separated. They wandered into the kitchen for coffee and conversation, and left the young people to fend for themselves. At first, the kids broke off into established camps, based on familial ties or friendships. They huddled together chattering away like a bunch of hens trying to fix the pecking order; then separated into small protective groups based on class and social pretense. Since I was a foreigner here, having no rightful claim to any of these groups, I found myself standing alone. Feeling unusually conspicuous, I looked for a secluded corner where I could hide.

Both friends and relatives, individually or collectively, asked Linda questions and talked of past experiences and generally made her feel the center of attention.

Finally, someone started the phonograph and people began to dance. Here was a chance, however brief, to have Linda to myself. When I approached she kicked off her shoes and taking my hand hauled me eagerly to the center of the room. Once I had my arms around her, I held her close. Feeling the soft touch of her cheek pressed to mine, I closed my eyes and shut out everything except her warm presence. Perhaps that made us conspicuous to the other partygoers and there may have been a buzz in the room as unguarded comments were passed from one to another. But Linda and I didn't notice. She whispered in my ear, "I'm sorry Michael. The party's great, but I wish they'd all go away so that we could be alone."

"Don't worry about it, I'm fine," I said. "Besides, this is your big moment, enjoy it."

Soon her cousin was tapping on my shoulder and I had to give her up. Then others came and made repeated demands upon her time. There were no private moments, no opportunities to present the tiny treasure that rested cozily at the bottom of my pocket.

The evening wore on and I became impatient and bored, but smiled bravely whenever Linda looked my way. It was apparent from whispered comments, which were exchanged between us as she passed by, that she was growing tired of all the attention and was more anxious than ever for the party to come to an end. A little after eight-thirty the adults began to hint that it was time to go and shortly they came to gather up their children. Going outside, they began to move in the general direction of their cars. The good-byes among the adults were prolonged and it was well past nine before all the guests had gone home.

At last Linda and I were alone sitting together on the darkened front porch while her parents were busy inside clearing away the debris left behind by the slatternly partygoers.

At first the sudden quiet brought a marvelous sense of relief. Side by side on a wicker love seat with the soft light spilling over our shoulders through the living room windows, the wonderful peace that surrounded us was almost palpable. The silence didn't last long, but neither did it shift back to the strident cacophony of the party that had blasted through most of the afternoon and evening. Instead, Linda disturbed the stillness by asking firmly, "Okay, Michael, what's up? You don't expect me to believe that you came here empty-handed. I mean, no gift—not even a card?"

"Hold your horses!" I said as I reached into my pocket. "When you've seen what's in here, you'll understand that I couldn't give this to you in front of the others."

As I offered her the package I could see that the pretty wrapping was crumpled from being in my pocket. But when Linda took it from me her face showed no sign of disappointment. All I saw was a wonderful smile of anticipation as she cradled it in her hands. I'm sure that by the size and feel that she already knew it must be jewelry, but she didn't say so. Instead she removed the small card and read the neatly printed message. I hadn't written anything profound. Just: *Happy Birthday, Love Michael.*

Carefully she untied the narrow satin ribbon and loosened the tape that held the paper in place. Her actions were restrained, as if she wanted to savor the moment, but she seemed too excited by the prospect of what might be inside. Suddenly the conflict became too much, and she hurriedly tore away the wrapping, freeing the furry box inside. She held it delicately, as if it were fragile, and gently lifted the lid. Pulling at the chain, she freed the golden heart and held it up in the fuzzy light that was coming through the living–room window. As the charm swayed in her unsteady hand the light glittered and bounced across her nose and cheeks, and her eyes widened with delight.

"Oh, Michael!" was all she could manage to say, but the passion in her voice said much more than any fancy speech. She fumbled with the box, trying to set it down on the wicker table in front of her without taking her eyes off the heart. Then she noticed the engraving, and turning towards me, asked what the letters meant.

"Michael, what's this?"

"It was Margie's idea." I said, honestly. "The L. is for Linda and the M. for Michael."

"I never thought . . . I never dreamed. Oh Michael, it's lovely!"

"I hope this will be a keepsake, to remind you of our summer together," I said.

"Michael, I really don't know what to say. No one has ever

done anything like this for me before. I won't ever forget. I won't forget this summer or us . . . or this," she said, holding up my gift. "It's, it's—oh Michael!" she said, breathless in her enthusiasm. Then, as an afterthought, "I only wish I had something to give you."

Dropping the necklace into her lap, she began to tug at a small silver friendship ring that refused to go over the knuckle of her little finger. Finally it slipped free and she nearly dropped it. "It isn't much and it certainly won't fit, but . . ." She didn't finish, instead she pressed the ring into the palm of my hand and closed my fingers over it.

No girl had ever given me a gift before and it was obvious that this silver band was meant to be a special symbol of Linda's love for me. Pulling out my wallet, I tucked the ring into the corner and put it back in my pocket.

"Michael," she said thoughtfully, "there is one thing . . ." She paused and I heard her cough as if she had something stuck in her throat. "The summer is nearly over and when it ends you'll go away—and I'll go away. Then what? What will become of us?"

"I don't know—I wish I did," I said, feeling a knotty constriction that made me feel like coughing too. "I want to believe that everything will work out. That no matter what the distance between us, we'll still find some way to be together."

"So do I!" Linda said, tugging absently at my shirt collar the way my mother did when she thought it looked crooked.

"But I really don't think it's going to work out that way."

"That's not what I wanted to hear," she said, pulling harder at my collar as if she were trying to choke out a better answer.

"I don't want this to end. Somehow there has to be a way for us to be together. I just haven't been able to figure out how."

"You make it sound so hopeless," she said, biting one of her nails.

"I'd do anything to make it otherwise," I said.

"Can't you kiss it and make it better?" she asked with an exaggerated frown on her face.

Her frown made me smile and I gladly threw my arms around her. I knew she was begging for comfort, but I didn't have any to give. Kissing her gently, I enjoyed the cool wetness of her lips. I don't know if my kiss did any good, but as often happened her mood shifted, and she turned her back and pleaded for help with the tiny clasp on her necklace. After searching in the folds of her skirt, she had picked it up again and was trying to fasten it around her neck. "Michael, can you help me put this on?" Reaching up, I soon had the catch locked in place. She looked down to see the shiny metal resting neatly between her small breasts. "Now your heart is next to mine," she said.

The tone of her voice when she made this pronouncement implied that she wasn't just talking about that cold metal cutout. I couldn't help feeling that she wanted to put my real heart next to hers. And if she had, she would have felt it pounding very hard.

"Thanks," she whispered, as she turned to touch my face. Then she dragged her finger along the edge of my lower lip and held it there. At that moment I was so happy it hurt.

"Let's get out of here," she said. "Let's go down to the beach."

We cast off our shoes and set them side-by-side under the loveseat. Then, descending the porch stairs and following a natural pathway through the tall saw grass, we headed towards the water. When we stepped out onto the long sloping shore we came upon a dinghy that someone had left moored high up on the beach. It should have been turned bottom up, but instead it stood with its keel firmly planted in the sand. The boat was white with a heavy rope bumper tacked along the edge of the gunwale, and the stern board, which faced the sea, had the name "FOUR WINDS" painted on it. It was a pretty little craft: the interior was highly varnished, and the dark mahogany trim contrasted sharply against the lighter natural oak frame.

We decided to sit inside. Stepping in just ahead of the center seat, we dropped down onto the slatted bottom and rested our backs on the starboard gunwale. Curled up together, arm in arm, we found ourselves in a cozy little world, under a star–brightened sky—a perfectly lovely romantic setting, in which to spend a few private moments.

I nibbled playfully on Linda's ear and brushed my cheek roughly against hers. Then turning, I embraced her, and kissed her. Encouraged, she returned my kiss with hungry expectation.

****

In the beginning our kissing had been occasional and brief. A natural shyness kept us from going too far. But soon a sweet familiarity led us to more feverish encounters that became more reckless and dangerous. And what had once been uncomfortable stirrings in private places had now blossomed and expanded into a disturbing level of sexual potency. Still, these rising passions were not unbounded. When these fires began to burn too hot, something always pulled us back. There seemed to be a kind of unspoken understanding between us of what was acceptable.

Nevertheless those boundaries were getting a little shaky. It was like an old bumper jack that inched up a notch every time you pumped the handle—the higher you got the more it wobbled and threatened to fall.

Because of our sense of commitment to each other, and with it an increasing level of trust, sexual experimentation became more compelling and less frightening. One of those experiments involved slipping my hand under the hem of her T–shirt or blouse to caress her bare back. Usually I would creep slowly upward until I had moved far enough to touch the little hooks that held her bra in place. Though I would never have had the audacity to undo them, the possibility was an exciting one.

****

Tonight I kept going higher and higher until I realized there was nothing there! "What's this?" I asked.

"What's what? She answered, coyly.

"Shouldn't there be something here?" I said, thrumming my fingers on the spot between her shoulder blades.

"Not necessarily." She smiled, and something about that smile shook me. With ungracious suddenness I dropped my hand. I didn't entirely withdraw it—that would have been rude, but I did bring it shakily to her waist.

"What's the matter?" she asked.

"Oh, nothing."

"Does that make you nervous?"

"Nope!" I said, but the high pitch of my voice was a little too clipped and unnatural.

There had been times while laying together on the beach that Linda would rub my bare stomach, and since my swim–trunks were always a little droopy she generally took the opportunity to poke her finger into my navel. Then she would stir it around playfully, which was often very ticklish.

This evening, nestled together in the bottom of the boat, she began to tug on my belt. Popping the catch, she slid the tongue through the buckle and then she started pulling on my shirttail, freeing one side and then the other. I thought she wanted to rub my stomach again; but once I was undone she pressed the palm of her hand hard against my soft abdomen and drove the ends of her fingers under the waistband of my undershorts. She didn't probe deeply enough to get into trouble, but I was already erect so she wouldn't have had to go very far. The muscles across my stomach contracted sharply (snapping taut as a drum), and every nerve was supercharged; one wrong move and I would surely cream my shorts. I didn't say anything, but the stillness and the tension must have been a clear signal that I was in distress. If she had moved even a half-inch further down, I was prepared to grab her wrist and leap out of the boat, which probably would have been a gross overreaction.

At first nothing happened, and I sucked in my breath in anticipation. Then slowly she removed her fingers and gently walked them upward, until they came to rest lightly against my ribs, just below my breast. I let out a low, wheezing sigh and wondered what she had intended. Was she just testing, and had my tense silence frightened her away? Whatever her purpose, I was immensely relieved that she had retreated.

We both tried these experiments. But, no matter how tempting it was to keep going we always withdrew to safer ground. Whether it was common sense or conscience that restricted our tentative efforts to explore such forbidden territory I couldn't tell, but up to now we had only been willing to sneak up on these things. Lately however, it was becoming more and more difficult to keep from crossing the line.

Tonight Linda had come a little closer than usual, which was a bit scary. But in spite of my misgivings I wasn't upset. In a way it was rather daring, which is what made this whole business seem so terribly wicked. It was like poking your arm through the bars of a caged tiger and taunting him—dangerous stuff—but it was all just callow pretense. We never expected to get close enough to actually get bitten.

Linda gave me a mushy kiss and I kissed her in return. Then I released her and fell back to rest my head on the small seat in the bow. In a moment I stretched out my arms, flung my hands loosely over the sides, and stared up at the bright stars. My breathing was heavy and irregular and I pushed hard against the passion raging inside until gradually it softened and diminished and finally I was in control again.

I heard Linda utter a long contented sigh, and glanced over to see an inner warmth radiating from her eyes that was disconcerting. And when I considered that I might be responsible for that special glow, it tickled my heart and lent a special boost to my young ego.

"Just look at those stars!" Linda said.

They were marvelous, and they sparkled with incredible clarity. I usually only saw that kind of sharpness on a cold winter's night, and I certainly didn't feel at all cold tonight.

The sweet mischief of the last few minutes had acted as a kind of panacea, and the problem of our future, though not entirely forgotten, no longer seemed quite so immediate.

CHAPTER 12

EVERY YEAR near the end of August, around the time of my brother's birthday, we would have a cookout on the beach. Even before we started to spend our summers at the cottage we would make the trip to the shore in observance of this unique Jablonski family tradition.

These summer's eve celebrations were family only, but this year I had asked permission to invite Linda. Dad understood that Linda was more than just a friend and after discussing this with Mom, they agreed to make an exception.

We always held these gatherings in the evening after the bathers had collected their gear and gone for the day. Like a battlefield forsaken by the soldiers who had fought there, the beach bore the scars of hundreds of feet, which had left tiny depressions everywhere. Here and there where the sand had been beaten down by a blanket or a giant beach towel, this rough pattern was interrupted by smooth spots, which looked like islands in the midst of a choppy sea. Now this desolate landscape, still hot from the afternoon sun, was all ours.

Though there was some degree of ritual involved in this affair, it was mostly informal. The biggest part was building the fire. And Dad, always mindful of safety, would go to the local fire station for permission, which in those days wasn't any more complicated than a verbal okay and a warning to be careful.

To begin with, we dug a pit in the sand about four feet wide and two feet deep, and then gathered a dozen or more large stones to circle it. Next, we spread out along the dunes looking for pieces of wood and other suitable fuel. Concentrating our search high up on the beach and wandering deep into the dunes, we found the sort of stuff that was likely to have washed ashore during a snowy nor'easter—part of a shipwreck, or a piece broken off some ancient pier—objects that might have been torn away during a tropical gale, and afterwards carried by the tides and currents until they found their way here to our little beach. We collected all this flotsam, large and small, brought it to the pit and stacked it into an imposing pile that stood several feet high. Dad struck a match and put it under the kindling and newspaper he had brought along and soon the flames were leaping skyward.

As the fire grew hotter and brighter it was rather breathtaking. I can't explain it scientifically, but something relative to the wood having soaked long hours in the salty sea and later being dried and bleached by the hot sun caused it to give off incredible colors when it burned. A fire of this size was exciting and my parents and my brother and sister and I sat nearby fascinated by its beauty.

The real festivities wouldn't begin until after seven. We had all come down earlier to build the fire, and while we waited for it to burn down to a more manageable size, Mom and Margie went back to the cottage to collect the food and other sundry items, which had been prepared for our cookout. It was a simple meal: hotdogs and rolls, homemade pickles, chips and soda, and the traditional marshmallows for roasting.

While they were busy with these preparations, I rushed off to find Linda and walk her back to our camp.

By the time Linda and I returned, the flames had dwindled to a respectable level and the family was beginning to settle in. Earlier I had found some relatively straight sticks and trimmed them with my pocketknife. Each of us picked up one of these and used it to skewer a hotdog.

It'd been unusually warm and sticky all day, with temperatures well into the nineties, so everyone had on light clothing. Linda and I had chosen to wear our bathing suits because we were hoping for a cooling swim after the sun went down. The sand was uncomfortably hot under our feet and as much as we wanted to cook our food, the fire was still too high to make that practical. Even though the breeze was light, we couldn't stand on the leeward side. The wind drove the heat and smoke into our faces, and forced us to retreat beyond the reach of our cooking sticks.

Considering the length of the flames, the fierceness of the fire and the number of people trying to get next to it, Linda and I decided it was better to withdraw, at least for the moment. Later, when the fire had burned down and it was less crowded, we'd return to renew our efforts. Taking our cooking sticks, with the hot dogs still in place, we pushed the ends deep into the sand. Then we headed down to the water's edge.

We continued onward until we reached a point where the sand was flat and wet from the falling tide. Here it was squishy and cool underfoot. For a moment we stood there pressing our feet down into the soft yielding surface, feeling the ooze squeeze upward between our toes.

The surf this evening was ineffectual, and lacked the force that we were accustomed to. But now and then a wave rushed up and washed over our feet, leaving tiny ripples in the sand when it pulled away. It was late enough in the season that the ocean water had finally begun to warm up. Usually in June, when you first went into the water, it would strike with a kind of bone-chilling cold that would make your feet ache. Now, in late August, especially after a hot day and with such a moderate sea, the water had a pleasant chill that was wonderfully refreshing.

Our disposition changed now that we had cooled off a bit, and we became playful. Running through the shallow surf, dodging and weaving, we sent water flying in all directions. We took turns chasing each other in a mock game of tag. Knee deep, we had to drag our legs through the water and the effort left us sweetly exhausted and giddy.

From the excitement of the game, and in the orange light of the setting sun, Linda projected a marvelous radiance. She was wearing a new swimsuit with a scooped neck, and there was a narrow, turned-up cuff around the legs, which made them look like short-shorts. A brilliant white, it presented a stunning contrast to her darkly tanned skin. Over the summer her hair had lightened considerably. Naturally thick, she kept it short and trim. And though often tangled by wind and water, it always smelled great, even after swimming in the ocean, when it took on the tangy aroma of dried seaweed and salt.

Now as she danced in front of me, I observed an impish sprite. Unrestrained in body and spirit, she seemed completely at ease, driven only by the innocence of youth, and the cooling indulgence of a lukewarm sea. At first I watched her with envy, and then taking her hand, I joined her. Churning the water into a foamy green soup, I let myself go—and she drew me willingly into her wonderful world of whimsy.

No one was watching us, but even if someone were, it wouldn't have mattered. It should have made a difference, and if I had been my old self it would have. But this summer with Linda had changed me. Whenever I was around her I became infected by her playful spirit, and I was suddenly ready to take chances and cast off convention. Her daring always played off my dull restraint—chipping away at my cowardice until she had converted it into a do-or-die kind of grit.

What was so remarkable about our relationship was the way that we fed off of each other. Like the egret and the hippopotamus, it was almost symbiotic. We came together as if I were the bone and she were the muscle—it was as if she were the other half of my heart. At sixteen I couldn't explain it, and even now it's not entirely clear, but somehow we were better off as a couple than we could ever be as individuals.

After our high-stepping dance in the sea, I picked up some brown wrack along the fringe of the backwash and started to pop the slippery bladders that kept it afloat. Linda tried to do the same, but found the skin too thick. It was all great fun. Oddly, the seaweed made me think of food, and I reminded Linda that if we expected to eat we needed to return to the fire.

Arriving back at the pit, we saw that the others had already finished eating. Observing the hot coals, I realized the fire had burned down too far for us to cook so I went to scavenge for more wood, and when I found a couple of pieces that had been overlooked on the first round, I returned to add them to the dying embers, and waited for the fire to rise again. Meanwhile, I began rummaging for something that Linda and I could eat right now. There were still chips and I found a couple of sodas soaking in a bucket of cold water.

Soon, we positioned our hotdogs over the growing flames and began to roast them, rotating them back and forth until the skins turned crisp and black. We put them into rolls that had been warmed on the hot stones at the edge of the pit. Then, dressing them out with mustard and relish, ketchup and onions, we devoured them with rabid enthusiasm.

Sitting there facing each other, legs crossed Indian-style, we passed the time with plain talk about our favorite movies, about the fire, about the comedian we had seen on the Ed Sullivan Show Sunday night. Then we started telling jokes and that progressed to vacuous ideas for crazy inventions. Most of what passed between us would have bored anyone else to tears, but we were perfectly happy with this silliness. We even argued about the specific shade of toasty–brown we wanted on our marshmallows. But when we actually started roasting them, we ended up burning them, or setting them on fire.

Surrounded by family, I was barely aware of their existence. All of my attention was directed towards Linda. Not that I didn't hear the sounds of chatter and laughter in the background, but no one seemed to notice us and no one came to interrupt. Perhaps they saw that it was hopeless to try and get our attention. Whatever they thought, they didn't attempt to break down the invisible barrier that we had unwittingly pushed up around us. And our self-imposed isolation didn't appear to dampen their spirits, or take anything away from their own personal enjoyment of the evening.

When it got to be nine o'clock, Dad took the bucket that had held the sodas and dumped the melted ice water over the fire.

Then he went back down to the sea and refilled it. Dowsing the pit a second time, he began kicking sand into the hole, making certain the campsite was secure and that every part of the fire was extinguished. Margie and Timmy helped my parents remove all the gear and food that had been lugged down earlier, and along with a bag of rubbish they cleared away all signs of the evening's festivities. I was only half aware of all this activity, until I noticed a sudden quiet.

All this time there had been a steady competition of sound and movement swirling around us and now everything was still. It was then that I looked up and saw that we were alone, sitting next to a cold fire, watching, as the last remnants of smoke slowly drifted away. Recognizing that the celebration was over, but reluctant to let the evening come to an end, we left the blackened fire–pit and began wandering north under the long shadow of the sea–wall.

After leaving the cottages and the wall behind we looked up to see that we were only a hundred yards or so from the Rock. We hadn't come this way all summer, not since the Fourth, and I wasn't sure why we were heading in that direction now. We stopped for a moment, and then without any discussion we altered our track and trudged up the sloping shore towards an aggregation of boulders that sat high up on the beach. They stood next to some twisted scrub pine, and beyond was a long stretch of weeds and brambles that grew all the way back to the road. The tangled saw grass and beach plum were so dense that nothing could get through except an old briar–patch rabbit that hopped back under a thorny bush as we approached. On the other side of the road was a salt marsh, and the only house we could see showed a single light that glowed in the distance like the evening star.

Other than the Rock, this was clearly the most isolated spot on the beach. Seven huge boulders, ranging in height from six to eight feet, stood in a rough circle that looked a lot like a crowded Stonehenge. In front, blocking our way, was a broad bed of broken seashells, polished slate and rounded pebbles. Linda and I skirted this line of debris, and stepping into the pathway between the two largest boulders we stole a quick kiss.

The hour was late and it was especially dark. Only a sliver of moon and a few dull stars illuminated the broad expanse of beach that stretched from our hiding-place to the water's edge. The blackness of the night made it seem cooler, but it was only an illusion. The sticky heat of the day still hung close to the shore, and there was only a sluggish breeze coming in off the ocean, which brought us no relief.

Standing between these pitted, red columns, I looked past Linda to watch the restless combers wash and pull against the wet sand–flats, and it reminded me that we hadn't taken our swim. Unexpectedly, I was possessed by the same brash spirit that had invaded my mind earlier, while Linda and I had played in the foamy backwash. It was a devilish idea, but I was in a reckless mood, and I translated that recklessness into action before I considered the consequences.

"Linda," I said, "let's go skinny-dipping!"

"Michael, are you serious?"

"Yes," I answered, instantly regretting my cheeky impudence.

"Okay—if you're up to it, so am I!"

Boy, you really stepped in it this time, I thought. But what could I do? If I dropped out now, I'd looked like a wimp.

Actually, I was really only half afraid. I would be perfectly fine once I was in the water. There, surrounded by the dark sea and obscured by the dimness of the night, I could bare all. But I wasn't ready to strip here by the rocks and walk all the way down to the water naked, especially in full view of Linda. Even in a bathing suit I wasn't comfortable with what people could see of my body, and what was still covered wasn't any more remarkable. My love for Linda had persuaded me to be bold and this was an exciting idea, but I wasn't sure if I was ready to be *that* bold. I suspected too that Linda wasn't quite as daring as she pretended to be.

"Look, I know it was my idea," I said, "but I feel kind of funny about this. I don't mind swimming—well, you know—naked. It's just that undressing here in front of you is too embarrassing."

"Aaargh," she said with impatience, "don't be a ninny!"

"Hold on, let me finish!" I interrupted, putting my hand up as if I were directing traffic. "I'm not trying to back out. We can still do this—with conditions."

"Conditions?"

"Yes. What if I promise to turn around while you take off your swimsuit and run down to the water? Then you look the other way until I can join you. Later, when we decide it's time to come out, we can reverse the whole thing."

"Michael, I can't figure you out! One minute you're full of adventure and the next . . . or is it me? Maybe you're just afraid to see my bony butt."

"No—well, yes in a way."

"So you think I'm too skinny then."

"No, that's not it at all. I've always thought that your figure was," I paused, searching for the right word, "well—bewitching!"

"Do you mean that?" she said.

"Yes, of course."

"It sounds a little odd," she speculated, "but—I like it."

"Believe me, you look great! The problem isn't you, it's me."

I couldn't think of anything more exciting, or more desirable, than seeing Linda naked. Which is exactly why I couldn't bring myself to encourage her. If she were to undress in front of me, and I did the same, I knew my body would react to the sight of hers, and that would be *terribly* embarrassing. Even the idea was enough to start a timid swelling, which was not unpleasant, but *was* unwanted. It only made me painfully aware that there were some things I couldn't control, and I wasn't about to allow Linda to be a witness to anything that personal.

"What's so wrong about being naked?" Linda asked ingenuously. "I certainly believe in modesty, but I wonder sometimes why we are ashamed of our own bodies."

"I don't think that I'm ashamed of my body," I said defensively. Although I suppose I really was ashamed. "But I've always been taught that it's wrong to expose certain parts of it." And right now, considering the continued expansion of what Tooey liked to call his third leg (because it was long and skinny like the rest of him), those teachings made pretty good sense.

"That's what I'm getting at. Why is it so bad for me to see your bare butt or for you to see my bubbies? Are we supposed to think that part of our body is ugly or evil? I find that hard to believe, and I don't think that's what God intended. I don't want to upset you, Michael, but I've *seen* it all."

"What do you mean?" I asked, wondering what—or whom— she had seen.

"I often baby-sit my four-year-old cousin, Joshua. He doesn't like clothes very much and he's a whiz at stripping them off. Usually I end up chasing him around, trying to get him to at least wear his underpants. And then of course there's my little brother who went through the same thing when he was four and I was eight. Besides—there *are* anatomy books, and not all statues have fig leaves. I've seen Michelangelo's "David". That fleshy thing isn't very pretty, but it's not all that frightening either. As a matter of fact, when I was twelve, a boy my age told me he had a name for it: he called it 'Freddy'. Then he went on about having a *chubby* or a *chunky*—something like that. I asked him what that was, and when he tried to explain, I started to laugh. He got *sooo* mad, but when I tried to picture what he was saying, it really broke me up."

"Jheez—I mean—that is so gross! Why would he—you just don't tell girls stuff like that."

"What's the big secret?" she interrupted. "I can't see how knowing about this chubby business is going to hurt me, can you?"

"I guess not. I *dooon't* know," I said, feeling as if I were drowning in quicksand.

"Don't you think that our parents are being too protective?"

"Maybe. But it seems to me that our parents have been around longer than we have, so they ought to have a better idea of what's good for us."

"Of course they do, but they can't always be right can they?"

"No, but how do you tell the difference?" I asked.

"I guess we can't," she said submissively.

"So, that means that we have to trust them, at least until we're old enough to figure these things out for ourselves."

"Michael, can we do it?"

"Do what?" I asked in a panic.

"You know—can we still go skinny-dipping—the way you said before?" she asked, looking at me with her head cocked to one side like a bird watching the worm it expects to eat for dinner.

"Yeah! If you want to," I said shuffling the sand with my feet.

"Of course I do; I just thought I might have talked you out of it. Michael—don't get the wrong idea. I mean, I've been taught the same things you have. It's just that once in a while I like to do something—you know—naughty. That doesn't make me a bad person does it?"

"No, I feel the same way—sometimes." I answered truthfully. "Like last night when I stole half a pie from the refrigerator, and snuck out to the front porch to scoff it down. I probably shouldn't have done it, but I can't believe that God's going to send me to hell for it."

"But isn't this a lot more serious?"

"I suppose so, but it doesn't have to be—if we're careful," I added with a sheepish grin.

The long stillness that followed made me nervous. And then when Linda reached out and physically turned me around, I knew what she had been waiting for. It wasn't necessary, in fact it was probably kind of dumb, but I closed my eyes while she slipped out of her swimsuit and made her run down to the water. Shortly, I heard her plaintive voice calling me from the distance. With quick nervous jerks I tugged at the waist of my swim-trunks, pulling from side to side until they were down at my knees, then let them fall. I stepped out with one foot, kicked them off with the other, and raced down the beach feeling a strange freedom of movement, now that there was nothing there to restrain me. As my feet hit the edge of the water and sent the cooling spray upward against my bare skin, I let out a goofy Tarzan howl, then dove in and came up at Linda's side.

And so it was that we got to go skinny-dipping in the cold Atlantic. Swimming with primitive abandon, we savored the slippery luxury of the water as tiny currents eddied and swirled past our naked bodies. We felt wonderfully safe and alive, but there was also a real sense of risk. The sudden possibility that someone might come along the beach in the dark and discover us added a special element of intrigue and excitement to our adventure.

The idea that this was new to us, that we were young and inexperienced, and especially that what we were doing was forbidden, made that night with Linda something unique. Even at that young age I knew it was an experience whose innocence and veracity could never be recaptured.

We kept a suitable amount of space between us and by unspoken agreement there was no touching or kissing. Only occasionally did we expose ourselves, when briefly a portion of bare skin, sometimes pale, sometimes tan, would rise above the surface as we played—jumping, and turning, and diving.

The water was the warmest that we had experienced all summer and we were having such a marvelous time that we hated to bring this to an end. But we understood, warm as it was, the Atlantic could be unforgiving, and that a sudden chilling of the body might lead to hypothermia, although we couldn't identify the problem in those exact technical terms. We simply noticed that our lips had turned blue and we started to shiver. So we made our preparations and left the water the same way that we had come in.

First Linda, and then I, returned again to dress behind the rocks. After the freedom of being naked, our swimsuits felt particularly restrictive; and without a towel to dry ourselves they soon became wet and clingy. But there was nothing that could dampen our spirits. Refreshed and exhausted, we walked slowly along the shore, heading south back toward the cottages. Finally, passing the sea–wall and the jetty, we stopped in front of the dunes near Linda's home. Lingering here for a moment, she kissed me affectionately and thanked me for suggesting this puckish adventure.

"Michael, I'm so glad we did this! For awhile I felt as free a bird—as wild as a child! Maybe that's why Joshua hates to wear his clothes."

"Maybe!" I agreed, as I tried to stifle a giggle that was just itching to get out. Linda giggled in return, only she didn't make any effort to hold it back.

She kissed me again, just a little buss on the cheek, and then turned away. Following the path that led between the dunes, she disappeared into the shadows. I waited until she made her way to the front porch. Once she had mounted the steps, and I could see her standing under the porch light, I waved and shouted goodnight. Satisfied that she was safe, I rushed home to my hot and breezeless room.

Timmy was staying with a friend this evening so I had the room all to myself. Changing into my undershorts, I lay on my bed and stretched out on the rumpled sheets. The entire experience of bathing together in that soft tranquil sea was characterized by such sweet innocence and joy that I could hardly feel any guilt, and as sleep overtook me, I found myself drifting away, floating into a dream world filled with watery scenes of Linda and me, swimming side by side, wearing (as my mother would say), nothing but Goosebumps.

CHAPTER 13

THE NEXT few days were lazy and uneventful. Any time spent with Linda was always splendid, but it was difficult to imagine how we might improve upon our last adventure. We spoke openly, but sparingly, of that evening—enjoying a kind of sweet afterglow that we were anxious to hold onto. What little we did say was honest and direct. Linda admitted that she would never have been brave enough to suggest the idea, but that didn't mean that she hadn't secretly thought about it.

"I've had some first-class fantasies, but they couldn't hold a candle to what we experienced the other night!" Linda confessed.

She said more than once that she was pleased; pleased with me for asking and pleased with herself for having the guts to turn at least one such dream into reality. There was never any hint of regret—from her or me. It would have been blasphemous to suggest it. We had this wonderful secret, something so special and unique that it couldn't be shared with anyone else. Those few minutes were so private, so intimate, so binding, that no one else could appreciate their meaning. This was very serious stuff and we tried to be sophisticated about it. Yet every so often a look or a smile would set us off and we would start to giggle. Then we would make ditzy little movements with our hands, thrusting them forward and dividing the air as if we were swimming in the deep. It was terribly childish, but we couldn't help it.

Currently, the weather was exceptionally hot and humid, and our sole entertainment was restricted to finding ways to stay cool. The humidity sapped our energy and we sought out the shade, and ice–cold drinks, and artificial breezes from an ancient electric fan.

I noticed that Linda wore my golden heart often, only removing it when she was fearful that she might lose it. I caught her frequently fondling the chain and rubbing the heart gently with her fingertips. Perhaps she was checking to see if it still hung freely in the hollow of her breast. Or maybe she just needed to reassure herself that it was as real as my love for her, and hers for me. The idea that she loved me, that she treasured this gift and that I was capable of stirring her passion, was an exciting one. I had never dreamed that I could have that kind of power over anyone, or that they might have a like power over me. It was wonderful, but it also seemed dangerous. What if that power were abused? But I couldn't imagine ever using it against Linda, and I was just as certain that she would never use it against me.

CHAPTER 14

IT WAS Friday. A week had passed since the fire and the cookout, and our late-night swim in the sea, and there had been no relief from the hot, humid weather. Today it was dark and overcast, and rain had been falling off-and-on all morning. Around noon, I went over to Linda's for lunch. Her mother had prepared an assortment of sandwiches. The usual stuff like ham and cheese, and corned beef, and something not so usual called watercress. The bread was sliced into neat little triangles and all the crusts had been cut away. There was potato salad in a clear crystal bowl, some kind of fruit drink served in tall glasses, each with a curly slice of lemon hanging over the rim, and a cut-glass compote with black olives and long green pickle wedges. The food was set out in the dining room with a real tablecloth and linen napkins. To Linda this was casual fare, but to someone like me; someone who was used to paper plates, this was awfully fancy.

At approximately one-thirty, her mother announced that she was leaving. A friend had stopped by and they had decided to go shopping. Because he made a scene and begged to go along, Mrs. Richards took Linda's little brother with them. Poking her head through the dining room doorway she announced that they wouldn't be back till five and she warned us to behave ourselves. Every mother said that, but I wasn't sure why. What did she expect us to do, burn down the house?

Now that we were alone, we decided to go into the den and play some cards. The air was hot and muggy, and a gray rainy mist hung about the house like a shroud, adding to the general feeling of listlessness. We soon became bored with playing cards and determined that we might find some small relief by sitting at the bay window in the upstairs hall. The rain had stopped for the moment, so we opened the windows wide and were pleased to find that a refreshing breeze was coming in off the Atlantic.

Sitting on a fitted cushion that covered the entire window-seat, we took up positions on opposite sides of the bay, and surrounded by pillows, we lay back lazily against the frame. Closing our eyes, we could taste the fresh smell of the ocean. Nothing was said. We just relaxed, quietly listening to the wind and the surf crashing roughly along the shore. After awhile, Linda got up and went into her room. Returning with a handful of books, she set them down between us and we began to read.

"Michael, look at this!" she exclaimed.

Leaning across the cushion, she offered me the book that she had been reading. She was wearing a short, white, loose–fitting top with a scooped neck. It was unrestrained at the waist and short enough to reveal portions of her abdomen whenever she moved or stretched her arms. As she bent forward, bracing herself with one hand against the cushion between us, the expansive top fell away, exposing her budding breasts. I was able to look into the neck and see out the other side. She had no bra! I knew that sometimes she didn't wear one, but knowing it and seeing it were two different things.

She was directly in front of me, which gave me a clear unobstructed view. It was impossible for me not to see every detail. And though I was embarrassed for her, I still found myself staring fixedly at her two small breasts. Pale white, with nutty–brown nipples—her bubbies (as she affectionately called them) hung soft and glorious from her skinny frame. And suspended between, on a delicate chain, was the small golden heart that I had given to her. I saw all this in an instant, yet even after all these years that image is just as sharp and just as sweet.

Linda looked at me looking at her, and recognizing her predicament brought her hand, book and all, towards her gapping neckline. Pressing the errant top against her body, she uttered a tiny gasp. Now feeling suddenly ashamed, I begged, "Linda, please forgive me. I didn't mean . . . I didn't expect . . ."

She placed her fingers delicately over my mouth in an effort to silence me. "Stop!" she said. "It's not really your fault."

Then, even though she was obviously embarrassed, I heard the high tinkling sound of her laughter. "If you could only have seen the bug-eyed expression on your face just now!"

"Awwww," I said with a meaningful sigh, "what am I supposed to do with you? You ought to be mad as hell and instead . . . How can you be so forgiving?"

"Well-l-l- " she said, "it *was* my fault. I'm the one who decided not to wear a bra, and I did get careless. But—you could have looked the other way. And admit it, Michael, your eyes were just about glued to my bubbies," she said waggling her finger first at me and then at her breasts.

"I know," I said, looking downcast.

"On the other hand, I suppose I ought to be flattered," she said, her smile full of promise. "I'm not Marilyn Monroe or some pinup girl but . . ."

"No, no, you were wonderful! That is, er—they were fine."

"I guess I would have been disappointed if you weren't interested, and you were obviously interested."

"Yeeeah," I answered, slurring the word and pulling at my fingers like some kind of 'Bashful Sam'. Indeed, I'd been totally captivated by the sight of her *bubbies*, but her frankness made my face run hot. While I sat there like a needless bump on a log, Linda was already putting this behind her. She gave me a stab in the chest with her finger that pushed me back against the cushions.

"Hey?" I said.

"Hey yourself," she answered and started to tickle me.

In an effort to escape, I slid off the cushion and onto the floor, pulling a couple of loose pillows down with me. Linda followed, landing on top of me, her face so close to mine that I could reach up and bite her nose. In fact I did give it a friendly nibble, which made her laugh, and I could feel her warm breath swirl across my face with the softness of a feather.

"Are you that hungry?" she said. And a giddy rasp in her voice made me shiver with delight.

"Yes." I said. "I'm starving!"

"I'm not something to munch on, you know."

"I'm not looking for food, I'm hungry for your kisses," I growled.

"Oh, really?" Her impish grin put tiny dimples in her cheeks and made it clear she was enjoying this silly banter.

Then, spilling her breath in a long low sigh that was filled with erotic meaning, she proceeded to kiss me affectionately. She began by gently pressing her mouth to each of my bushy brows. Then with my eyes closed and smiling at the magnificent tenderness of her touch, I felt her lips brush lightly against each lid. Continuing, she moved along the ridge of my nose, delicately dragging the fleshy edge of her lips until she came to the end. Stopping, she surrounded the tip of my nose with their soft fullness; tightening her mouth playfully and nibbling in mock hunger, she pretended to bite it. Finally dropping down, mouth open, she encircled my lips. Then she began pulling away and returning in a sucking manner that was wonderfully provocative and brutally stimulating. But it was such a tender and affectionate performance that I could hardly disapprove or object.

Impulsively I embraced her, pressing her closer. One hand moved aggressively to the nape of her neck, and pinching a short swirl of hair I drew her downward, forcing her lips to engage mine more passionately. In a tangle of arms and legs, we rolled over, ending in an uncomfortable heap on the hall rug. We had changed places and she was beneath me looking up. Breaking away slightly, I gazed deeply into her eyes and saw a glow there that I had never seen before. It was the kind of glassy brightness that comes to someone who is in a high fever.

"Get off!" she said breathlessly. "You're too heavy!"

Releasing her, I fell away, rolling onto my back—grateful for a momentary respite. Every sensitive part of my heart and mind and body had been rubbed raw. Hot blood was coursing through my veins and I felt it pulsating thickly. My breathing had increased and a throbbing at my temples made the edge of my vision seem a little fuzzy. Each time Linda had kissed me, or touched me; or each time I had done like things to her, the level of passion had risen exponentially until it was almost unbearable. One thing built upon another, accumulating in a kind of hard tension that made me feel that I was about to explode.

Rising to her feet, Linda extended both her hands, offering to help me up. I accepted, and as I rose up before her, she refused to let go. Instead, she started dragging me toward her bedroom door. Her face was possessed by the most beguiling smile, and that same glow that I had seen just a moment ago flashed and burned in her eyes. Powerless to resist, I was drawn, with some trepidation but not unwillingly, toward her room.

As we passed through the doorway, Linda freed one hand and quietly closed the door behind us. Leading me to the middle of a half darkened and stifling room, she turned to face me again. Still not speaking, her eyes staring intently into mine, we stood erect in the center of her room. Transfixed by her gaze, I was unable to move. Slowly she withdrew her hands leaving my own hanging in the air. Then, with a quick graceful movement, she unfastened the button at her waist and allowed her shorts to fall loosely about her ankles. She stepped out of them and with a practiced motion kicked the garment aside. With those gone, I looked down to see her dainty white–laced panties. Now, taking hold of the edge of her top, the same brief, loose-fitting top that in some way had precipitated all this, she lifted it effortlessly upward over her head, then let it drop casually to the floor at our feet.

Having done this, the cool whiteness of her young breasts showed starkly against the line of her bronze tan. What moments before I had seen only briefly and quite by accident, were now fully exposed. Fascinated, I took a moment to observe this wonderful manifestation—not just this one part, but all of her. The hot breeze coming in through her bedroom windows disturbed the ends of Linda's hair, pushing a few wispy strands across her cheek to touch the edge of her lips. Their earthy softness was just as natural and just as enticing as that first day when I had been so tempted to kiss them. Looking into her eyes, I saw that the pupils were wide and dark, nearly obscuring their bright color. Her satin skin, wet and shiny with perspiration, glistened in the gray light filtering through the windows.

Drinking in the details of her slender figure, I became intoxicated with its delicate beauty. Her small breasts stood out proud and firm with a fat, nutty-brown circle defining each nipple, and those were hard little buttons that begged to be touched. There was in fact such a powerful impulse to test their hardness that my fingers moved shakily in that direction, but when I was only a hair's-breadth away I stopped. I couldn't do it. Then dropping my hand, I did accidentally brush the pointy end. There was a tiny quiver as I watched the nipple spring back and I felt as though I had committed some terrible sacrilege. But when I looked into Linda's eyes I saw no hint of condemnation. Instead a puckish smile parted her lips and I was forced to grin and look away. I let my eyes drop to a point just beneath the creamy curve of her breasts. Here a small circle of ribs—a gentle ripple of bone and muscle flowed quickly downward, and in the middle was the inky shadow that filled her navel. Her waist was narrow; her hips, girlish and straight, were not fully formed. And from there her long willowy legs stretched downward to her feet. I could see her toes nervously pulling and curling in the deep nap of the rug, and having taken in every part I was afraid of what might come next— of what I might be forced to see next.

Just a single item remained, only her brief white underpants. And if that were to go—well—I mean, I'd never seen a girl naked before. Oh, there had been pictures in magazines, but this was different. Linda was real, she was flesh and blood, and what made it worse, she was someone that I had deep feelings for. Good Lord, I was in love with her!

But that last piece didn't go. Instead, she began to work upon me. Extending her hands, she brought them up under the edge of my T-shirt. She started by pressing her palms tenderly against my stomach, then she slipped her fingers seductively around my waist and traveled upwards along either side of my spine. As the fluid motion of her hands lifted my shirt, the feathery touch of her fingers caused me to shudder, but I still raised my arms and allowed her to bring the garment over my head. Once she had it in her hand, she sent it sailing through the air, and I watched it disappear into the shadowy recesses of the room.

During all this I remained trance-like, conscious of every touch and sensation, but unable to move or resist. Now I was nearly faint, battered by such fearsome desires and aroused to such a fevered pitch of excitement that it was nearly impossible to endure. Although I wasn't completely aware of what was happening to me, Linda's intentions were clear. If she had her way we would both soon be as naked as a jaybird. I felt like I was tottering on the edge of a narrow wall, and whichever way I fell it was bound to be disastrous. There was this nettlesome churning in my gut, telling me that if I did nothing to stop this I would soon be in terrible trouble. I imagined being pushed down into a Kafkaesque world filled with pain and joy, my chaotic emotions plunging me deeper and deeper until all my childhood illusions about love and romance were destroyed. This was so adult that it was beyond my understanding, and it was such an overtly bizarre image that frankly I was frightened.

Things were advancing much too quickly. Linda was now working on my trousers. Having already loosened my belt, she was fumbling with the top button in an attempt to undo me. Soon, I would only have my undershorts to protect me.

Finally, I felt the troublesome button let go and she began pulling cautiously on the zipper below, as if she were afraid of what she might uncover. In another moment I would be standing there in my shorts. Only the thinnest piece of fabric would remain. And if I allowed her to pull those away, exposing that shy member, which was now so grossly enlarged—I would truly be undone.

A cold chill hit me bluntly in the chest, where my warm heart should have been, then plunged heavily to the pit of my stomach, and a tiny voice that up to now had remained silent screamed: *this is wrong!* This was not a lark; not just some giddy escapade carried out on a dark night in a warm sea.

Up to this point I had been swept along by my own inexperience. What Linda expected me to do next would put me into a slippery pink world—a soft downy region, secret and forbidden. A place I had never been before. To put it bluntly, sex was a mystery to me. Frankly, I didn't know *how* to be physically intimate with a girl, and I suspected that Linda was as much in the dark about this as I was.

Apparently she had moved blindly along, trusting that somehow when it came to the important stuff, I would know what to do. And truthfully there was an incredible urge to do whatever it took—whatever was necessary to find relief. Every part of my body was in torture—every nerve rubbed raw—every muscle hard and quivery. But in spite of that urgency I couldn't find a solution. Even if we did stumble through this, if by trial and error we figured out how to make things work—get one part to fit the other— we still weren't ready. And in some curious manner, I sensed that I was on sacred ground; that I was in danger of defiling a kind of private sanctuary that shouldn't be entered.

It wasn't ignorance alone that was frightening me, but the feeling that sex was much too important to be taken casually. Before things progressed this far, there ought to be a greater commitment. A declaration of undying love wasn't enough. According to the standards of my world, we were supposed to be man and wife. At least that was the conventional wisdom, and I wasn't prepared to argue with that wisdom. Even if my body was at odds with those ideals, my mind and spirit were still convinced of their correctness.

I reached for Linda's hand to stop her, but it was too late. My trousers rippled past my hips and descended, bunching up around my ankles. Now I was in the same condition that she was, with only a single piece of clothing left. Taking a step closer, she put her arms around my waist. She wasn't being fair; how was I supposed to keep my resolve under these conditions? We were not pressed together, but near enough for me to feel the pointed firmness of her bare breasts rubbing lightly against my own. Her added height did not put us eye to eye and she needed to lean in to brush her lips along the bridge of my nose. I felt her warm moist breath disturb my lashes and my resolve melted away. Wrapping my arms around her, I placed my hands into the hollow of her back just above her underpants, and briefly crushed her waif-like body into mine. Certain now that she must feel an unfamiliar hardness between us, I worried about her reaction. She had to know that I was swollen and erect; would she understand, or would she be offended? But she said nothing. Instead she closed her eyes and kissed me gently on the cheek just below my right eye. And then, cocking her head a little to one side, she moved downward to delicately touch my lips. There was such a wonderful innocence in this tender action that it was completely disarming. In that instant, I could hardly believe that anything earthly was capable of separating us, or that anything heavenly could possibly condemn us. I whispered softly that I loved her and heard her repeat the same sweet words back to me. The deep breathy sounds that came to my ear swept aside the last of my defenses.

Linda, withdrawing an inch or two from my embrace, let her hand fall down my sweaty back in short staccato movements until it rested upon the waist of my shorts. As her thumb searched the edge and slipped under the band, she used her free hand to take hold of my arm and draw it around her middle. There she let go and my hand dropped limply over the back of her panties. No one could have any doubt about her meaning. And when she tugged at my shorts, and they started to give way, I panicked.

Throughout this entire process my emotions had been tossed about, flying first in one direction and then another, traveling from simple reason to unbridled passion, from incredible joy to fearful anguish. At last I came to the realization that things had already gone too far. Because of my reluctance to act rationally when I could have, whatever course I chose to follow now would very likely hurt Linda. But I had already faltered once and I knew that if anything was to be done, it had to be done quickly. Grasping her hand by the wrist (the one that was pulling at my undershorts), I lifted it and swung myself away, pulling free from her embrace.

"I can't do this," I confessed. "It's not that I don't want to . . ." A look of shock swept across her face and I heard a low groan as if she were in pain. Bending down I took hold of my trousers, which were still hung up around my ankles, and pulled them up. Gathering the ends together with one hand, I used the other to take back Linda's and pulled her toward the bed. There, sitting precariously on the edge, I looked up at her like a child seeking forgiveness. "Linda, I love you. And if you asked, I would do anything to prove it. But I can't do this." Forgetful of my condition, I let go of my pants to take her other hand. The top fell open in a crooked V, but they didn't drop any further because I was sitting on them.

"I know this is a crappy thing to do, but if we keep going, however good, however wonderful this may seem now, it will come back to haunt us later and we'll end up hating each other. I can't explain how, but all the sweet joy—everything—everything we've shared will be lost . . ." Pausing, I saw that none of this was getting through to her. "I'm not making any sense, am I?"

As I sat there searching her face, waiting for an answer, the last of that dewy–eyed innocence, which a moment before had set her aglow, drained away as if the spirit inside had suddenly died.

Roughly she twisted her hands free, and spinning away from the bed she stooped to pick up her top, which lay abandoned on the plush carpeting at the center of the room. She crushed the top in front of her, using it like a shield to hide her breasts. Then, moving off to the far corner, she found my T-shirt, which was lying on a low chair. Bending she scooped it up, and returning to me forced it into my hand. Now for the first time she spoke. "I think that you'd better go," she said, her voice full of cold indifference. The words were simple and direct, and I took her sharp dismissal painfully.

I fastened the top button of my trousers, and leaving her by the bed, moved rigidly to her door. I opened it and slipped into the hallway beyond. Walking with a deliberate gait and a stubborn determination to hold on to my pride, I made my way down the stairs, through the front foyer and out of her home. At last, when I reached the beach beyond the dunes, I broke into a run. An incredible pain in my chest and a tightness in my throat made breathing difficult and I wasn't able to run very far. By the time I made it to the jetty along the outer shore, I collapsed. It wasn't the running that had worn me down. I was literally choking on the hopeless despair that was tearing at my heart. It was so painful that it frightened me, and I was trying hard not to give in to it. But I couldn't hold it back, and when I finally let go the sobs came so quickly and so harshly that they were gagging me. And before I had a chance to stop it, my lunch spewed out onto the sand.

I had gone too far, and now I was suffering the consequences. If I had just shown some moral courage, I might have abandoned this situation before it became so disabling. After falling so deeply into her sweet trap, I knew that my sudden decision to withdraw had hurt Linda. Was that decision based on a sense of honor, or did I do it out of fear, because I was too chicken–hearted to pull it off? Then I thought—*She started it!* But that wasn't fair—hadn't I gone along willingly? And after all, wasn't she just demonstrating that her love for me was more important to her than anything else, even her virtue?

Tormented by these feelings of remorse and self–doubt, I had lost all track of time. I may have been kneeling in the wet sand for as much as an hour, when the rain started again. And though it was a crazy idea, I found it comforting to imagine that this wasn't just more rain. I wanted to believe that heaven itself was so moved by this tragedy that the angels had come to weep with me. It was weird; even under these genuinely painful circumstances I couldn't seem to keep myself from wallowing in melodrama.

The rain came down lightly at first, then descended with greater intent until it became torrential. I was too miserable to worry about getting wet, but when I saw the crooked flashes of light near the horizon and heard the roll of thunder that followed, I knew I had to find shelter.

I may have lost Linda for the moment, but I wanted to live long enough to at least try and win her back. When another bolt of lightning streaked across the sky, I offered a desperate prayer. "God, help me!" I shouted, and started off along the beach, pumping arms and legs in a mad dash back to the cottage. Mom and Timmy weren't at home and I left a puddly trail all the way up to my room. Soaking wet, I threw myself down on my bed and surrendered to the lonely ache that was cutting my heart in two.

CHAPTER 15

MORNING CAME after a sleepless night, tossing and turning, unable to think of any rational solution to my problem. How was I to demonstrate to Linda that I was worthy of her forgiveness, that I still loved her, and that I was utterly miserable without her? One thing for sure, I couldn't convince her of anything unless I was able to speak to her again. Waiting for what I hoped was a reasonable hour, I picked up the phone and tried to call.

Her mother answered the telephone. "No, Linda is taking her bath right now," she said.

"Will you tell her it's me?"

"Yes, Michael," she replied. "I promise I'll have her call you, as soon as she's out of the tub." But she didn't call back, and when I called a second time, her mother said that she wasn't available.

"Do you mean she can't come to the phone, or that she isn't there?" I asked. When her mother hesitated, I suspected that Linda was probably there, but unwilling to answer the phone. Now I had reason to believe that she might not talk to me at all. What else could I do? I wasn't prepared to give up. Somehow I had to find a way to reach her.

The next logical step seemed to be to go to her house. Maybe if I was at her door—but it made no difference. Her mother answered the bell, and she was obviously at a loss when Linda refused to come down. She even went up to her room in an attempt to find out what the trouble was. Returning to the front door, she seemed more confused than ever. I tried to enlist her help in getting Linda to change her mind, but it was useless.

"Michael," she pleaded, "you're a wonderful young man and I'd like to help, but for some reason my daughter is very upset with you. I won't repeat what she said, but she made it perfectly clear that she doesn't want to see you. To put it kindly, Michael, your name is mud."

"Did she tell you why?"

"No, she won't discuss it with me."

"Somehow I have to talk to her," I begged.

"Michael, I can see that you're miserable and obviously Linda is suffering too, but as much as I want to help you—both of you—I'm powerless to do anything."

"I understand," I said, "I really do, but I'm desperate. If you can influence Linda in any way, PLEASE, Mrs. Richards, do it!"

"If she would only talk to me, maybe I could straighten things out. Otherwise, my hands are tied. Give her some time, Michael. Maybe she'll get over it."

As I left, defeated, I thought to myself, Linda won't get over it. And this is definitely not the kind of thing that you can discuss with your mother. Whatever I decided to do about this, I wasn't going to include my mother, or my father. It was too personal. And I was sure Linda would feel the same. Besides, if her mother ever discovered the real reason that Linda was so mad at me, she would never let me see her again.

There was just the tiniest glimmer of hope when I got the bright idea that I could write to her. After littering the floor of my room with crumpled paper—all failed attempts—I discovered that I couldn't write anything more than an opening line. When I looked at what was scribbled on the page it was rambling and incoherent. I just couldn't find the words and I soon realized that writing to her was hopeless.

I wanted so badly to proclaim my love, but wanting wasn't enough—wishing wasn't going to do it. My feelings for Linda were real, but yesterday when we decided to play in the adult world, we had come to disaster. Even though we hadn't gone all the way, everything had gone terribly wrong, and both of us ended up deeply hurt. This was not a game that you simply won or lost, it wasn't that easy. And now Linda hated me.

What could I possibly *do* to get back in her good graces? For three days I struggled to find an answer. Finally, when I had tried every solution that I could invent, I decided to talk to my older sister Margie. She had been there before when I was in trouble, and I could hardly approach Mom or Dad. There was no way that I could give Margie all the details, but maybe if I presented this as a *hypothetical* case, and asked her to give me a girl's point of view, she might be able to help. I had to admit that this was far more complicated than any of the problems I had brought her in the past, but I was desperate and Margie seemed my only hope.

Like a cat stalking its prey, I pounced upon her early in the morning as she headed to her room after her shower. Wrapped in a towel, water still beaded on her legs and the back of her shoulders, she was loaded down with items that were supposed to make her look beautiful. She hated her hair, which was a mousy brown, and naturally straight. Most of the time she put it up in rollers or used a curling iron; once she tried a permanent wave, which filled her room with the stinky smell of chemicals. Mom let her get away with that, but when she dyed it black, mom put her foot down. She made her cut most of it off, and when it grew in it looked horrible. Margie had several boyfriends, so someone thought that she was attractive, but I couldn't see it. Her coke-bottle glasses made her look pretty ditzy. They magnified her eyes and the distortion was comical. Which is why she hid them the moment she got out the door. But she wore them at home to keep Mom happy, and that was the face I saw most often. Without them, she probably looked fine.

I came up behind her just after she stepped though the bathroom door into the kitchen and begged for her help.

"Give me a break, Michael!" she protested. "I just got out of that damn shower, I'm not dressed and I'm freezing!"

"So—my timing stinks. I still need your help, Margie. You know I wouldn't ask like this, if it wasn't important."

"Okay! Okay!" she said. "Let me have thirty minutes, then come knock on my door and we'll talk."

I was there pounding noisily on the wall next to her door, exactly thirty minutes later. She wasn't ready.

"Michael!" she hollered through the folds of the shabby curtain that barred my way. "Do you have to take me so literally? You know it takes me more than a half-hour to get myself together. Go away. I'll find you when I'm ready. Whatever it is that has you so hot and bothered can wait a few more minutes. Now get lost, before I really get mean!"

Downstairs, I found a box of raisins on the shelf, and sitting at the kitchen table I started to munch. All this worry and tension was making me hungry. During this frustrating ordeal, I had eaten a lot of food. On the first day I made such a pig of myself that my mother was openly concerned. "You shouldn't eat like that, Michael. Every time I see you you're packin' it in; this morning it was a bag of chips, then a jar of pickles, and now . . . what have you got?"

"Marshmallows," I mumbled with my cheeks full.

She complained, but it didn't seem to occur to her to ask why. When she saw me devour even more the next day she didn't say anything. Instead she gave me that funny look that she used to warn me that I was stepping over the line. It must have been obvious that I was in some kind of trouble, and yet she never tried to get me to tell her what it was. Maybe her instincts told her that I wasn't ready to share this with her. And I wasn't, but I still wanted her to ask. Whatever was in her mind, she permitted me to go on sadly moping about the house. Even as recently as last night while she watched me finish off the last of the ice cream; and again less than hour later when she found me on the front porch eating dry cereal, devouring handfuls of corn flakes straight from the box, she still kept her peace.

Now I was at it again. Returning to the fridge, I pulled the cap off a bottle of milk and finished it (something that was strictly forbidden). Next came a banana from the top of the breadbox. When that was gone, I started foraging for some Ritz Crackers©, sure that I had seen the box recently in the cabinet above the stove. Logically, all this should have turned to fat. But all my worrying was creating a nervous energy that appeared to burn away the calories as fast as the food hit my stomach. In fact I wouldn't be surprised if I had actually *lost* weight.

After another fifteen minutes, during which time I repeatedly checked the kitchen clock, Margie fulfilled her promise and came looking for me.

"Well, brother Mike, what's happening?" she asked casually.

"Jeeze, I can't talk to you here—it's too personal!" I said, angered by her flippant attitude. But then, how could she possibly guess at the dismal state I was in? Reminding myself to be more forgiving, I took her arm and hustled her out to the front porch. Dragging her along, we descended the stairs to the beach and sitting on the bottom step, I pulled her down beside me.

"Now that you've got me where you want me, what's up?" she asked.

"It's not that easy, Margie. I don't know how to start this. I mean, it's kind of embarrassing," I said, nervously twisting my feet into the warm sand.

"Michael, don't make me drag it out of you. Just say what you have to, and be done with it," she ordered.

"Well—I've got this friend and he's having trouble with his girl and . . ."

"Stop! Stop!" she shouted. "Don't give me this *friend* crap. Whatever's going on here, it has to do with you and Linda."

"How'd you know?" A foolish question, but then everything about my approach had been foolish. Margie knew me too well.

"Michael, I'm not blind and I'm not stupid either. It's obvious that you and Linda have a thing for each other—the two of you have been inseparable. The most I've seen of you all summer is a blur as you rushed out the back door. For the last few days you've been walking around here with a face so long your chin has been dragging on the floor. And now you're sitting here with me. It doesn't take a genius to figure out that the two of you have had some kind of a fight. Now tell me, what's the problem."

Leaving out as many of the details as I dared, I explained why

Linda wasn't speaking to me. I told Margie about the rainy afternoon that we had spent together. Without being too specific, I went through the progression of events, which somehow had led me to Linda's bedroom. I couldn't tell Margie that we had started to undress, or that we nearly ended up having sex. I just explained in general terms that from there on the situation had expanded into something more than I had bargained for, and at last my good conscience and home training won out and I told Linda that I couldn't do it. I let Margie figure out what *it* was.

"When I tried to explain, she got mad and kicked me out. Now, she won't have anything to do with me. I've called—but no matter what I do, she won't talk to me."

"I have a feeling, Michael, that you're not telling me everything, but it's not hard to imagine what you've left out. If it's any consolation, I think that you handled yourself admirably; Mom and Dad would be proud. Whatever you do, Michael, don't shoot yourself down for doing the right thing. I know some adults who wouldn't have handled this half as well. Still, I'm sure you've had some doubts, especially considering Linda's reaction. It would have been so much easier to give in, but you would have had a hell of a time dealing with the guilt that comes afterward."

It was nice to know my big sister thought that I was the good guy in all this, but that justification didn't do anything to heal my broken heart.

"You really stepped in it this time, Michael. It was a lot easier when you came to me with kid stuff, like a black eye, or a skinned knee," she said, touching the scar on my leg. "I may be a couple of years older than you, but I'm hardly an expert on romance, or as they say—matters of the heart. And something like this is a real bum-buster." She said, putting her elbows on her knees and pressing her chin into the heels of her hands. "I honestly don't know what to do."

"Pleeeze Margie, you hafta' try!"

"IF—and I mean if, I can get the two of you back together even for a few minutes, you're going to have to do some pretty fancy talking. It seems to me that Linda was willing to go all the way, and you walked out. Pardon me for saying so, but if I were her I think that I'd be pissed off too!"

"Margie!" I squawked. Even during our worst fights I'd never heard her use that kind of language.

"Okay, okay, I shouldn't have said that, and I don't want to give you the impression that I'm on Linda's side, but . . . Michael, you've got yourself in some serious trouble, this is *grooown*-up stuff. No, it's more than grown-up."

"Which is why I came to you."

"Yeah sure, like who else. I can just see you trying to tell Mom about this," she said, judiciously.

"All right, so you're not exactly an adult, and I admit there isn't anyone else. But can you help me?"

"Who knows? Look, Michael, maybe Linda was wrong, but she trusted you, and in a manner of speaking you let her down. If you can get inside her head for a minute, maybe you'll understand why she's so angry."

"I do understand, I just don't know how to make it up to her."

"Well in a case like this I'm not sure you *can* make it up to her. But that doesn't mean you can't ask her to forgive you. Have you tried to write to her?" she said, looking at me as if she'd had a sudden inspiration.

"I wrote all kinds of letters, but I tore them up, crumpled them into little balls, littered the floor with them—even made airplanes out of them."

"Okay! I get the picture. Don't write some long flowery letter—send her a note. Something brief and to the point. Just tell her that you love her and that you have to meet and talk. Look, you write it, and I'll see to it that she gets it," she said, with sisterly determination.

"Do you actually think that will work? It sounds too easy. What if she doesn't read it? What if she just tears it up?" I protested.

"What if—what if—you worry too much! I'll see that she reads the note, and if she objects I'll tell her she owes you more than that. I'll tell her that she shouldn't be so quick to dump you without at least giving you a chance to explain and ask her forgiveness."

"Would you really *do* that, Margie?"

"Of course I would. You're my brother, aren't you? Okay, so you're a pest, and sometimes I'd like to ring your neck, but I know you're hurting and I don't enjoy seeing you like this. Besides, if anyone is going to make you this miserable, I think it ought to be me," she said, driving her elbow into my ribs.

"Ouch!" I complained. "Cut it out!"

"You mean like this," she said, pinching my leg. Then I pushed her and she pushed me, and rising from the steps I stumbled and fell on the sand. I picked myself up and we started fighting back and forth until she got the best of me and I ran up the stairs to get away.

"It might work," I speculated, as I went back inside. My efforts so far hadn't brought me any success, so what did I have to lose? I went to my room and wrote the note exactly as Margie had dictated, and she carried it to Linda just as she had promised. Surprisingly, it did work!

According to Margie's report when she returned, she got past Mrs. Richards, somehow convinced Linda to read the note, and then talked her into giving me a chance to apologize for my insensitive behavior—although I wasn't sure *how* I was being insensitive. But it really didn't matter as long as I got to see Linda again.

Margie had persuaded me that a little unvarnished humility would go a long way towards softening Linda's heart, and what did I know about the peculiar logic that infects a young girl's mind? After all Margie was one of *them*—a girl that is—which is why I had gone to her in the first place. Besides, how could I argue with her? Where all my efforts had failed, she had succeeded. She came back with a message from Linda, telling me to meet her on the Rock. "She'll be there at one tomorrow afternoon."

"Hallelujah!" I shouted joyously.

"SOOO—what do you say now, brother Mike?"

"Thank you—thank you—thank you!" I said, with heartfelt gratitude, as I dropped to my knees and started kissing her hand.

"Get up, Mike, and stop being silly. You're very welcome. It was worth it, just to see that goofy smile again."

CHAPTER 16

AS THE appointed hour approached, I left early and headed down the beach, hopeful that I would arrive before Linda. Walking along the shore, I thought of the last time we had been on the Rock: the fireworks, the light from the newly risen moon, our first kiss. That night, I recognized that the love I had for Linda was real and not just some promising fantasy. Right now, that seemed like a long time ago. During these last few weeks everything had been so perfect. I'd been lulled into a wonderful sense of security where nothing seemed to go wrong, where anything seemed possible. How could I guess that I would come to face this awful moment, where our whole relationship might depend on a few well-chosen words? Absorbed by these reflections, I suddenly realized that I was nearly at the base of the Rock. Stopping, I looked up and saw that Linda was already sitting on the summit waiting for me. There was no way for me to know what that meant, but I wanted to believe that she had come early because she was anxious to forgive me. That might not be true, but it was too demoralizing to consider any other possibility.

Full of purpose, I plunged into the shallows, and began to climb with eager anticipation. Soon I was at the top. I noticed that while I was hurrying to reach her, Linda had moved. She was now on the other side, sitting in the same spot that we had occupied the night of the fireworks. Facing away from me, she sat staring out over the harbor. She must have heard the slap of my bare feet against the rock as I rushed to her side, because she turned to face me the moment I stepped up behind her. She looked tired. But she smiled bravely, as she commented on my own haggard appearance. "You look like hell!" she exclaimed. Then squeezing my wrist she ordered me to "Sit".

Scooching in next to her I looked away toward the sea. I couldn't figure out how to begin, and I was afraid to meet her gaze. Linda sucked the salty air deeply into her lungs and I heard her let it out in a long sigh. It was a mournful sound, filled with such terrible sadness. But it was something more than just the expulsion of sound and air; it seemed to bring her some needful relief. Whatever she had suffered, whatever anger she had harbored towards me during these last few days must have been exhausting, and now I sensed that she had let go of that anguish. As I glanced her way, she greeted me, letting a smile slip quietly across her face in a thin line that suggested it was not freely given. It was not her usual smile, but it was enough to give me the courage I needed to begin.

"Linda, I know that I hurt you and I'm sorry." The tightness in my throat told me this wasn't going to be easy, but now that I had taken the first step I prayed that my timid resolve wouldn't desert me. "When I saw the pain in your eyes—the anger—I couldn't . . . I never meant to hurt you like that. For the last three days I've been trying to find a way to make things right again," I paused, but she remained silent.

"It's not as if I didn't know what was up when you dragged me into your room last Friday. Once your top came off it was pretty obvious where we were headed, but—it didn't matter—not to begin with anyway. It was as if something had grabbed hold of me and wouldn't let go. At first I tried to get free and then I wasn't sure I wanted to be free. But it all went a little crazy and in the end I couldn't decide . . ." I stopped again, unsure of how to end my sentence, but Linda said nothing and her silence was scaring me.

"Believe me, I knew what you were offering and I really wanted it to happen, but I just wasn't ready. I only wish that I had pulled out sooner, before we both got hurt. Please don't misunderstand; it wasn't because you weren't desirable or—or that I wasn't tempted."

Where this was coming from, I couldn't tell, but after days of self-abuse, it was a relief to finally get it out.

"Michael," she said, her voice soft as the breeze that stroked the wispy ends of her hair. "I gave myself willingly—I was ready to sacrifice everything, and you pushed me away. Do you have any idea how that made me feel? I mean—I hated you, or at least I tried to hate you. But I couldn't—and believe me I worked hard at it. When I finally cooled off I realized that you were right, having sex would've been a humongous mistake. It would have changed everything!"

"Things have already changed," I said, thinking the trust that we'd had for each other was no longer absolute.

"True, but it could have been much worse. Michael—if you hadn't . . ." She took a moment to pick at a small scab on her leg before she looked up with a challenging gleam in her eye. "Standing in my bedroom, with your arms around me, it was like swimming in molasses, everything seemed to be running in slow motion. Everything felt so right. It was so good—so incredible—that I was willing to do anything—*any*thing to keep that feeling alive. All summer long we've been playing at this—getting closer and closer to—well, you know."

"Yes," I answered. I did know, but I couldn't say it, not out loud.

"What if we had—Michael, what if we'd done it? Arrrrggh," she groaned, pressing her fingers to the corners of her eyes and rubbing as if she were trying to erase that image.

"It might have been exciting," she said, switching to a more speculative tone. "Hell, it probably would have blown my socks off! Except I wasn't wearing any," she added, with a laugh that was kind of a hiccup. "Or—maybe not. Maybe it would have been *awful!* But . . ." She paused for a long time. Somehow I sensed that she wasn't finished, so I kept quiet and waited.

"But—awesome or awful, if we'd done the deed, it would have ruined everything," she said, sadly. "It could never be the same— all that—all the neat stuff that we've shared together, would be gone. Well, not gone, we'd still remember, but it wouldn't have the same meaning anymore. I know that sounds crazy," she said, rubbing her hands down her thighs and over her knees. "Michael, I want to get this right—I need to say it so that you'll understand, but it so hard to find the right words."

"You're doing fine," I said. Not that everything she said was perfectly clear, but I had struggled through the same mangled process, and because of that, I knew what she meant.

"Three days ago, in my room, none of this seemed very important." Linda continued. "When I had my arms around you and the two of us were nearly naked—I—I had this incredible desire to swallow you up—to pull you down inside me. I don't understand how, but I wanted the two of us to become one. That probably sounds pretty weird, but it—it was more than just a physical thing, you know? No, I suppose you don't—I—a*aaaargh*!" she groaned.

"Linda, it wasn't easy for me either. You were—your skin—and the look on your face—it was incredible, but I was scared to death!"

"I know—but I wasn't thinking about that then. My stomach was in knots, my heart pounding—I felt hot and cold at the same time. It was all so crazy, and yet I was so into it—so energized, I could hardly stand it. And then when you pushed me away—I mean, you can't just throw a switch and shut that kind of thing off!"

"I'm sorry!"

"Forgive me Michael, but when you walked out—I wanted—I swear when that door closed behind you, all I wanted to do was tear your heart out. First I cried, and then I cursed you, and then I wished that you were dead. Then I wished *I* were dead. But I couldn't keep it up. Lord knows I tried. But no matter how hard I worked at it I couldn't change the fact that I was—that I *am* in love with you. So, when Margie came with your note I had already relented. She just gave me the excuse I needed to come and see you."

"I didn't mean to hurt you." I said. "That day in your room, I wanted so badly to give in, to just let go and allow you to—what was it you said? To let you *swallow me up*. But I didn't know what that meant, or how to make it happen. Then something took it all away. I don't know what, maybe it was fear, or conscience. Whatever it was, it made me stop. I tried to explain, but you weren't listening, and . . ."

"What did you expect?"

"I don't know," I said flatly. "I guess I just wanted you to understand."

"I *do* understand, Michael. It took me a while, but I *do* understand," she said turning her face back towards the sea.

Moving my hand shakily, I let it fall over her knee. It was designed to be a gesture of peace and she might have pushed it aside, but she didn't. "If you want to punish me," I said, "it's too late. You couldn't possibly make me feel any more miserable. These last couple of days have been torture. All I could think about was that I would never see you again. If you could only forgive me . . ."

"Michael, I have—*I have* forgiven you," Linda insisted.

"Last night," she continued, "I had a bad time of it. After I talked to your sister, I started worrying about what I was going to say. Who was right; who was wrong; who should apologize. It was all crap—just a stupid waste of energy. After tossing and turning for hours, I finally left my room and went up to the attic. I don't know what time it was—maybe three. We keep the dormer windows open, and in the early morning hours when the air outside is cooler, and the wind has picked up, it's really nice up there.

"Standing in front of one of the windows, suddenly I knew. Michael, it wasn't you, it was me. You weren't *taking* me anywhere—I was pushing. I didn't know where I was going, but it didn't seem to matter." She covered the hand that I had put over her knee, "Near the end I shut everything out, nothing else existed, not even that niggling little voice that tells me when I'm headed for trouble. It was just you and me," she said, squeezing my fingers and looking straight into my eyes. "Michael, you said you wanted me to forgive you, but—maybe it should be the other way around."

"Are you serious?"

"Yes," she answered calmly.

"Then you're forgiven."

"Michael, can I add one more thing? If we had gone—if we had taken the next step, I honestly would have been lost. I didn't have a clue. I guess I was counting on *you* to lead me through it."

"*Me?*" I protested. "I was in over my head as soon as you took your top off! It doesn't seem fair, does it? We've got all the right equipment and yet we have no idea what to do with it."

"True," she said, smiling. "But after last Friday we certainly know a lot more than we used to. The problem is, what are we supposed to do with that knowledge?"

"Nothing. When we get older—when we're married . . ."

"Married? Michael, are you saying you want to marry me?" she gasped.

"Yes—well someday. Why, is that bad?"

"No. I just hadn't thought about it. I hadn't looked that far ahead."

"Well, it's not goin' to happen right away," I said wistfully. "I have no job, no license, no car, I'm still in high school, you're only sixteen . . ."

"Stop!" She said. "You're depressing me again! If it's really that hopeless, why'd you even bring it up?"

"Nothing's ever hopeless," I said.

"Well at least we can still be friends," Linda said.

"Friends? Does that mean like—no kissing, no hugging?"

"I wasn't suggesting THAT, Michael. Gawd, I couldn't be around you and not get a little lip–lock once in a while, or at least a hug. But—if that's the only way we can be together."

"No way! We'd both go nuts!" I said.

"Good, because if we can't at least share a kiss . . ."

Before she could finish I leaned in and touched my lips gently to hers. She responded by opening her mouth slightly and closing it over mine. Then she pulled away. I could still feel the wetness of her lips as the breeze cooled my hot face, and once again I felt a familiar rush of blood stirring in my veins.

We sat there on top of the Rock, quietly basking in the afternoon sun. The sweet innocence of youth had persuaded us to tickle the tiger and it had nearly devoured us. But we were lucky; after a few days of suffering and introspection, we had managed to close up the wound. And happily, even though there were a few stitches still showing, we had come out as good as new—maybe better.

CHAPTER 17

THE DAYS that followed were enchanted and idyllic, pleasant times filled with easy, carefree events. We started each day early in the morning and ended reluctantly late in the evening, sometimes past midnight. We did the same kinds of things that we had been doing all along, but now they took on a new urgency. We knew the summer was nearly over, that we were measuring our time not in weeks, but in days and hours, and every moment spent together was golden.

Late at night we sat on Linda's front porch swing and kissed. In the afternoons we went swimming and stretched out afterwards to bake in the fiery heat of the August sun.

During the cool morning hours we played a simple game. It was something that we thought we had invented, which I'm sure had been played by others, ages before we discovered it. But we were naive enough to believe that we were the first.

Linda would lay face down and pull her shirt high enough to expose the lower half of her back. Then with my finger I traced letters on her bare skin. Only three or four letter words were allowed. She was supposed to guess what I had written. If after three tries she couldn't come up with the right answer, we changed places. It was a ticklish game that sent waves of goose bumps racing along my spine, but the playful brush of her finger against my skin was exciting and I felt that I could endure hours of such gentle torture. Sometimes her touch was deliberately light and feathery, which made me wiggle and squirm, until I'd lost all sense of what she was writing. But whether I was lying under her hand or she was lying under mine, it didn't matter; win or lose, the experience was still magnificent.

Occasionally we would take long walks out on Driftway Road to the Strawberry Point Bridge. When the tide was running we would sit on the concrete bridge-rail and watch the currents as they eddied past the abutments. Between the tides, when the water was calm, it was clear enough to see the bottom and we would try to count the horseshoe crabs sitting in the mud.

In the early evening after supper we often went to the Variety Store on Egypt Road. We'd buy a Popsicle, or maybe spend a dime for a cold soda from the chest cooler out front. Hires Root Beer and Canada Dry Ginger Ale were our favorites, but once in a while we would sort through the bottles until we found an Orange Crush. That tangy bite swirling over the tongue, the wonderful coolness and the electric tingle of carbonation as it went down really hit the spot. There was nothing else quite like it after a hot sticky day. Usually, coming back from the store, we would climb the sea wall, drink our sodas and talk, or just sit quietly and watch the sea.

There wasn't anything extraordinary about these events, yet they were extremely important to us. We wanted desperately to create lasting memories of carefree moments. But somehow all that desire for happiness was self-defeating. As much as we wanted to be together and as hard as we tried to inject a certain romantic vitality into all our activities, we were still plagued by periods of boredom, bored by what we were doing or not doing, and even occasionally bored with each other. It's not that we didn't want to share every minute that remained of our vacation, but just being together wasn't enough. What we needed was something to do—someplace to go. That's when we decided to plan a trip to the lighthouse on the other side of Satuit harbor.

Once we had a place to go and something specific to look forward to, Linda and I threw ourselves into the process: the planning, the anticipation, the hope of a day on our own; the challenge of exploring new ground and sharing a new experience. It might turn out to be a simple uneventful day that is soon forgotten, but we held real expectations of the sort of day that could be recorded in the book of life and that would be important, at least to us, for many years to come.

Again we needed transportation and again I turned to Earl and Tooey. But this time I was asking them to let us have their bikes for a whole day. They weren't happy about that. They rode their bikes everywhere, even when it would have been more practical for them to walk. And Tooey was a little touchy about having a girl ride his bike, as if somehow Linda might contaminate it. That peculiar idea hadn't occurred to him a few weeks ago when Linda had used it to go to the movies. But now, even though he couldn't say why, he seemed genuinely troubled. I tried to reassure him, "Linda's not contagious; it's not like you're going to catch anything from her if she rides your bike."

"I know that!" Tooey said, disgruntled.

"Then what are you worried about? She won't break it. Unless you're afraid that she'll put some kind of a curse on it?"

"Nooo."

"What—do you think if you sit on the same seat your banana will fall off, and you'll start talking with a squeaky voice?" I said, with a waggish irreverence.

"Don't be stupid!"

"Then why are you being such a bonehead?"

"Just for that, maybe I won't let you have it at all," he warned. I really couldn't blame him; I had gotten kind of nasty. But honestly, sometimes he could be a real putz. He finally gave in after I offered him a two dollar bribe. That was a mistake, because Earl came by an hour later and wanted to know why *he* wasn't being paid. I had to give him my last dollar and a half.

****

The Friday before Labor Day, Linda met me at the cottage. It was early when she arrived. The sun had only just cleared the horizon. She and I worked together in the kitchen, preparing our lunch.

"Under the sink you'll find a large thermos. The lemonade's in the fridge, the ice cubes too. You can put that together, while I'm mixing the tuna-fish." I directed.

"If you say so." Linda agreed, and gave me a wink, which suggested that I was being too bossy.

Hidden by the refrigerator door, she called out over the top, "Michael, I can't move this ice tray. Have you got something I can use to pry it loose?"

I reached into the drawer and handed her a flat butter knife. "Here," I said, "this usually works."

"Damn it!" she said, when the knife slipped and she caught her knuckles on the edge of the tray. "Sorry—I cut my hand. Have you got something I can use to stop the bleeding?"

I went to the bathroom for a facecloth and ran it under the cold water. Then while she pressed the cloth against her knuckles to staunch the bleeding, I pulled the tray free and put it in the sink. After a moment I cracked it against the side of the counter and Linda reached to take it from me. For the first time I got a good look at the deep cut on her knuckle. It was silly, really; we were way beyond holding hands, but when I moved to touch the spot with my finger, there was a tiny charge. Not static electricity, but a subtle exchange of energy as if something had passed from spirit to spirit. We looked at each other, Linda smiled, I smiled, then I turned away to find a bandage. She put the tray on the counter and I unwrapped a Band–Aid strip and gently covered the wound. We both went back to work, but a quiet excitement seemed to fill the air. Even after all the time we had spent together, just a touch, just the knowledge that she was in the same room, breathing the same air, seemed to arouse my senses and make me glad to be alive. When she wasn't looking I watched her movements, not because they were different or remarkable, but just because they were hers. For the rest of the time we were in the kitchen together, there was an economy of words. Only yes, or no, and in between there was a wonderful, palpable silence.

Finally we were ready to leave and we stepped out the back door and headed for Earl's house to pick up our borrowed bicycles. It was seven when we arrived at his doorstep. Tooey had spent the night, leaving his bike at Earl's so that we wouldn't have to make a separate trip.

Apparently we woke Earl. His eyes half-opened, he looked groggy when he came to answer the door. I wanted to laugh when I saw the condition of his hair and the ugly torn T-shirt he had obviously slept in. With a tight smile I listened to him grumble when he handed me the key, and I tried not to chuckle when I heard him slur his words. The bikes were chained to a pipe on the side of the house. Afterwards, returning the key, I gave him a quick thank-you and heard him grumble again as he closed the door.

The weatherman had promised us a great day. There were no showers in the forecast and no thunderstorms had been predicted for late afternoon, which often was the case. We had no reason to expect any repetition of the disaster that had struck at the end of our last trip.

Following the same route that we had taken before (when our tiny caravan had traveled to the local theater) we made our way to Main Street in Satuit.

Taking a break, we stopped and poked around for a while, looking into store windows and admiring the items on display. None of the stores were open at this hour, and that was just as well, since Earl and Tooey had cleaned me out. Linda admired everything, and said so, but that praise never turned into a request.

Once we left Main Street, it was necessary to make a few twists and turns before we could find our way to the Sandhills Road. From Main we turned onto Brewster Avenue, then north along the frontage road to Cedar Swamp Avenue, and finally east, till we reached Sandhills Road and started moving out onto the peninsula. More than two hours had passed since we left Earl's. Taking our bikes along the narrow road that led to the lighthouse proved to be an intriguing adventure all by itself. In a snake-like fashion the road wound back and forth following the pattern of the shore, threading its way between boulders, hugging the rugged rock walls and passing below overhanging ledges.

The rocks were irregular and in certain places the shear face was split and broken, leaving crevasses and shelves, which sometimes looked like chiseled steps. The coloring on these steep walls varied from slate gray to warm earth tones: burnt umber and raw sienna, and here and there something that looked a little like rust. Coming around a wooded turn in the road, we saw a deep cut in the rock, and we rode our bikes between two walls that formed a miniature canyon. We followed this briefly, marveling at the closeness of the nearly vertical sides, which crowded the narrow pavement and made us feel almost claustrophobic. Then, coming out the other side, we headed toward the water.

The road here ran parallel to the bay, only twenty or thirty feet from the sea and just inches above the high-water mark. Fat cedar posts with wooden rails bordered the road and formed a rustic guardrail. All along the route, wherever there was any room, scrub pine and blighted hardwood trees grew at odd and twisted angles. In those places not covered by trees and brush, there was a crazy profusion of coarse grass, colorful weeds and wildflowers. The effect of all this chaotic undergrowth and wild misshapen trees was an otherworldly, almost alien landscape, a place of fairy tales and dreams. As we wandered through this maze, we discovered that we had entered a twisted forest, which surrounded us and totally obscured our view. When we broke free of these woods an electrifying vista of the harbor jumped up before us, and we were momentarily stunned by its tranquil beauty.

Then, glancing to our left, we were treated to an even more captivating sight. Just above, sitting high on the rocks with the sun gleaming off its white tower, was the lighthouse. Almost like a storybook castle guarding some ancient coastline, the bright vision of the tower and the keeper's cottage was worth all the effort we had expended to reach this isolated point.

Straddling our bikes and gazing first at the lighthouse and then at the harbor, with its tall-masted boats rising and falling on the gentle swells, we could almost imagine that this was some kind of Eden. The scene before us was so magnificent, so perfect, that it defied description.

Pushing my bike a little nearer to Linda's my leg brushed against hers and I felt a gentle rush. Again I was amazed that Linda's closeness—that the lightest contact, nothing more than rubbing my trouser leg against hers—could give me the tingles. It was interesting to see that love didn't always represent itself in the sort of eruptions that made the earth move beneath your feet. Sometimes it could sneak up on you quietly. And when it came that way, its sting was often sharper, because it was so unexpected.

Linda reached for my hand and we stood there concentrating, as all our senses came under attack. We absorbed the color of the sky, and the rocks, and the sea, the brilliant white of the lighthouse tower, and the rippling reflections of the boats on the water. We inhaled the smell of the dry seaweed on the beach, and with it the salty air and the piney aroma of the stunted trees. We heard the sound of the water teasing the stony shore, and the noisy calls from a raft of seabirds that were flying above us.

A wonderful sweet ecstasy seemed to infect the air, and this heady atmosphere made us feel a little giddy as we walked our bikes across the sand to the base of the rocks. Dismounting, we laid them down and moved off toward a long set of wooden stairs that zigzagged from one landing to another up to the lighthouse. At the bottom of the stairs we looked up and saw the light-keeper waiting at the top. He stood high above, on a platform that hung over the beach like the railed pulpit on the bow of a fishing boat. As we stepped out onto the landing he seemed angry, and we were chagrined because we knew that we were trespassers.

"You kids don't belong out here. It's dangerous, and I don't need the aggravation," he said with a surly growl.

"Can't we look around? There must be a lot of history to this place," I said, and he appeared to soften somewhat when he heard me mention 'history'.

"Well," he said, hesitantly, "I could tell you a couple of stories that would certainly make your hair curl." Rubbing the stubble on his chin, he seemed to reconsider his decision to send us away. "Ummm, I guess if I showed you around—I mean if I kept my eye on you, that'd keep you from gettin' into trouble. C'mon into the kitchen for a minute and meet Maude. By the way, my name is Abernathy." He stuck out his weathered hand, and we introduced ourselves. Then he spread out his arms and herded us toward the backdoor of his cottage. "My wife and I have been tending this light for thirty years. But all that's about to come to an end. See that metal gismo over there?"

Stopping outside the cottage entrance, we looked in the direction that he was pointing. About a hundred feet beyond the light tower was a hollow looking configuration of pipe and angle-iron bolted together like pieces of a giant Erector set. All this was anchored to a concrete base that had a steel door mounted in the side. On top was a glass beacon and between was some kind of mechanism that was obviously designed to turn the light back and forth in a simple arc.

"That contraption's supposed to replace this lighthouse," he said, tossing his hands up, to frame the original tower. "All automated, don't you know. The Coast Guard expects me to keep an eye on that thing while they run their tests. If it breaks down and I can't fix it, then I crank up the old light until they can get a technician out here."

"It's an ugly thing isn't it?" I observed.

"You said it kid," he answered. "Strictly practical, no room for beauty or grace."

"How long before they close this place up?" I asked, indicating the old light tower.

"If the Coast Guard has it their way, we won't get to spend another Christmas here. The engineers put that gadget up last October and it's been running pretty near perfect since. Only broke down once during an ice storm last winter. Damn shame too, it's been a good life for me and the Mrs."

The light-keeper took us into the kitchen, and after a cordial introduction his wife offered us a glass of cold water. Mr. Abernathy explained that the water came from a cistern deep in the rock below the kitchen. He opened a trapdoor fitted into the floor and showed us a black hole that plunged into the solid rock. The daylight from the room only penetrated a foot or two into the inky darkness. But when he flipped on a switch next to the refrigerator, a number of bare bulbs that followed the shaft downward came on and we could see a steel ladder that led all the way to the bottom.

Maude sat us down at the table and handed us a couple of fresh peaches. They were honey-colored and furry, and still covered with droplets of water from washing them off under the hand pump. They were sweet and succulent and along with the cold water wonderfully refreshing after the long hot ride out here.

We ate and drank quietly, and when we were done, the keeper led us out of the kitchen and down a granite–walled passageway that connected the cottage to the tower. Every few feet there were tiny slits, which allowed a dull light to penetrate into this gloomy chamber. And the breeze coming through these same openings combined with the musty dampness and rushed past our ears with the whispery sound of the surf striking the rocks below the point. Other than the quality of mystery that such a place might suggest to a young, imaginative mind, this was obviously a very convenient way to travel from the keeper's living quarters to the light.

When we reached the end, Mr. Abernathy opened a heavy door and we stepped into a circular room at the bottom of the tower. In front of us was a thick wooden column, rising from the center of the stone floor. The post was more than a foot in diameter and was scarred and split with age. It was now covered with a dreary battleship gray, but in places where the paint had chipped away there was evidence that it had been painted many colors. Fitted into the post were narrow iron treads, each with the same decorative pattern stamped into the surface. They were long and pie–shaped, and one after another spiraled upward toward the landing above.

With our heads back, craning to see into the dim recesses of the heavy iron beams that crisscrossed beneath the platform, the keeper asked: "Would you like to go up?"

Linda gave a childish squeal of acceptance and I heard the

clatter of her loafers as she mounted the stairs ahead of me. And while I hurried to catch up, Mr. Abernathy followed behind.

When we got to the last step and climbed through the hole in the iron flooring, the size and complexity of the lenses that towered above us was mind-boggling. They were made up of concentric circles of glass mounted on a delicate metal bracing that extended out from the center like a giant web. There were three of these lenses, forming a triangle, and in the middle was a large gas–fired lantern with a gauzy mantle on top.

After explaining the inner workings of the light (in technical terms that were nearly impossible for us to understand), Mr. Abernathy suggested that we step outside and take in the view. Although that seemed a little dangerous, it didn't hold us back. And as soon as he showed us the square door, hidden in the low wall below the sweep of the lens, we bent down and stepped gingerly out onto the narrow catwalk.

The first thing I noticed was that I could look straight down through the slotted grating under my feet. The metalwork looked strong enough, but its openness made me queasy and my legs felt a little rubbery when I stood up. Linda wasn't doing any better and I wasn't surprised to see how tightly she clung to the rail. Freeing one hand, she clamped her fingers over mine and began to squeeze them painfully. Her viselike grip was uncomfortable, but I didn't dare complain; in fact, the pain was distracting enough to bury some of the panic that was beginning to rise in my gut.

Clutching the railing, we stood there rigidly and looked straight ahead; any downward angle was too unnerving. The view in front of us was of the open sea. It was wide and vast, and even in the warm sun it looked cold. Next to the horizon the blue sky was nearly purple, and we could see the hazy outline of a freighter heading north towards Boston Harbor.

Before Mr. Abernathy had the chance to call us back in, I choked down my fear and persuaded Linda to move slowly around the circular grating. She would only push her feet along in little shuffling steps, but that was enough to get us from one spectacular view to another. At the entrance to the harbor we watched a small powerboat cutting through the water, leaving a white, frothy wake behind. Beyond the boat was First Cliff, and just below, darkly silhouetted against the sparkling ocean was the Rock—the same Rock where a few days ago I had begged for Linda's forgiveness.

Finally we came around to face the shore. Now we could look back along the rugged route that we'd traveled to get here. But the view stretched well beyond that, and we could see inland to the crest of the low-lying hills. We even spotted the old fire tower that stood in the middle of what was called the Town Forest. From so far away the wooden frame looked weak and flimsy. It was like a bunch of matchsticks stuck together in a crisscross pattern, with a boxy cabin stuck on top.

Wherever we stopped along the rail the view was splendid, but when Mr. Abernathy called us in, we were more than happy to comply. Continuing her skittish steps, Linda led the way cautiously back to the doorway, and into the relative safety of the glass enclosure.

Once inside, Mr. Abernathy directed us to the stairs and led the way back down. He took us through a short fat doorway cut deep into the side of the wall, and emerging into the sunlight, we squinted against the sudden brightness. Staying on the walkway that surrounded the base, we came to a stone bench, and he invited us to sit down beside him. Then, as promised, he began to tell us some of the history of the Satuit station.

He was a skillful storyteller, filling our minds with vivid images of frightened sailors and courageous sea captains, of violent storms and trembling seas that rose up to engulf the light. There were stories of clipper ships and schooners, whalers and lobstermen. And of course, the sad accounts of the widows and lovers left behind. He spoke of possible treasure lying on the ocean bottom just a few hundred yards offshore, of attempts by salvagers to reclaim it, and how some of them had lost their lives in the process.

We heard about the dreadful hurricane of 1938 and the devastation that it caused all along the coast from Long Island to Boston. Seventeen children drowned in a school bus at Jamestown, Rhode Island. People climbed on the roofs of their cars in Providence as the turbulent floodwaters rushed down the city streets. Cottages along the beaches were reduced to rubble by winds that blasted the shore at a hundred and twenty miles per hour. Cars and boats were destroyed and a railroad bridge was washed away at Wareham, Mass. Here in Satuit, a schooner was washed up on the Minot Beach Road. Linda and I remembered seeing part of the keel sticking out of the sand high on the beach, and now we knew where it had come from.

Continuing, he recounted a fascinating story about the wreck of a Greek freighter in 1947 during a February blizzard. The ship was driven up on the rocks not a hundred yards from the shore, on the windward side of the lighthouse. With a broken rudder, it had lost steerage, and was pushed by the sea and wind until it struck the rocks, hitting them broadside. In an hour, several holes had been smashed in the hull next to the keel. One of them was at least eight feet long. Minutes later, a rogue wave lifted the 7000-ton freighter sixty feet into the air and let it come crashing down on top of the undersea barrier that had been tearing it apart. The crew of thirty was rescued by breeches buoy. Working in high winds and snow, the rescue was accomplished without losing a single seaman. In the early morning hours as the storm moved out to sea, the ship began to break up, and piece by piece it slipped off the rocks and sank to the bottom.

At last, Mr. Abernathy brought this stirring chronicle to a close, by telling us the story of a ghost who appears on the point during December storms. Those that have seen this ghostly apparition believe that he is the spirit of a mariner who was found washed up on shore during a winter nor'easter back in 1916. It was two days before Christmas when the light-keeper and his son discovered the body wedged between the rocks. It was a gruesome sight. He'd been in the sea for too long and no one could identify him. For some reason, they never located any wreckage from the ship he was on. Since it was wartime, people thought he might have been a victim from a freighter torpedoed by a German U-boat.

Witnesses say that he has appeared on the point often, especially during December, always when a winter storm is coming in off the Atlantic, and particularly when it's snowing. Typically, he is described as wearing a watch cap and a dark sailor's peacoat. He stands on the rocky shore at the tip of the point in the area where they originally found his body, which is directly below the promontory at the far end of the compound. Usually he vanishes, as the high waves from the storm break over him, taking him back into the sea.

One evening, he appeared on top of the promontory and was spotted by the keeper from his cottage. It was a cold night, with driving rain, and thinking that the man was in trouble, he started out to try and help him. It was a dangerous process and he wasn't able to get very close, so he shouted against the wind and rain, calling out a warning. The ghostly vision turned to face the terrified keeper and then melted away, evaporating into the foggy spray of a breaking wave.

No one knows why he haunts the point, but some think that he's upset because he wants to be identified and is unhappy about resting in an unmarked grave in a lonely corner of the churchyard.

It was well past two when Mr. Abernathy finished his account. He told us we were free to explore the area around the light as long as we stayed away from the edges, especially on the side next to the open sea. He had been a great host, and his stories, filled with detail, were marvelous to listen to. The ghost story was the perfect ending, and we thanked him over and over, until he begged us to stop.

When he got up and headed back to the cottage, we were left sitting on the stone bench, wondering what we should do next.

Our first concern, as it turned out, was food. After all, we had only had a light breakfast and that was hours ago. Moving down the walk to a grassy knoll that had a tall white flagpole planted in the center, we settled in the only spot on this rocky fortress that was green. Opening the backpack that we had brought with us, we spread out our meager lunch and began to fill up on the goodies that we had prepared earlier that morning. The meal was eaten eagerly, with only a little light chatter between mouthfuls of chips and tuna-salad sandwiches.

Afterwards, we wandered about the compound until we found a spot under a flat granite slab that hung over the south side of the promontory. Crawling into this hidey-hole, Linda and I scooted back, to take advantage of the shade. Facing the harbor and watching the sailboats and cabin cruisers straining against their moorings, we listened to the steady rhythmic slapping of the sea against their hulls. I had not felt this content for days and it was a feeling that I wanted desperately to hang onto.

All summer long we both seemed to have been haunted by the same shadowy specter. It was an elusive creature, always just out of reach; hobbling miserably in the background, it constantly threatened to destroy our happiness. Up to now we had managed to push it back, refusing to let it in, but today this moody spirit was more persistent. Cautiously it crept out of the shadows, and now it pounced upon us with unexpected harshness. In three more days I would leave for home, and two days after that Linda would be back in Stoughton. Would this forced separation tear us apart, or would we find some way to save our friendship and the love that had become such an essential part of who we were?

I can't remember how, but we both saw that this problem couldn't be ignored any longer. And once again it was Linda who stepped into the fray.

"Michael, you're leaving on Monday. What happens to *us* after you've gone?"

"I don't know. It's goin' to be awfully hard to see each other when we're more than fifty miles apart. I have no car and it's not likely that I'm going to find anyone to drive me. My parents are bound to put the kibosh on my calling because it's long distance. We could write, which is something I'm not very good at. Maybe we can arrange to see each other at Christmastime, or during spring break. That means we'll be apart for—what—three or four months at a time. How will we survive when we hardly get to see each other?" I asked, stricken by my own grievous disposition. "I can't imagine not being able to touch you or hold you—not being able to kiss you. But then, I don't see that we have any choice."

"You're scaring me, Michael. Should we give up—say goodbye and pretend this never happened?"

"No way! It did happen. It happened to you and it happened to me, and separation or not, we can't erase that as if it didn't exist. My Gawwd, Linda, I love you!" I cried.

"I know that, Michael. I love you too, but what can we do?" Linda asked.

I could hear the desperation in her voice, and I was just as desperate, but there didn't seem to be any solution. "I don't *know!*" I said. "I just don't want this to come to an end. Are we being punished?" I asked painfully. "Have we done something wrong? How can that be? We fell in love; what could be so awful about that? It's not fair!"

"No, it isn't fair, Michael. It stinks—it just friggin' stinks," she said bitterly.

It was like being held in a vise, unable to move in any direction; it seemed that we were incapable of doing anything that might save us. We were caught up in an inevitable series of events that we were powerless to change.

"It's not as if I haven't seen this sort of thing before," I concluded.

"What do you mean?" Linda asked.

"Nathan, one of my friends at school, was really hot for Susan. I mean it was more than just going steady, he had even given her his class ring. She put a big chunk of tape on it so that she could keep it on her finger.

"Then her parents got involved; they decided that things were getting *too* hot. Since they had money, they sent Susan to a private school, hoping that the distance would help to cool things off."

"Did it work?" she asked.

"They tried to stick it out. There were daily phone calls for awhile. But eventually her parents got their wish."

"If you're telling me all this to make me feel better, it ain't working." Linda said, punching me in the arm.

"You don't know the half of it," I answered mysteriously. "Last night my dad gave us the worst possible news. He told the family that we wouldn't be returning to the cottage next summer. The president of the company has told him there won't be any raises, and no bonus this year—for anybody. Two of their accounts canceled and until they can be replaced everyone suffers. Sooo, Dad decided we had to tighten our belts too.

"I was hoping that no matter what happened this winter, we would still get to spend one more summer together before I had to go off to college. Now, even that's gone."

Linda didn't answer. Scrunched together in this cozy hiding place, I twisted around to see that she was close to tears. I continued watching, until they began to escape and gently roll down. Reaching out, I took her into my arms, and with her head buried in my shoulder, we both started to weep. At first it was soft and restrained, just the sound of sniffling and an occasional whimper, as her warm tears slowly soaked through my light summer shirt. Tenderly, I lifted her head, and with an easy motion I moved her away just enough so that I could examine her face. With my palms cupped over her ears, I used my thumbs to carefully sweep aside the wetness. Then I kissed her delicately on her forehead, and gently pressed my lips to the crest of each cheek.

My intention was to comfort her; instead it had the opposite effect. She began to cry more freely, and when I saw what I had done, I thought my heart would break. Gulping spasmodically, I started to cry with her. This uncontrolled blubbering rose and fell in a kind of wailing lament that echoed loudly in that close chamber, and was awful to hear. For several minutes we were both inconsolable. It seemed that all the wonderful brightness that had filled our day was gone, and we were drowning in this dreadful black melancholy.

The two of us sat there, huddled together in a knotty tangle, trying to climb inside of each other in the foolish hope that once we made that mystical connection nothing could possibly separate us. Finally we relaxed the fierce grip that we had upon each other, and seeing the dusty streaks that marred Linda's face, I reached into my pocket and removed my handkerchief. Something my mother insisted I carry, but that had never made much sense to me until now. Haltingly, I began to dab at her face until Linda plucked the soft linen cloth from my hand and finished the job. Forgetting my good manners, I hauled my shirt-tail from under my belt and brought it up to rub away the stickiness that I could feel under my eyes and in furrows on either side of my nose.

During the next few minutes we gathered up our things and went to tell Mr. Abernathy that we were leaving. It was obvious from our reddened eyes that we were upset, but he said nothing. Instead, he thanked us for coming, and told us that he had enjoyed our company. He even expressed the hope that we might come again and visit him; which was really nice of him. But under the circumstances, it wasn't likely we would have any chance of returning.

The ride back was slow and tiresome, and few words passed between us. Only the sober reality of our pending separation accompanied us as we pushed heavily against the pedals.

Arriving back at Earl's house well after five, and leaving the bicycles, we thanked the guys and headed down to the beach. Removing our shoes, and holding one in each hand, we walked along until we came to the dunes in front of Linda's house. Here, standing in the rough sand, we kissed. I enjoyed the moist softness of her lips pressed against mine and knew that I would miss that softness. Because our hands weren't free we didn't embrace, but leaning in we stole one more kiss before parting. As Linda stepped away, I promised to return after supper. Then I ambled off at a rugged pace, angrily kicking up sand in front of me as I headed toward the cottage. It had been a splendid day, but because it ended with such awful sadness, it would be a bittersweet memory.

CHAPTER 18

SATURDAY AND Sunday passed quietly, and though we were together we couldn't shake the general sense of despair that pervaded everything we did. Apparently the tears which were shed Friday afternoon while we were under the protection of that shady ledge had finally forced us to face reality. When my parents closed the cottage on Monday, we would have to deal with an uncertain future. All summer long we had enjoyed a relationship that had taken us to such sweet and dizzying heights, and which now threatened to plunge us into the most crushing despair. Even if it were possible for either of us to find this kind of love again, we would never be able to recreate the unique events, or the special innocence, that had made our first experience seem so incredible.

This year my family didn't celebrate Labor Day, we were too busy cleaning and packing to leave. Besides, no one was in a holiday mood. We all knew that this was our last summer—that we wouldn't be coming back next season. We expected to leave by noon on Monday. Mom and Dad would pack us into the back seat of the car, and then after leaving the keys with the owner on the other side of town, we would return to our winter home in Wakefield.

Linda and I agreed to meet at nine on the beach near the seawall. As I approached her, I wondered, would I have expended all this time and emotion, would I have allowed myself to fall so hopelessly in love, if I had been able to look into the future and see this moment? What would I have done if I had known how awful it would be to leave Linda behind, with no prospects for tomorrow, or next month or next year, with the real possibility that I might never see her again? I decided that it wouldn't have made any difference. Somehow I was convinced that this was predestined, that we were kindred spirits, and whether we had come together this summer or next, on this beach or somewhere else, eventually we would have met, and loved, and left. Although, if this had happened at another time and place, would it have ended the same way?

    Standing there, shifting her feet in the sand, she looked as attractive and desirable as ever. What passed between us in those few minutes was cold and artificial. We promised to stay in touch. But secretly I was convinced that neither of us had the tenacity or endurance that it would take to continue our romance in a passionless world of phone calls and letters. I felt an onerous sense of foreboding as I looked longingly into her eyes. What I saw behind their wet brightness was hurtful, and I lowered my head. Quickly Linda's fingers came under my chin and brought it up to confront her sweet smile. We embraced, holding onto each other with cruel desperation. For a long time we didn't move, then at last we kissed. It was quick and eager, but not particularly passionate. Afterwards Linda broke away and ran down the beach. She looked back only once, as she reached the jetty. Then she continued along the outer shore until she had disappeared beyond the dunes. I followed her progress, watching her until the end. The strong ocean breeze cooled my hot face and disturbed the grass along the top of the dunes, but there were no tears. Not today.

CHAPTER 19

I WENT back home; back to school and friends, back to the same boring and familiar routine. Linda and I did try to stay in touch. We wrote letters and talked on the phone. But there was no real substance to what passed between us. Nothing in our correspondence compared to the depth of experience that we had shared during the summer. There were discussions about school and friends, and hopes for college, and sock hops and parties and glee club, and the National Honor Society. Unfortunately, I didn't know her school, or her friends, or her teachers, or the places she referred to, and she didn't know any of the people or places that I spoke of or wrote about.

It was my last year, my senior year of high school, one of the best and in some ways one of the worst years of my life. Both of us were busy, our lives filled with activity, and yet none of these events, simple or complex, exciting or boring, were being shared. And neither of us was willing to resurrect memories of the kind of intimacy that we had enjoyed during our summer together; it was too disabling. So, gradually we stopped calling. We had less and less to talk about, and the awkward silences that punctuated our conversations were horrible to endure. We didn't discuss this. It doesn't seem that either of us came to any conscious decision about ending those calls. It just happened.

I suppose that I might have tried harder. Maybe I could have bummed a ride from a friend and gone out to Stoughton to see her. Looking back, there were probably a number of ways that I might have kept our relationship alive. But it didn't happen. I was young and foolish, and the possibilities that I see now weren't clear to me then.

That wasn't the end of it—not entirely anyway. Linda was too much a part of me. I thought of her often, usually at the oddest and most inconvenient times. While writing a school paper, a certain phrase would remind me of something she had said, or a line she had read from a book of poetry. Shopping in a store one afternoon, a sales girl looked up at me from the other side of the counter and when she smiled I thought I recognized the same easy expression that I had seen on Linda's face. The one she used whenever she caught me scrutinizing her good looks.

On a frigid night in December, I was sitting on my porch steps waiting for my father to warm up the car and pull it out of the garage. My head was tipped back as I stared up at a cloudless sky, full of stars. Unexpectedly the thought of that night we had lain together in the bottom of the dinghy rushed back to haunt me. The image was as vivid and crisp as the cold air around me, and the stars were just as clear and bright as they had been on that warm summer's eve. A piercing ache cut into my heart and a terrible sadness made me feel suddenly empty.

I had incredible dreams, situations so real I thought that they had to be true. And then I would wake up, open my eyes and those delicious images evaporated into the blackness of my room. These visions were bittersweet, a mixture of biting sorrow and exquisite joy. Even so, I longed for those dreams and the opportunity they brought to relive old passions. Time clouded over some of the details, and when I was awake it became more and more difficult to describe Linda's face or remember her touch. I had not fallen out of love, but the feelings were no longer as sharp and intense as they were when I was wrapped up in her arms. Which knocks the hell out of the idea that absence makes the heart grow fonder.

CHAPTER 20

GRADUATION DAY came and with it the end of old dreams and the beginning of a new adventure, one crowded with responsibility and fashioned by doubts and fears about what the future might hold. Of course I hoped for a destiny full of success and happiness, a future full of possibilities and no real prospects for failure, or at least none that I was willing to consider. Not very realistic I know, but I would have to face reality soon enough.

I graduated in 1958, a National Honor Student, at the top of my class or very near the top. With an A/B average there was never any doubt that I would go on to college. But I didn't have the money, and since I had to find a way to raise those funds myself, I knew that my entry into those prestigious halls of ivy would be delayed

During the summer I found a full-time job in a grocery market, and I worked part-time, Friday nights and Saturdays, at the foundry where my father was an accountant. It was hot, heavy work, but it paid twice as much as the store. Nevertheless, even with two jobs, I knew it would be a year before I had enough saved. It was a busy time, but not so crowded that Linda didn't creep into my thoughts. Even so, those gentle intrusions never turned into any kind of action.

****

Now, with only a few days left before I went off to college, I decided to try and contact her. It had been more than a year since any word had passed between us; but I suddenly had the urge to see her again. Maybe it was because I would soon be hundreds of miles away.

When I phoned, the operator told me that the line had been disconnected.

What happened? Where had she gone? Borrowing my father's car, I drove out to Stoughton to see if I could find out. When I finally got to her block, it took two trips up and down her street before I located the right house. Seeing her home was intimidating. Built in a French provincial style, it was made of brick, with limestone blocks decorating the lintels and sills and running in staggered lengths up the corners. The ivy climbing the sides was thick, and green, and grew up the walls in random masses that added to its bulk and made the building seem even more imposing. Linda had never mentioned servants, but this was the kind of place that certainly should have them. I felt out of place here, and I was hesitant to pick up the knocker and announce my presence. What if Linda didn't want to see me?

At last I pounded heavily on the door with my fist, and heard the sounds reverberating through the house. I braced myself for whoever might come, but when the door finally opened there was a stranger standing there. A diminutive little woman who looked smaller still as she stepped into the massive doorframe.

"Do the Richards live here?" I asked, once I'd overcome my surprise.

"No," she said. "We bought the house six months ago."

"Do you know where they've gone?"

"I'm sorry," she said. "I have no idea."

I tried the neighbors, but they couldn't help me either. It was disappointing, but I didn't have a lot of time to brood over it. There was so much to do before I got on the train. I was dying to know what had become of her, but I couldn't put aside my plans in order to try and track her down.

It was the fall of 1959 and I was getting ready to start my freshman year. I had been accepted at a small college in the Midwest. St. Paul was a fun place to be; and even though it was a city, it was nothing like Boston. It had a small town quality to it, and the people I met were polite and friendly, easy to talk to. They often struck up a conversation while waiting in line at the bank or at the checkout counter where I went to buy soda and snacks.

Choosing to live off campus, I found a couple of rooms to rent in a quiet, clean neighborhood that was within walking distance of the campus. By sharing expenses with two other guys, I was able to afford an apartment in a friendly old Victorian that was set well back from the street. The middle of the street was divided by a wide strip of grass, and that divider and the sidewalks were shaded by long rows of ancient elms. The branches fanned out in an interlocking canopy that changed dramatically from season to season. A pale leafy-green in the spring, mottled ocher in the fall, and lacey white in winter. The winters were bitter cold, and there was an abundance of snow, which to me was delightful, especially at Christmas-time. Of course I didn't have to shovel, and for the first two winters I didn't drive, which made the constant snowfall less wearing. The frigid weather would have been intimidating back home, but the people here seemed to like it. And although everybody talked about the weather and complained about the cold, generally winter was a cause for celebration among these hardy citizens.

The campus had less than six hundred students, which offered some distinct advantages. With smaller classes the professors were more accessible, and when the work got to be a little overwhelming it was easier to ask for help. Some of the assignments were long and confusing, and required extensive research, which made it difficult to complete them on time. When that happened, I often trooped down to my professor's office and begged for an extension. If he thought I was making an honest effort, he was usually more than willing to come to my rescue.

Miles from my home in Massachusetts, I was totally on my own. There was no one here to drag me out of bed in the morning, or remind me that I had an early class, or badger me about studying for an upcoming exam. The courses I took were demanding and there were long stressful hours of homework, but most of the time I managed to keep up. This wasn't like high school; getting good grades here was a whole lot more exacting. It took concentration and effort to master these new concepts and it wasn't easy to hold onto those ideas, especially when I was trying to take in so much at once.

It wasn't all hard work. There were dances, and rallies and sporting events. Live concerts and plays were held at the auditorium, and the college had a number of different clubs and organizations that catered to individual interests. I signed up as a reporter for the "New Leaf", which was the college newspaper. And I became a member of the chess club: I wasn't championship material, but I played a pretty mean game. In my last year, I decided to take a life drawing class. I had a little bit of artistic ability and I thought I could handle some figure drawing, but the class was a disappointment. The guys told me that all the models posed nude and I was curious. The closest anyone came to naked was a girl in a lime–green leotard. I still did all right—I got a C+! After that I took a class in ceramics and made a couple of lopsided bowls on a foot–powered pottery wheel.

As for sports, I enjoyed them; I just wasn't talented enough to qualify for any of the teams. But I was an enthusiastic fan and attended most of the games; at least the ones played at home.

I made a number of friends, including my roommate Paul, who became a second brother to me. The campus provided an excellent opportunity to exchange ideas with a variety of people whose views were very different from my own. Some of the students were from foreign countries and that gave me a chance to learn about their language and customs. It was fun to be able to swear in German; although there was never an exact English translation. And Abydos filled me in on the latest in Greek philosophy, which had more to do with his ideas on romance than they did about Plato. I find it amusing to think that we had access to all that cultural diversity long before it became politically correct.

I did have a social life, though it was limited and not terribly exciting. No matter how busy I was with my studies, I still hadn't lost my interest in pretty girls. I can't remember why, but for some reason there were more of them than there were of us—more girls, that is. And my studies threw me together with several young maidens who were very attractive and very agreeable. Of course I wasn't any more courageous then than I was at sixteen, but when I did get up the gumption to ask, mostly they said yes. Still, until my last year, these dates were few and far between. Time was part of the problem (there was too little of it), but it was also hard not to compare every girl I met to Linda. That probably wasn't fair. It usually meant that I only went out once or twice with the same girl. But fair or not I couldn't seem to avoid making the comparison.

By my fourth year I finally relaxed that standard, and there were two girls in particular that I met and dated who were more than just casual acquaintances. They developed into relationships that required some earnest effort, and each started with the promise of blossoming into a genuine romance.

My roommate Paul introduced me to Rebecca in the fall of my senior year; and for three months we shared some fanciful and loving experiences. She was really quite a pretty girl, with classic features, pale skin and dark eyes. Quiet and conventional, she was always pleasant, never aggressive. The kind of perfect young woman that every good parent wishes for; the sort that they refer to as a *good girl,* the type that you can marry and grow old with. Which was fine, but I wasn't comfortable with that kind of perfection. I needed someone a little less saintly; I wanted an earthly creature whose spirit was grounded in substance and reality. Someone who would demand to see the real me and when she had discovered who that was, would love me anyway.

Besides Rebecca wasn't as perfect as she seemed. On the surface she was everything anyone could wish for, but I soon discovered that that image wasn't real. She was like an elaborately painted Easter egg: everything bright and showy, but inside that fragile cover it was empty. All the thick sticky elements—all the rich ingredients, all the meaty substance that held the promise of life—had been sucked out.

There was never a time when Rebecca spoke with conviction about anyone or anything—she never defended a cause or stood her ground on any weighty moral issue. It was apparent that she worked very hard not to offend, and it wasn't possible to draw her into a debate, because she would always end up taking your side.

Rebecca was like a little child. She was always trying to please, and very much in need of personal approbation. After we had dated for a time I came to realize that she was easy to be with, always sweet and agreeable; but she was *too* agreeable. Her quiet acceptance of anything that I suggested made me angry. Just a little conflict once in a while would have been a welcome diversion. I sometimes said things that were obviously wrong, just to get her to correct me, but she wouldn't take the bait. Even when I admitted I was wrong she would just say: "I'm with you," or "If you say so." "That's it?" I would challenge, and her response was always: "So—what do you want, blood?" That was as close as she could come to an argument, and even that was always followed by: "I'm sorry."

At last I came to the conclusion that Rebecca was only a reflection of whoever she was with at the time—a mirror of the person from whom she sought approval. I could see all the parts: a piece of her girlfriend Carol, something of my moral inhibition, or the philosophy of her favorite history professor, Mr. Hassler; but the parts changed. They were only as constant as her friends, and her friends often lost interest in her. Once I came to recognize that Rebecca wasn't any more or less than a collection of such bits and pieces, it became clear to me that she wasn't meant to be my soul mate.

So one evening, after an amiable discussion, we decided that though we had become good friends, something was missing, and we agreed that there was no reason to continue this courtship. We had no future, at least not one that included marriage, which was something that was very important to both of us. It probably seems old-fashioned today, but at the time I always looked at the girls I dated with the idea that I was choosing a partner—that our relationship would ultimately lead to love and marriage. To me, that was the object of the game.

However, things were changing; and the college campuses were the foundation for the early stirrings of a new sexuality. As I looked around me I could see the loosening of old Victorian standards—the beginnings of a generation that sought to redefine the meaning of sex. Living together became more important than marriage. That way, if things didn't work out, you could just walk away. I had a hard time with that; I had a hard time with all the new ideas that were being thrown at me.

The guys that I lived with, and some of those in my classes, talked about meeting girls at a frat party, or off campus at a bar, and by the end of the evening they were in bed together. It was a kind of casual sport, like a quick game of tennis, something that provided a little exercise and a little sweat, and then it was over. Soon they were seeking a new partner—a new conquest. It was a your-place-or-mine attitude that transformed love into something purely physical, something totally devoid of substance or commitment. It was hard for me to deal with this new social standard. In fact, I couldn't deal with it at all. It took away all the mystery and destroyed the magic that had always made getting to know a girl so exciting. My classmates often talked about foreplay and how important it was to good sex. My interpretation of foreplay was something else. It wasn't the kind of thing that you did for a few minutes before you played hide-the-weenie. To me, it was the whole process of dating, which could take weeks or months or even years. To me it was romance, and the object of all this horny effort wasn't to get a girl into bed, it was to bring her to the altar.

My friends told me that such old-fashioned ideas were part of a tight–collared, repressive religious philosophy that was designed to keep people from having fun. They argued that sex was natural and wonderful and ought to be enjoyed openly and unashamedly by everyone. Besides, they said, I was hundreds of miles from home. If I decided to experiment with sex, or drugs, or booze, what was to stop me? Who would know?

"I would know," I answered, and they laughed.

My father had taught me that real character was built around the principle of doing the right thing. Then he qualified that by adding: "That means doing the right thing even when no one else is watching."

My roommates and others made fun of me, but eventually they left me alone. That was hard too, because they didn't just stop trying to convince me of the equity of this new philosophy, many of them stopped talking to me altogether.

Into this unsettling period of moral uncertainty came a young woman of such a capricious nature, someone so distracting, that she left me totally unbalanced. I met her in the spring of '63 just before graduation. Her name was Sandy and she was a part of this new age. A nymph, a spritely pixie, a rebel, someone who thought the old ways were outmoded and obsolete, she objected loudly to the restrictions of a society that was driven by Victorian prudery and Christian hypocrisy. She wasn't a hippie or a flower child, but she was definitely heading in that direction.

Our first encounter was at the campus library. While doing research for a school paper I accidentally bumped into her. Loaded down with books and trying to claim the same table, we both came crashing out of different aisles and collided. The impact sent books flying in all directions and both of us landed awkwardly on a hard and unforgiving floor. My selfish rush to get to the empty study table in front of me had knocked Sandy on her keister; and she ought to have been mad as hell, but she wasn't. Instead, she began to laugh, and then to blame herself. Apologizing, she showed such eager concern, asking again and again if I were all right, that frankly I was dumbfounded. And then she begged for my forgiveness. Her candor and her unabashed interest in my welfare left me utterly defenseless.

Beautiful would not fairly describe her. There wasn't anything very remarkable about her looks. Yet she *was* attractive. There was a bouncy exuberance, a brightness in her eyes, an infectious smile, an abundant personality that made you want to be around her. I felt a need to bask in that brightness, and to feed off that energy. She had a pleasing figure, short and trim, what one might call petite. And there was a certain solidity to her tiny form. She was robust and apparently not a stranger to regular exercise. Though I never measured her, I'm sure she couldn't have stood more than five feet tall, and to reach that, she would probably have had to stand on her toes. Her hair was long and straight, falling nearly halfway down her back and it seemed to be in constant motion, which was wonderfully distracting. She was so unaffected, so pleasant and friendly, I felt encouraged to ask her out the very afternoon that we met. Her answer was quick and spontaneous: she not only accepted, but she made me believe that she was anxious to spend more time with me. I couldn't guess where this was going, but judging by the butterflies in my stomach, it certainly was a promising beginning.

She met me at a place on Grand Avenue, called Piccolo's, where we split a double-cheese pizza and talked. Then we went to see *The Apartment*, with Jack Lemmon and Shirley MacLaine, which was playing at an old movie theater near Fairview. It was the kind of movie-house that still had a balcony. Rococo and fancy scrollwork decorated the walls, and the seats were covered in red velvet, with hard mahogany armrests. We climbed up to the balcony because Sandy said she thought it would be exciting to sit near the rail and look down on the other movie-goers. There were only three rows of seats, and searching the darkness I found only one other couple sitting in the back corner. That made the possibility of romance seem very hopeful, but nothing much developed other than holding hands.

By the time that I dropped her off, after a long evening that lasted till past one in the morning, we had become good friends. There was even a bubbly little kiss before we parted. It was impossible for me to decide what sort of person Sandy really was. Her lavish free spirit confused me. It was too soon yet to know if I was falling in love, but I could see that her generosity and openness would probably make that very easy.

Over the next few weeks, we saw a lot of each other. Sharing assignments, doing homework, having lunch, going to local theater performances, even attending a free concert. It was not a deeply passionate relationship: a touch, a tender kiss, holding hands; nothing more familiar passed between us. Even so, the closeness that Sandy and I did share was enticing and it was pleasant being in her company. I didn't feel the need to practice any pretense. Both of us seemed totally at ease.

Never before had I met someone who had such limitless confidence. Her sense of security astounded me. She was so completely sure of who she was and what she wanted out of life. College was only the beginning; she said she wanted a career in advertising and public relations. She was very active politically and had already expressed some hope of running for office. Maybe not as high as Congress, but something. She thought that there was a lot wrong with the world, and she believed that government was best equipped to persuade people to do what was right.

Though I couldn't imagine anything that I might do or say which could possibly embarrass or shock her, she continually shocked me. She often acted on impulse and no subject was too sacred or too intimate. There was nothing foul or vulgar in her manner, but she talked openly about sex, and even shared the details of her sexual experiences. All of this was usually described in clinical terms rather than street language, but it was still very embarrassing. Since Linda was the only person that I had ever come close to being intimate with, Sandy's experience was considerably more than mine. Not that she *slept around,* but she had definitely had sex with her last boyfriend. She told me so; and she was very clear about when, where and how. I wasn't used to having a girl share such things with me. True, Linda had discussed some personal thoughts (about sex), but always with a shy reticence. With Sandy it was very different. She seemed to assume that I was comfortable with her directness. If she had asked I might have objected, but the subject always came out of nowhere, and before I could say anything, she had already moved off in another direction. Yet with all of her talk, Sandy had never shown that kind of interest in ME! Even on those rare occasions when she slipped into slang, like *dick* and *beaver*, and *getting it on*, she never suggested that we should cozy up or diddle around. In fact we hadn't done anything other than kissing, which was ruddy and eager, but not particularly hot. It was hard for me to decide if I wanted more intimacy. What would I do if Sandy *did* try to jump my bones? Not that I didn't have feelings for her, but . . . And it was the *but* that worried me.

****

In the middle of May, just before the semester ended, after a grueling week of finals, Sandy and I decided to drive all the way out to Bass Lake in Plymouth, which was west of the Twin Cities. It was unseasonably warm and sticky, with the temperature above eighty degrees. We drove out on County Road 10, arriving late in the afternoon. To get to the shore, we turned off on a gravel road, and after following a gentle curve through a thick stand of trees, we came out into a clearing and a circle of cottages. These were recently built and brightly painted, but they weren't very large.

The few people who had been enjoying the water were already leaving. Some, after pulling their canoes from the water's edge, were loading them onto the roof of their cars. Three or four of the others went into one of the nearby cottages.

Late as it was, we were determined to borrow a boat and row out on the lake to cool off. My roommate, Paul, had a friend who lived on the shore. With my roommate's written directions, we soon found this man's home. It was about a quarter of a mile further along the gravel road. This was not a cottage and not something that had been thrown up recently. It was a shingled two-story building with dark green shutters. It looked like something from the 20's, and the house and the shore and the tall pines reminded me of a scene from an old-black-and white movie. The sort of place the kidnappers would have used as a hideaway.

The man who answered our knock was big and swarthy, with an infectious smile that never seemed to leave his face. He introduced himself as Kevin and we explained who we were and who had sent us. His smile grew wider still as he invited us to come into his living room. After bringing us a glass of cold lemonade, he excused himself while he went to check on his dogs. They hadn't stopped barking since we drove up, and he said he wanted to quiet them before he brought us down to the dock. When he returned, he took us along a well-worn path to the boathouse. As we stepped out onto the wooden dock a blue-gray kingfisher plunged into the water ahead of us. Pointing at a twelve foot lapstrake tied across the far end, he told us we were welcome to take it. But he did warn us not to stay out on the lake after dark.

Sitting low in the water, with an eight-or-nine-inch freeboard and a beam that was almost five feet across, she looked safe and dependable, but more than that she was 'yare,' which loosely translated refers to something quick and responsive. And maybe, like the hourglass figure on a girl, it describes the graceful beauty of a well-proportioned boat. I don't know if Sandy could appreciate any of this, but I certainly did. During my four years at school I hadn't looked at a boat or been near the ocean, and this sweet little craft reminded me of what I had been missing.

Once we were on board, I pushed gently away from the dock and started rowing slowly towards the middle of the lake.

By five o'clock we had made it to the far side. Along the shoreline was a wooded area that was free from houses. At this hour all the other boaters were gone. And while the late afternoon sun shone on the lime-green leaves and gave a special brilliance to the tender new grass along the water's edge, we drifted sluggishly through the beginnings of Canadian pondweed and flat lily pads. The heavy humid air, the timid breeze and soft wispy clouds, the flutter of waterbugs and the splash of a bass breaking the surface ahead of us, created a relaxed languid mood, a kind of lazy somnolence that nearly put us to sleep. Enjoying the tranquillity of this secluded cove on the north side of the lake, and listening to the gentle slapping of the water against the hull, I leaned across and took Sandy's hand. Apparently she saw this as a signal to cozy up and do a little petting; and being careful not to tip the boat, she moved over to join me on the center seat. Putting her arms around my waist, she embraced me lovingly, and gave me a sweet kiss, nothing intense, but extremely charming and inviting. Then, as often happened, her disposition changed and she announced that she wanted to have a swim.

"We're not dressed for swimming!" I protested.

"People don't dress to swim," she said. "It's just the opposite."

Sandy was wearing a fitted, white cotton shirt with the name of the college printed across the back and a pair of plaid Bermuda shorts. And, in what was becoming the style of the 'new woman', she was without a bra. They weren't burning them yet, but some were discarding them as a form of protest. I was casually dressed in dungarees and a light-blue button-down shirt with the sleeves rolled up. Sandy slid off the seat into the bottom of the boat and started to remove her shoes and socks. Once she had decided on a course of action, there was no way of changing her mind. She seldom thought things through or considered the consequences. For her, if it felt good or seemed right at the time, then she did it. So I wasn't terribly surprised when, having already stepped out of her shorts, she pulled her shirt up over her head and, bare-breasted, slipped over the side of the boat into the water.

"Hoo–boy, this water is cold!" she shouted back at me.

"What did you expect? It was solid ice only a few weeks ago!" I answered. "It takes more than a couple of warm days to take away the chill!"

"C'mon, Michael, join me!" she invited playfully, as she came alongside.

"No way! You just said it was too cold!"

"Aww, it's not *that* bad," she reported; then reached up to rock the boat.

Somewhat reluctantly, I removed my shirt and trousers, hauled my undershirt over my head and jumped in with only my shorts on. I thought that after swimming in the Atlantic no cold could shock me, but there was something very different about this. It was a relentless bone-chilling kind of cold that attacked my body with a terrible piercing pain. I knew the minute I hit the water that I didn't want to stay in here very long. I hollered loudly and then started to laugh at myself and at the absurdity of the situation I was in. Sandy, who had been splashing rather wildly, began to laugh with me. I really think that all that reckless thrashing about was more than just good fun. It was probably designed to help keep her blood moving.

Moments later, I was dragging myself out of the water. It was difficult getting back into the empty boat without capsizing it. After a couple of attempts, it became obvious that climbing over the side wouldn't work, and I went around to the stern, where I gingerly tossed my upper body over the edge, and squirming and twisting, wriggled back into the boat.

Kneeling, I grabbed the edge of my boxers and began to squeeze out the excess water. Then realizing that this was a wasted effort, I dropped down in the bottom of the boat, gave my shorts a quick yank to drag the waistband past my hips and slid them off, one leg at a time. Sopping wet, I leaned over the gunwale to wring them out. With my legs still spread wide over the slatted decking, I looked down and saw that my penis had shriveled away to a wrinkled little nubbin and my testicles had nearly disappeared into my groin—and I thought: the ocean, even at its coldest, had never caused this much damage. First I poked the end timidly to see if there was any feeling left. Under the pressure of my finger it moved a little, then sprang back when I let go, which proved that the flesh wasn't actually frozen. Then I reached down to cover myself, hoping that the warmth might save me from frostbite. That's when I discovered that the whole business fit into the hollow of my hand, and I wondered: What if my poor little 'doogie' never recovers? The best solution seemed to be to get my clothes on. So, using my dry undershirt as a towel, I wiped away some of the wetness and dressed quickly in my shirt and pants.

Then turning my attention back toward the lake, I immediately started to encourage Sandy to come out of the water too. It didn't require much convincing. She wasn't as brave as she pretended to be, and soon was at the side of the boat begging for my help to pull her on board. As she fell back into the boat, her body was no longer buried under the murky surface of the lake, and without that protective covering she lay there nearly naked. Her paleness contrasted sharply with the dark gray interior of the hull, and she was breathing heavily and shivering. The brief underpants that she had worn while swimming were drenched. Whatever the material, it was very thin, and the water made it almost transparent.

Her body was beautiful, and she seemed proud of her nakedness. There was no feigned modesty—no hurried effort to dress herself. Under different circumstances, this erotic display would have been a definite turn-on. But we had no history of this kind of intimacy and instead of being excited I was embarrassed.

Whether it was the prolonged silence or the expression on my face, or both, she soon realized that I wasn't happy. Her openness hadn't brought the reaction that she expected, and I could see that my cold response had made her uneasy. She shrugged her shoulders and with a sullen air of disappointment started to pull her shorts over her water-soaked briefs. The dry-wet combination made that difficult, and the struggle made her breasts jiggle, which only added to my discomfort. Then she reached out to retrieve her shirt. But when she pulled her top down, the wetness of her body was quickly absorbed, and the sodden material clung to her like a second skin. The circular shape of her nipples bled through and seemed darker and more conspicuously erect than they had before she'd covered them.

The sensual impact of all this was explosive, but more than anything else I felt angry. And I wondered: *Why?* Was I ashamed? Was this a matter of prudery? I wasn't sixteen anymore, I knew the difference between male and female, and I understood how those parts were designed to come together. It was all a very natural process. But somehow this didn't seem natural—this wasn't just happenstance. Sandy had chosen to strip off her clothes and had never once asked how I felt about it. Even now her manner seemed much too provocative. The signals here were all wrong. A sudden queer feeling overtook me—a deep in-the-gut kind of ache—as if someone had reached inside and torn something out. Was it shame, or disgust, or some kind of disillusionment?

STOP! I said to myself. *You're not being fair!* As troubling as this was, I hadn't been totally honest with myself about Sandy's motivations. She could be scatterbrained and impulsive, but she wasn't depraved, and her exhibitionism certainly wasn't meant to be indecent. Two hours ago, she probably wouldn't have thought of taking her clothes off in front of me; and tomorrow she would very likely regret it. Whatever the outcome, I was sure that Sandy wouldn't have played this game if she didn't think it would please me. And now, what she had so freely offered had been rejected.

I looked at Sandy and saw her discomfort. She had folded her arms to hide her breasts, and legs together she sat ramrod straight. For the first time I saw a shadow fall across her bright face, and I knew she wasn't as invincible as she pretended to be. Shaking her head, she sent out a spray of water in all directions, then she bent forward in submission and let her heavy tresses form a shameful curtain between us. I should have at least tried to explain my feelings, but I couldn't do it. I had all these thoughts churning around in my head, but I couldn't get them out. My mouth was dry and my tongue immobile, and it was impossible to translate those feelings into words.

Sandy swung around and moved to the narrow seat in the bow. It was clear that this was meant as a dismissal. The moment had passed, and any opportunity to repair this rift between us had passed with it. Picking up the oars, I slid them into the locks and started rowing slowly toward the dock. The trip across the lake was quiet, and in the car, whenever I started a little polite chitchat, all I got back was a sullen yes or no. When I finally dropped her at her dorm, she rushed away without even a goodbye. The next day she was herself again, bright and pleasant, but no mention was made of the lake. And when I tried to bring it up, a quick gesture of her hands cut me off. She just wouldn't talk about it.

During the next several days, I began to consider whether or not this friendship was apt to become anything more. Consciously reflecting upon the wonderful experiences that we had shared together, I discovered that I liked Sandy, she was really a marvelous person, but we had very few things in common. We didn't believe in the same values and I couldn't easily discard all the teaching and standards that I had grown up with. I wasn't prepared to accept the idea that freedom meant a complete lack of discipline. The concept that you could do whatever you wanted just because it felt good was just too radical for me.

Sandy had become a good friend and we agreed to keep that friendship alive; but we both knew that it couldn't be anything more than that. Actually, the time that I spent with Sandy, even after we stopped dating, was beneficial. The fact that we had conflicting ideas about the meaning of life and argued constantly about that and other weighty issues helped to crystallize in my young mind what was important to me, and what it was that I really believed in. Those friendly confrontations helped me to determine what direction I would take, and who I would finally become.

CHAPTER 21

WHILE I was away at college, the world that I grew up in changed. All the ancient ideologies and values seemed to be under attack. Young people everywhere began to question all the old standards, especially on the college campuses. The hippies or flower children of this counter-culture were suspicious of everything that had come before and had learned to distrust every institution. They were particularly at odds with their parents, believing that they were responsible for creating a world that was corrupt and full of greed. I will agree that not all was right with the world. Some of our history was flawed and some of our leaders were less than honest. By the time that I graduated from college in June of '63, it was becoming apparent that the government couldn't be trusted and some very scary things were happening around the world.

During the years following that joyless parting, between Linda and me on the beach in Ocean Bluff, a lot of startling and unpleasant events had taken place. Castro overthrew Zalvidar Batista and turned Cuba into a Communist State. The Supreme Court passed a ruling to desegregate the schools, which was supposedly a good thing, but which led to rioting and demonstrations, and racial polarization. Gary Powers was shot down in May of 1960, by a soviet surface-to-air missile, while flying a U-2 spy plane over Russian territory.

At first President Eisenhower denied the existence of such a plane, but when the Russians produced the pilot and pieces of the wreckage, the U.S. was forced to admit that they had been flying missions over the Soviet Union. The fact that the President would lie to the American public was disturbing to me. It may have been terribly naive, but I had an unquestioning faith in the Presidency, and I trusted Eisenhower in particular. Like so many others at the time, I saw him as a hero, and heroes were supposed to be of mythological proportions—strong and brave and true.

In 1961, John F. Kennedy was inaugurated as the 35th president of the United States, the first Catholic to hold that office, which had caused a good deal of controversy during his campaign. Personally, I didn't care about his religion; I was more concerned about whether or not he would keep us in Southeast Asia. There was a lot of controversy about whether on not we belonged in Vietnam. The draft was a scary thing and if the U.S. expanded the war, I saw the very real possibility that Uncle Sam might put a gun in my hand and ask me to kill someone. Under different circumstances I wouldn't have objected to that, but the whole idea of *this* war was pretty foggy. And I didn't want to risk my life for something I really didn't understand.

In that same year, we had to deal with the disastrous Bay of Pigs invasion, an unsuccessful attempt by Cuban exiles to take Cuba back from Fidel Castro. Approximately a week later, President Kennedy came forward and took full responsibility for the fiasco.

The following year, we were forced to confront the worst crisis since 1950 when the North Korean People's Army crossed the 38th parallel and captured Seoul. The President went on national television, and showing graphic aerial photographs, announced that the Russians had installed missile bases on the island of Cuba. Ninety miles off the coast of Florida, our avowed enemies had positioned nuclear missiles aimed at the U.S. mainland. People were certain that we were headed for a nuclear holocaust. I was one of them, worried sick that this might be the end. I had seen the movies of the Bomb going off and buildings being blown away. I had grown up with the Russian nemesis, bomb shelters and civil-defense drills. Up until then, it hadn't seemed very real. As kids in grade school, we had often joked about the absurdity of saving ourselves by crawling under our desks and putting our heads between our legs.

Fortunately, through diplomatic efforts and the use of an American naval blockade, the Russians backed down and agreed to dismantle the bases.

CHAPTER 22

EVEN WITH the Russian threat, and the civil rights movement causing riots in the streets, when I graduated in June of '63, I was still hopeful that America would survive. But a much greater tragedy lay just ahead, one that would torment the national soul and shatter public confidence. On November 22, 1963, John F. Kennedy was assassinated by Lee Harvey Oswald in Dallas Texas and the entire nation came to a standstill.

Anyone who was alive at that time, and isn't too young to remember, can recall in detail where they were and what they were doing when they first heard the news. Even now, the harsh images and the tear–choked words of the news commentators, the sadness and shock on the faces of everyone I saw, are fixed in my memory.

Over the years since, there has been continual controversy about who was actually responsible. Theories about a high level conspiracy. Questions about the gun, and whether there was a second shooter—confusion about witnesses and the man that was seen on the grassy knoll. There have been very few answers. But on that day I had only one question—

Why? Why would anyone shoot the President of the United States?

Yes, I had been on a college campus, I had witnessed the rebellion, the outcry against perceived injustice, but I still believed in my parents. I really thought that they knew what was right and what was just—but this? This was insane!

There was a terrible sense that this was more than just the murder of a great leader. Somehow I felt that I was witnessing the death of the nation. It was as though from this point on everything would be defined by this singular event: that the history of the country would be divided into a *before* and *after* with Kennedy's death being the point of separation.

For me, nothing would ever be the same.

****

When I left college, I went back to my summer employer while I continued to apply to several companies in Boston for a job as an accountant. On this particular day I was working at Carlton's Super Market. Around noontime, the store got busy and I was called from the stock room to come up to the registers and help out bagging groceries. As a convenience to our customers, we would bring the bags out to their car and load them into the backseat or the trunk. As near as I can recall, it was about one o'clock when I noticed that something was out of whack.

Generally Friday afternoons were busy. In those days Friday was also payday and so it was a logical time to go shopping. But this afternoon, even though the store was filled with the usual people, there was a strange and chilling quiet. At first the cause of this stillness eluded me. Then, as I headed back from the parking lot to the front entrance, I saw several people standing next to a car. The door on the passenger side was open and it was obvious that they were listening to the car radio. I thought this seemed odd, and wheeling my grocery carriage over, I asked one of the listeners what was going on. He looked at me with an ashen face and said flatly: "The President has been shot." During my lifetime I have had to face a number of traumatic situations. All of them were painful, but none ever hit me harder than those few words did on that bright, sunny November afternoon. Nothing in my life up to that time had prepared me for something as emotionally charged as this.

As I stood there with the others, listening to the sound of disbelief in Walter Cronkite's voice, the reality of what he was saying hit me as if someone had viciously cracked a two–by–four across my chest. My emotions always seemed to hang too close to the surface, and the smallest tragedy could bring me to tears, which was often embarrassing. But today I wasn't alone. And I wasn't embarrassed when those emotions clawed their way up, looking for release. A hot, stinging sensation irritated my eyes and turned into a watery blur. And when it finally spilled over I didn't try to hide it, or wipe it away; I just let it happen.

For the rest of the afternoon I walked around only half–aware of what I was doing. Looking back, how I managed to function at all is a mystery to me. I suppose that if my work had involved anything dangerous, I would have been at risk. My thoughts kept going round and round, but they always came back to the same question—

Why?

Over the next couple of hours until my workday ended, people came to me with sketchy accounts about what was coming in over the airways. Most of this information was fractured and disjointed, and it did nothing to dispel the cheerless cloud of sorrow that seemed to engulf me, and everyone around me.

At five o'clock I punched out and headed for home. But I didn't go home; instead I drove out to the reservoir. At night, it was a place that was frequently used by the kids to make-out, but during the day or in the early evening it was also an excellent spot for some solitary reflection. At first, I sat in the car, listening to the radio. All the stations had something to say about the shooting in Dallas and every word seemed to plunge me deeper and deeper into despair. I've always been religious—not a bible-thumper, and not always a churchgoer, but most definitely a believer. Now, with this tragedy weighing so heavily upon me, I turned off the radio and sitting in the darkened car I began to pray.

In the beginning the words came haltingly. This was not my first prayer, but I hadn't had a lot of practice and I felt awkward. I spoke aloud, faltering, not able to find the right words. Then, as I became more contrite, the essence of my prayer changed. I wanted God to give me some reason for this insanity. If there was supposed to be some purpose in this madness, what could it be? I had come for answers, but that's not what I got. God didn't seem to have any, or at least he wasn't giving them to me. Then suddenly it wasn't about Kennedy anymore, it was about me, and I poured out my doubts and fears.

Who was I? Why was I here? I couldn't imagine that anything I had said or done in my life up to now had ever made any difference. And I hardly expected that anything in my future was going to change that. Yet here was a man who *had* made a difference, and who could say what greatness he might have achieved if his life hadn't been swept away by a bullet smashing through his skull? And so I rambled on and on, like a tank driving deeper and deeper into no-man's-land, until I finally broke down. I never felt like I got any answers, and yet when it was over I finally felt at peace.

Those few moments of prayer, those bitter tears shed, were not wasted. I still didn't know why Kennedy was dead—and I still didn't know if my life had any purpose. But I did feel that I was important to someone, and somehow that brought me a certain justification of spirit and gave me the subtle courage I needed to face the future, at least my own future. In the days that followed I had to deal with some disturbing questions, and there were times when I seethed with anger and indignation, but I never had to address the kind of passion that had torn me apart that first evening while I sat alone in my car next to the reservoir.

I've been told that "Real men don't cry." There seems to be a special mythology that requires men to be stalwart and unemotional in the face of any catastrophe. Bull! A lot of grown men cried that day. My father was one of them, and I had never seen him demonstrate such raw emotion before. Something was lost that terrible day. I'm not sure that I can define it, but somehow the peace and security of the world that I grew up in was shattered. Even worse, I began to doubt that it had ever existed.

Under this bewildering cloud of discontent I began to resurrect memories of the vacations I had spent at Ocean Bluff. Lying on the bed in my drab apartment, at the end of another lonely Sunday afternoon, I recalled those lazy summers when everything seemed so right. I longed to reclaim the sweet innocence that made my childhood world safe and full of hope. And suddenly I had an overwhelming desire to go back—back to the cottage, back to the beach, back to the halcyon days of my youth.

CHAPTER 23

WHEN THE warm summer weather had come again to the harsh New England coast, I made my preparations to return to Ocean Bluff. College was behind me now, and following a year of searching, I had finally landed my first job working for a small firm in Boston. After all these years of work and school, I was about to take my first paid vacation. Still not wealthy enough yet to afford a better car, I was driving my beat-up '47 Ford two-door sedan. It was a faded green, with lots of rust, but with a little care it had served me well through my college years and was still able to get me where I needed to go. I packed an old leather suitcase into the trunk and headed south out of Boston on the old Chief Justice Cushing Highway towards Satuit.

Vacationing on my limited budget wasn't easy. After seeking advice from friends and relatives, I had discovered a lovely guesthouse in Sea View, which was a tiny community only about a mile from Ocean Bluff—kind of a suburb of a suburb. The house wasn't on the beach, but it was within walking distance. Built on a prominent hill that rose sharply from the road below, it sat high enough above the trees and nearby cottages to offer an unobstructed view of the open sea.

This beautiful old home was not a stranger to me. I had seen it many times before, but had never been inside. Long ago, it belonged to Isaac Pierce, a local sea captain who had made his fortune in whaling. Now, with six spacious bedrooms, the stately mansion had been converted to a cozy inn that provided comfortable lodging at a modest price. You could rent a room for as little as eight dollars a night. I was paying nine, because I wanted to have a private bath. At these prices it was a luxury that I could afford, and I didn't like the idea of waiting outside in the hallway for my turn in the shower. I'd done enough of that at home and away at college. Besides, the price also included a real breakfast. Not one of those bland continental things, but the works: eggs, pancakes, hash–browns, ham and bacon, pastries and fruit. All laid out on a buffet so that you could take as much as you wanted.

I needed to make this trip; I wanted to make this trip; but what I expected to find by returning to Ocean Bluff was a mystery to me. Maybe I was trying to escape from a world gone mad—to return to better times—to recapture lost innocence—or maybe to escape from the dreariness of living alone in a cold water flat next Ashmont station. The trains made the walls vibrate and if I wasn't sitting in the chair it walked slowly across the floor. Ever since leaving college my life seemed flat and shapeless. It was nice to have a good job but what was I working for?

When I was sixteen, I thought that at twenty-three I would be old—well, old enough anyway to have a few answers—but that wasn't so. I was living independently and working to earn the money it took to pay my expenses, which is what I expected to be doing at that age; but those adult obligations weren't enough for me to declare that I was *grown up*. I still didn't have any answers to the mysteries of life, or at least to the mystery of *my* life, and I had no idea how I was going to find out.

As I drove under the leafy elms on Main Street, I could see that little had changed since I left seven years ago: a new coat of paint on Hewitt's Hardware store, a few shakes missing from the shingled walls of the movie theater, a bigger sign on Call's Drug-store, a second gas station at the corner of Allen St.. The rest was the same except that some of the stores looked a bit worn-out.

What impressed me most was that nothing seemed to be quite as big as I had remembered, except for the elms, which had obviously grown larger. I expected that, after all they were trees. But the buildings and the streets couldn't have changed, they couldn't be larger one day and smaller the next. Maybe because I had seen more of the world, this small part of it had shrunk or at least I was forced to see an image, which was somehow diminished from the grandeur of the limited world that I had once believed in.

Driving across the Strawberry Point Bridge, I realized how glad I was to be back. It was exciting to be on familiar ground, and even though I had some vague doubts about the wisdom of trying to resurrect the past, I was filled with hopeful anticipation. The objects flying past my window had awakened memories of hot afternoons lying on the beach, cold soda from the variety store, collecting baby crabs and starfish in the tidal pools, movies at the Playhouse—the misery of adolescence and pimples, and my first attempt at dating. I was thirteen. It was my first summer at Ocean Bluff and Tooey asked me to sit beside his cousin while we were at the movies. We met in front of the theatre. When we got inside I thought I should hold her hand, but I was afraid to do it. She was too pretty, though even if she had been plain, I wouldn't have had the courage.

Glancing up at the street sign, I saw that I was passing Minot Beach Road. This would take me out to the cottage, but I wasn't prepared to go that way—not yet. Instead, I continued on to Massapoug Avenue and turned up the hill to the Sea View Inn.

After checking in with Mrs. Haggerty, the proprietor, I went to my room. I scooped the things out of my suitcase and tossed them into the top drawer of the bureau, then went into the bathroom. While I was splashing some cold water on my face, I looked at the condition of my beard and decided to shave. Then I felt hungry, so I left, and headed over to North Scituate to the Fish Shack, hoping to enjoy some of their fresh clams.

Once I'd had all the fried clams I could eat, I returned to the inn. Stripping off my clothes I stepped under a luxurious stream of cool water and let it wash away the dirt and sweat of a long day.

Afterwards, I came out in my boxers and wandered aimlessly around the room. Full of nervous energy, I studied the pictures on the walls, adjusted the windows for fresh air and rearranged the furniture. Finally, sitting down in an easy chair that I had positioned next to the window, I tried to read the paper. The flash of headlights from a car pulling up the road, the sound of crickets in the grass, a sudden breeze that sent the curtains billowing into the room, an itch on my back that couldn't be reached, destroyed my concentration and I finally threw the paper aside and went to bed.

I tossed back and forth, while a chaotic mixture of thoughts and images bounced around inside my head and kept me awake. Sometime after midnight these troublesome images slipped away and I fell into a deep dreamless world that made the night pass quickly. Startled by the noise of my own snoring, I sat up in bed and opened my eyes. I couldn't remember dreaming, but swirling around on the fringes were the notes of a familiar voice, calling out my name. It was disturbing—I tried to put a face to the voice, but it wouldn't come together. The harder I worked, the more it alluded me. So I gave up. Once I let go the answer came like an explosion of light inside my head—it was Linda's face and Linda's voice. Why, after so many years had she come back to me?

Wrapped up in my sheet, which had pulled free and left my feet uncovered, I suddenly caught the pungent odor of the sea. Ahhh, I thought, how sweet it is to be in this warm bed, sheltered by the routine sounds and smells of the shore. When I was young and these things were with me every day, I had taken them for granted, and now they seemed to have a whole new meaning. They were all part of the distant memories that I had come back to reclaim. And it was those unique details that brought me comfort and filled me with a gentle sense of renewal.

When I finally deserted the comfort of my bed, I threw on some loose-fitting trousers and a light shirt. Bending over, I rolled my pants up, and barefoot left the Inn and wandered down the hill toward the Atlantic. Walking along the road, I saw that salt-stunted pitch-pine, bayberry and cord grass were packed together tightly enough to bar my way. And it took some searching before I located a spot where I could get through to the beach

Following a crooked path between sharp blades of grass, I came to a pebbly berm that had been carved out by the action of the tides. Once I jumped off this narrow ledge onto the soft wet sand below I started looking for a dry place to sit. Trudging along I felt a pleasant coolness under my tender feet as they left mushy footprints in the sand. I picked out a high spot that had not been reached by the rising tide and sat down to watch the progress of the sun as it continued to climb above the horizon. Sunrise or sunset, the patterns and shapes, the billowing clouds, the magnificent array of color, the constant movement, always created an incredible display. Whenever I'd had the opportunity to watch the sun rise or fall, it was never a disappointment, and today this colorful pageant brought a soothing balm to my uneasy spirit.

The wind from the sea had intensified and I was conscious of a full, deep sound as it rushed past my ears. Sitting there quietly, while the wind tossed my hair and gently pushed it upward away from my face, I wondered why I seldom found time to appreciate these simple indulgences. How was it that I didn't often notice my mother's smile, or the way she pushed her damp hair back behind one ear whenever she was hovering over a steaming pot of her best stew? Why did I rush headlong through a spring shower and not find some pleasure in the gentle rain as it trickled down my face? How often did I stop to smell the freshness of newly cut grass, or the wonderful woodsy aroma of burning leaves? Why couldn't I take a moment to enjoy the sound of water rushing along a stony brook, or like today sit and listen to the ocean and feel the wind against my face. Then with a sudden sharpness I remembered another special luxury, one that I had not enjoyed for a long time—the cool wetness of a soft kiss. Not just any kiss, but the sort of quick buss that comes unexpectedly from the one you love. And for a moment I could almost feel the sweet touch of a young woman brushing her lips gently against my own. But it wasn't just any young woman who came to mind.

Even though she'd not been an active part of my thinking since just after I awoke, it was Linda's face that emerged, and its unforeseen return startled me. Ocean Bluff was bound to bring back memories of her, but I wasn't prepared for them to come with such biting sharpness. I had kissed or been kissed by others, and I can't say that they didn't stir my blood, but none ever made it rush quite as fast or run quite as hot as Linda did.

It'd been seven years since I last saw her. All that time helped to soften the influence she once held over me, but I was still in bondage, still a slave to the recollections of the wonderful summer we had spent together. The love we shared was the best and most exciting of all the good memories I had carried away from this place.

I came here looking for answers; but so far every answer seemed to lead to another question. Who was I supposed to be, and how did I fit into this new world? It was not the world I grew up in—it had all turned upside down—and I couldn't see the future, or at least I couldn't see one that included me. War, assassination, rioting in the streets; everything had gone crazy. The only thing that I could see ahead of me was loneliness. Oh, I had my parents, and Margie and Timmy, but I needed more than that. Maybe that's why everything seemed so bleak.

In the end, this aimless speculation was only depressing me, and I decided that I'd had enough. After all, the purpose of this trip was to make me feel better, not worse. I stood and brushed the dry sand from my trousers and headed back to the Inn.

Mrs. Haggerty had whipped up a sumptuous breakfast and I piled on generous portions of scrambled eggs and ham; then added a couple of slices of toast and took a large glass of orange juice. The eggs were especially good. They were made with cheese, salt and pepper and some sort of spice that I couldn't identify. The combination created a flavor that played so deliciously on my tongue that eating them seemed almost sinful.

Using my fork, I pushed the last few morsels onto the crust of a piece of toast, popped it into my mouth and shoved the empty plate aside. Then, taking a final swig of orange juice, I left the table and returned to my room to change into swim trunks. Wearing a baggy T-shirt and taking a large towel, I got into my car and drove off, hoping to see the cottage and then take a dip in the ocean. At ten in the morning the weather was warm, and with low scudding clouds and a steady breeze it was a perfect summer's day.

Coming along the narrow lane that approached the cottage, I could see that the years had not been kind. Obviously, no one was living there. The windows were boarded up, and the doors barricaded with two-by-fours. The wooden walkway had collapsed, shingles were missing and some of the panes in the oversized window under the back gable were broken. Not in pristine condition when we had occupied it years ago, now it was terribly run-down. Even though it had never been a grand home, it was sad to see it in such an awful state.

As I stepped around to the side of the house, I bent to look under the building. The pipes had been disconnected, the wires cut and stripped away, and the cedar pylons had shifted, making the house look slightly cockeyed. Judging from the soda and beer bottles near the front porch, there had been more than a few parties held here since it had become derelict. Standing at the bottom of the front stairs, I could see that several of the treads had been torn loose, and since they weren't anywhere nearby, I imagined that they had either been used for firewood or washed out to sea.

Whatever its condition, I was driven by a morbid curiosity to see the inside. But looking at the precarious angle of the house, I had some concern about how safe it might be. Studying the matter for a moment, I decided that if I could get up the stairs I would probably be able to pry open the front door. Climbing slowly, one step at a time, skipping the missing treads or using the narrow stringers for support, I could feel the structure tremble and the rotting wood complain under the unfamiliar weight. At last, I made it to the relative safety of the porch. The board barring the door was no longer secure. The salt air had rusted the iron nails and the wood was split and weakened from cold winter storms. Grasping the board firmly, I worked it loose and tossed it aside. The latch and door-hinges were weak, and when I pressed my fingers against one of the raised panels the rusty hardware failed and the door gave way. It fell to the floor inside with an explosion that echoed through the empty building. I knew that I was trespassing, and that technically I was breaking in, but I honestly didn't care. I entered with a free conscience, convinced that I had a special right to be there.

Once inside I needed a moment to adjust to the darkness. Glancing around the room, it was apparent that here too the elements had taken their toll. The place was thick with dust; and the debris from other visitors, both human and animal, were scattered throughout. The door crashing to the floor had disturbed the dust and the air was saturated. Tiny motes were visible wherever the sun found its way through the cracks. Moving toward the front window, I had a sudden vision of the evening that Linda and I sat here together wearing fresh dry clothes, staring out at the storm. Side-by-side, we watched the rain and wind lash against the walls, and I remembered thinking how safe I felt inside—how safe I felt with her. Now, looking at the broken glass and the sun streaming through the cracks in the walls, I was filled with sadness. It was as if I were looking at the bleached bones of an old friend. Someone who had died long ago, and whose remains lay abandoned and unmourned. Over the years I had polished my memories of this place to a crystal brightness that was far removed from reality and now I stood there wrestling with my emotions.

Whatever anguish I was suffering, I was in no hurry to leave. Shuffling through the rubble, I crossed the room and pried open the door to the stairs.

Stopping on the landing, I looked through the open doorframe into my old room. The windows on this level hadn't been boarded over, and the sun shone brightly through the dusty panes and cobwebs into the empty space. Not everything had been removed. A rusted metal bed-frame was still there, and in front of me was an old wooden nail keg. Picking up the keg, I moved it over and set it next to the window. Brushing away some of the accumulated dust, I sat down and looked out at the Atlantic. Again I thought of Linda, of that first night after Earl and I had met her on the beach.

I remembered how difficult it was to sleep, my thoughts cluttered with visions of this enigmatic young girl.

I recalled those few nights when I was sure that she would never speak to me again. How I had grieved over the idea of losing her, my mind filled with confusion and self-recrimination! If Margie hadn't intervened, Linda probably would never have given me a second chance, and it all would have come to a bleak and miserable end. I wouldn't have had those last few days—and the lighthouse. But it had ended nevertheless, and now all I had left were memories.

How could I have exhausted all that energy and emotion, building a relationship that I thought would last forever and then let it go? I suppose it had a lot to do with timing. We were too young and immature, and when circumstances tore us apart I didn't know how to fix it. Some would call it fate, but I wasn't sure I believed in fate. Right or wrong, I wanted to think that I could control my own destiny.

Whatever the cause, whatever the circumstances, there was no doubt in my mind that if I were faced with that same opportunity again, I wouldn't allow *fate* or anything else to get in my way. On the contrary, unless heaven and hell conspired against me, I would ask for Linda's hand, and if she would have me, I would marry her.

****

As one day followed another, the time swept by in a wonderful gut-rush of activity. I went swimming and thought of Linda. I imagined her riding the waves, the way she had that day when I had doused her hair with seaweed. Walking along the shore I remembered the hot muggy night when Linda and I stripped among the rocks and ran down the deserted beach to go skinny-dipping. I climbed to the top of the Rock and recalled the night that Linda and I had watched the fireworks, and then created a few fireworks of our own.

It seemed that no matter where I went or what I did, Linda

was a part of it. Her intrusion into every action or thought was not unpleasant or unwanted, but it was disconcerting. When I had considered making this trip back to the beach, I never anticipated that Linda would occupy such a disproportionate share of my recollections. I understood that she had been an important part of my experience here at Ocean Bluff—especially that last summer—but she came so frequently to mind that I began to wonder. Was she a part of the problem, a part of all the confusion and distress that had brought me back to Ocean Bluff? If I knew where to find her, maybe she could answer that question. But I had no idea where she was.

Over the years, whenever I had come home on vacation, I often thought of going to look for her. But there was no place to start, and once I was out at school in Minnesota, I was too busy to even think about where she might have gone. Other than that one attempt in 1959, just before I left for college, I hadn't made any effort to locate her. And as time went by I gradually lost interest.

CHAPTER 24

IT WAS Friday, which could be a good day or a bad day, depending upon your outlook. If you're working, it's the end of the week and you have the weekend to look forward to. If you're enjoying your vacation, it's the end of the week and your holiday is nearly over. Unfortunately, I was facing the latter. My time here had been well spent, filled with many pleasant experiences. I had found a degree of peace, a kind of peace that had eluded me for a long time. Nevertheless, the final solution had escaped me, and I was more certain than ever that somehow Linda held the key to this troubling impasse.

Late on Friday afternoon I drove into Satuit. I hadn't been back at all, since driving through to get to the guesthouse at Sea View a week before. As my vacation was winding down, I discovered that I had run out of things to do. When I awoke that morning, and lay in my bed daydreaming, it dawned on me that I might like to see a movie. I had no idea what was playing, but then I really didn't care. Now, chugging slowly down Main Street, holding on to the shift lever so that it wouldn't pop out of second gear, I realized that that low growl wasn't coming from the transmission. It was my stomach. I was hungry. Turning onto Otis Avenue I parked my car behind the theater, and walked down the alleyway to the ticket booth. Looking across the street, I remembered that Call's Drug Store used to serve food—all sorts of unhealthy junk, like hot–dogs and hamburgers, and greasy fries—and there was always ice cream and pie to go with it. The movie wouldn't start for another hour and this looked like a convenient way to fill my empty stomach.

Stepping off the curb, I checked the traffic, and made a dash for the other side. I could hear the hinges complaining loudly as I pushed open the door and it occurred to me that a little oil might be helpful. The inside was basically unchanged, and I went to one of the booths and found a place to sit. Gingerly picking up a food-stained menu, I noticed that the selections had remained the same, except for the prices, which had gone up. Few improvements had been made, and generally the place looked kind of dog-eared, like an old newspaper whose pages have been soiled and torn from too many readings. The seats were patched with tape, and the plastic top on the table had lost its checkered pattern in several spots from constant scrubbing. The service wasn't very good either; after fifteen minutes, no one had approached to take my order. Looking around in search of a waitress, I glanced over at the counter. There were a number of customers sitting on stools drinking coffee, with the remnants of their dinners scattered on the countertop in front of them. At one end was a youngster trying hard to finish a banana split.

That's when I first noticed the waitress serving them. Harried and a bit disheveled, she moved about efficiently, obviously trying to handle more than any one person could be expected to deal with alone. A sudden chill washed over me as I realized that *it was her!* Trembling with excitement, I studied this young woman more carefully. There had been changes, but it was definitely Linda.

I wanted so desperately to go over and wrap my arms around her and never let go—ever!

Restraint! I had to use restraint.

No longer interested in satisfying my hunger, I shoved my trembling hands into my pockets and watched. Her apron was stained with grease from the grill and she seemed to be trying so hard to catch up. My heart went out to her and I fought the temptation to join her behind the counter. I wanted so badly to help, but it couldn't be done, not without an awkward scene, and I couldn't do that in front of this audience of strangers. Though I had no doubt that they would find such a scene very entertaining. Without knowing or even guessing at what her reaction might be; and not wanting to embarrass her or myself, I stayed put, hoping that the right opportunity to speak to her would present itself. And I wondered, when that moment came, what would I say to her?

Since I couldn't answer that question, I continued to direct my attention to Linda and began to scrutinize her face. Her hair had been tied back in a short ponytail, but it wasn't cooperating, and parts having come free from the ribbon that she used to keep it in place now fell alongside her face. Nervously, her hand would rise to her cheek to push the errant strands of hair away. She looked unkempt and weary, which seemed to come from something more than just the hectic pace that she was keeping. Though her uniform was not particularly flattering, I could see that her figure had matured. She certainly looked very different from the skinny girl I first saw sauntering down the beach when she was only fifteen. The thought of her age was suddenly disturbing. Although it didn't seem so at the time, she was sooo very young. But then, so was I—hell, I was a child. And considering my inexperience, it was a wonder that we had gotten together at all.

At last, finished with the customers that she was serving, she glanced up and realized that she had someone waiting at one of the booths. Hurrying around the end of the long counter, she approached me with a businesslike stride, carrying a glass of ice water and a wet rag to wipe down my table. Without really looking at me, she gave me a quick smile, not the real thing after such a chaotic day. Only a fleeting automatic curl, which parted her lips and showed some of her straight white teeth. Since it wasn't genuine, it did nothing to enhance her pretty face. Somehow it just made her look more exhausted. Setting the glass to one side, she apologized for keeping me waiting. Then, leaning over in front of me, she started to clean the surface of the table. Now, only a few inches away, the smell of her tired body (a mixture of sweat and old perfume) filled my nostrils. It wasn't a pleasant odor, but it *was* Linda, and being this close to her again was almost euphoric.

She started scrubbing vigorously, trying to remove a particularly stubborn spot of crusty food. That action caused the necklace she was wearing to fall loosely from the collar of her blouse.

I was startled to see a miniature heart, with the letters *L & M* still clearly engraved upon it. The finish was scratched, and the bright polish had long since disappeared from years of wear. In the harsh fluorescent light it reflected a dull satin glow, and I swallowed hard as I recognized this tiny charm and realized the significance of its timeworn condition. Linda hadn't forgotten. She had kept her promise. She had kept this tiny charm and cherished it; and had worn it at least often enough to tarnish its golden finish.

"Linda—aren't you going to say hello?" I said steadfastly, though my heart rate and blood pressure belied the calmness in my voice.

The energetic motion of her arm stopped abruptly and she turned slowly until her eyes were staring directly into mine. Those same incredible blue eyes, that had raised my temperature and wreaked such havoc when I first saw them, were once again focused upon me; and the effect was just as devastating. I could feel the color rising to my face and I felt like a schoolboy who's just been kissed by the girl sitting next to him. But as that warm flush painted my face a bright red, I saw all the color drain from Linda's. She stumbled briefly and I thought that she was about to swoon. Instinctively, I rose up and reached out to steady her; then gently eased her onto the patched red cushion of the seat opposite me.

She sat quietly, trying to compose herself. Slowly her color began to return, then her mouth fell open and she seemed about to speak, but at first nothing came, and then, "Michael, is it really you? How did you find me?" she asked in a breathy gasp.

"Yes, it's me, and I didn't actually find you. I had no idea you were you here until I looked over at that counter a few minutes ago."

"Are you living in the area? How long do you expect to be here? Can we get together and talk? I can't believe this. I've thought of you so often, wondering what had become of you. We have to meet. I can't stop now, but I'll be off in fifteen minutes. I quit at six. Can you wait for me?" She chattered on like a busy squirrel, without giving me the slightest opportunity to interrupt. Finally, stopping to get her breath, I saw a chance to jump in.

"First of all, calm down! I'm staying at the Sea View Inn. And yes, I'll wait till you finish your shift," I said matter-of-factly. Then more tenderly, "Linda, I've wished and wondered and hoped for just such a chance as this, and now that it's here I can hardly believe it!"

"All right—okay—uh—OH!" she stuttered. "I came over here to take your order. What would you like? I mean, do you want to eat?" I watched her hand shake as she pulled a pad from her apron pocket and started a frenzied search for her pen.

This was the girl who was always so confident, so much in control. I'd never seen Linda this flustered before. It was very flattering, especially if I were the cause of it. Certainly no one else had ever been this distracted by my presence. I took her unsettled condition as a good sign. Indeed, I was hopeful that this disjointed performance was another indication that she still had some real feelings for me.

"If I *was* hungry, I'm not anymore; just bring me a small soda," I said, trying to be easy on her. Whereupon Linda stood and hastily departed, ostensibly to fill my order; that is, if she didn't forget what I had asked for by the time she reached the counter. She didn't forget, but she wasn't very precise about the size. Returning shortly, she brought me a very large frothy glass of root beer. As she presented it to me, I reached out and touched her hand. When my fingers connected with hers I noticed that the glass started to wobble and I shot forward with my other hand to steady it. *Incredible! Absolutely incredible!* I thought, as I took the drink from her and set it on the table. All through that summer Linda had been in charge and I was the one falling all over myself. Now, we seemed to have changed places.

As Linda went about her work I continued to observe her, but now there was a difference. Her confidence seemed shattered and the cool efficiency that I had seen earlier was gone. There were constant minor errors, silly little blunders that could easily be corrected, but that ought not to have happened in the first place. Once she dropped an empty cup and saucer that she had just taken from the counter. They didn't break—they fell into the dishwater in the sink and sent up a soapy geyser. Somehow she brought her hand down on the bowl of a spoon and flipped it into the air. Turning quickly, she caught it before it went clattering to the floor. Then she looked sheepishly in my direction to see if I were watching. And when she saw that I was, she gave a little wave with the spoon and went back to work. Once she tried to dig a scoop of ice cream from the chest behind the counter; and because her attention was directed at me instead of her work, she missed the cone in her hand and the dollop of ice cream fell back into the cooler.

At five o'clock she disappeared through a door at the back of the pharmacy that led somewhere into the dark recesses of the building. When she emerged fifteen minutes later, it was clear that she had worked hard to improve her appearance. The dirty apron was gone and she had removed the ribbon and pins to let her hair down. Cut in an even line just above her shoulders, it was longer than I remembered. She'd taken the time to straighten out her uniform, and with fresh powder and lipstick the transition was remarkable. Of course it could be an exaggeration, or selective memory, but at sixteen everything about her had seemed attractive. So it was hard for me to accept the idea that the woman approaching me had somehow grown even more beautiful. When she looked tired and disheveled, I felt I had the advantage; now, looking more like her old self, that advantage began to dissolve, and I wasn't certain about what to say or do, once she stood close enough for me to act.

"Where shall we go?" she asked anxiously, as I scooted over to let her sit in the booth beside me.

I hadn't given any thought to where we might go—I was far too distracted. Glancing out the window, I noticed a vacant park bench beneath one of the large elms that shaded Main Street. "What about right over there?" I said, pointing.

"It seems a little public, but why not." She gave me an ingratiating smile and rose to lead the way out of the store.

Watching for traffic, which was particularly hostile at this time on a Friday evening, we crossed to the grassy island that divided the road. We sat down on the bench facing each other, and Linda, who seemed even more anxious than I about this reunion, started a lively conversation. This time when she smiled it was genuine, not just a narrow curve, but open and enticing, spreading wide enough to make her eyes crinkle at the edges. And when she laughed it was bright and sure, filled with the sound of happiness.

"Michael," she said, "I can't believe it—I can't believe you're here!"

"I'm not sure I believe it either," I said, feeling a little woozy from the joy of having found her.

Where have you been?"

"Mostly at college."

"Which one?"

"Augsburg Business College in St Paul," I said. "What about you?"

"In school—Bridgewater State. Two more years and I'll have my teaching degree. I want to be with the little kids; the elementary grades seem a lot safer than high school."

"You look incredible." I said, knowing that that had nothing to do with the subject, but unable to keep from saying it anyway.

"Come again?" she asked, her eyes wide as she tried to stare me down.

"You heard me," I said. "That first time I saw you on the beach—well—what can I say? And now—now, you're more beautiful than ever."

"Get serious," she said, tossing her head to get the hair out of her face.

I knew it was an unconscious gesture, but that quirky little movement (one that I'd seen her use so many times that summer) seemed to be designed to give me a better look, and a chuckle rose up from my stomach and tickled my nose as it escaped in an embarrassing snort.

"What's so funny?" she asked.
"Nothing."
"Cut it out!!" she said, laughing. "You're embarrassing me." Then she pushed roughly against my shoulder to emphasize her discomfort.
"How did we let this happen?" I asked. "How did we lose each other?"
"Did we lose each other, Michael?"
I was silent. I knew the answer, but I couldn't say it. Suddenly Linda changed the subject For a while we exchanged histories and caught up on the years we had spent apart. Then we slipped back into something more personal.
"Who are you seeing now? Dating, that is?"
"No one."
"Oh, right," she said, cocking her head and giving me a doubtful look.
"My last date was over a year ago."
"Oh," she said again, only this time her voice dropped a couple of octaves. After a quiet moment I asked her the same question, and she said "No one." And this time I said, "Oh."
"I *was* engaged," she said. "I broke it off in March."
For a very long minute I said nothing. Then we both started to speak at once. "You first," I said. "No you," she countered. I wanted to ask how serious and how far this relationship had gone, but instead I shifted to safer ground. I questioned her about family, school, work—the talk was simple, light, and animated, and often interrupted when she touched my cheek, or pressed her hand over my knee, or demonstrated some other significant sign of affection.

Any careful observer viewing this scene might have come to the conclusion that we were two lovers engaged in an intimate rendezvous. There was no public display of passion—nothing more intimate than holding hands What passed between us, seemed amazingly subtle, yet it was very real and far more fiery than any scene acted out on stage or screen.

"Do you ever miss this place?" Linda asked.

"All the time, but it's not this place, it's . . ." I stopped in mid–sentence, afraid to finish.

"What?" she encouraged.

"It's you." I hesitated. "It's you I miss the most."

"We did promise each other that our love would last forever, didn't we?"

"Yes," I said, "we did. Was it real, Linda, or did we make it all up?"

"It was real to me," she answered with conviction.

"Nothing else ever came close—nothing else ever had the same magic," I said, reflecting on my other relationships.

"Well, doesn't that prove it?"

I didn't answer, I didn't quite know what she meant. Instead, I shifted nervously and my leg rubbed against hers. She didn't pull away. She reached over and picked up my hand, drawing it into her lap. Carefully she turned it over and with her finger traced the lines in my palm, first in one direction and then another, as if she were a gypsy looking into my future. But she never told me what she saw and the ticklish movement made me giggle.

Darkness had fallen. We were alone, the streets quiet and empty. The only light came from a distant street lamp. I sat there studying her shadowy form, her hair shading her lovely features from the distant light behind, and I could see how I had come to love her—knew that I still loved her. Not with the rash and unseasoned love of adolescence, but now, cultivated by experience, my love had taken on a gentleness that I wasn't capable of before. The eager yearning was still there, but it was buried deeper, and what once seemed so impetuous and so out-of-control had taken on a softness that was far more powerful than the frantic passion of my youth.

I couldn't help wonder if all the confusion and ambivalence that had plagued me over the last few days was somehow tied up in this sweet memory of love won and lost. Circumstance had driven us apart and now circumstance had brought us back together. Whatever else might come from this fateful encounter, I knew that I didn't want to lose Linda again. The overriding question now was what to do next?

"Linda, I know we've both changed, at least we're not children anymore, but after this evening it hardly seems as though we've been apart."

"I feel the same way," she admitted.

"Still, we've missed so much."

"I know," she said sadly. "It's as if we've torn a piece of cloth away from some ancestral tapestry and now we have to decide if we can piece the frayed ends back together."

When she said this, there was a catch in her voice that was sweetly disconcerting because I thought that I could guess the reason. If I could only tell her how much I loved her, but again the words wouldn't come. Instead I took out my wallet, opened it, and dug deep into the corner. In a moment I had it. Reaching for her hand, I tucked a small silver band into the palm. It was the friendship ring that she had given me on her sixteenth birthday. She looked down to see what it was.

"Michael—I—I—you kept it ," she said, shaking her head as if she couldn't believe it.

"Didn't you think I would?"

"At the time I did, but after a while I kind of forgot about it." She brought the tip of her finger down to touch the ring, scratching the surface with her nail as if she were testing its substance. "Aaaaaah," she sighed, and then fell silent.

After a moment I turned my eyes up from under my furrowed brow to peek at her face, but it was too dark to read her expression. Then, as I was about to speak, the raucous shouting from some young people in a passing car destroyed the mood. And as Linda pulled back her hand to check her watch, the scene seemed to collapse around me.

"Oh my gawd, look at the time!" she said in panic. "My parents must be frantic! My dad usually comes to pick me up, but I never called to let him know where I was. Unless he drove by and saw us, he'll think I've died or something! Can you drive me home, Michael?"

"Sure! My car is behind the theater. But—" I faltered. "I don't know where you live."

"Don't be silly, Michael. I live in the same house behind the dunes. Well, at least during the summer—the rest of the time I'm away at college."

The tone of her voice told me: *You should have known that*, but I never would have guessed. I did feel a little foolish when I realized how easily I might have found her. For some reason, all week long I had fought the idea of visiting her old summer home.

As we drove back over the familiar roads, we sat beside each other in the car and said nothing. We had talked for so long about so much, it wasn't necessary to say anything more. Besides, we had always been comfortable with these long silences, and that hadn't changed. As usual, it was enough just to be near her.

Pulling into her drive seemed odd to me. Whenever I had come before, I always approached the house from the beach. Shutting off the engine, I made no move to help her out of the car. Of course she had to go in, but I was dreading the thought of her entering the house and passing from my sight. I wanted desperately to kiss her, but as sure as I was of my own feelings I had no idea where she stood, and it seemed impossible to imagine after all this time that her feelings for me had remained the same. Certainly the right moment would present itself and I would jump in and . . .

But Linda didn't have the patience to wait for me to figure out when that would be. She scooted across the bench seat, closing the space between us, dropped one hand in my lap, put the other over my shoulder and kissed me. It certainly wasn't the kiss of an old friend, and as I slipped my own hands around her waist, the primitive stirrings that had raised such havoc when I was a teenager returned with a vengeance.

I held her closely, breaking away once to breathe, and then after another long kiss I stopped. I didn't separate or move away, I just sat there considering the possibilities. Again neither of us spoke. With her chin resting on my shoulder I could feel her hair crushed against my cheek, hear her soft breathing, and smell the sweetness of her body. Her long fingers rubbed against the back of my neck and played casually with the bristly hairs, brushing them upward and letting them spring back. Her other hand pressed firmly into my hip and her forearm rested lightly across my lap. There was nothing sensuous in this sweet interplay, nothing suggestive in the delicate stroke of her hand as it dropped gently between my shoulder–blades, no urgency in the way she held onto me; yet there was something so familiar and so wonderfully erotic that I felt a sudden arousal—a wayward expansion, which grew so swiftly it took me totally by surprise. Linda must have felt it too, because the arm she had lying across my lap jumped. Quickly drawing away, she smiled at me. Then, before I had a chance to consider the meaning of that smile, or decide how embarrassed I ought to be, she turned, popped the door open, slipped from the front seat, and stepped out into the night air. After a hurried goodnight she made her way up the stairs to the back door, and I leaned out of the window to shout: "Can I see you tomorrow?"

"I have to work again, but pick me up here at seven and we'll go somewhere." When she answered, her voice registered a new self–confidence. She sounded terribly pleased with herself, and I suspected that her happiness was somehow connected to the fact that her embrace—her kiss—could still have such an obvious affect on me.

CHAPTER 25

FROM THE moment that I recognized Linda behind the counter I had begun bit by bit to organize a plan. I didn't have all the details; it wasn't clear to me yet how, or when, or what I would do, but I was determined not to lose Linda again. With that in mind I could see that the next twenty-four hours might be the most important of my life. Sleep did not come easily. I made the effort because I knew that I needed some rest if I expected to finish my preparations and be ready for our seven o'clock date. The simple stuff was easy enough to arrange; it was the ultimate purpose of the evening that would require the most meticulous planning. Somehow before the evening was over I was going to ask Linda to marry me. There was the very real possibility that she might say no, but however it turned out I was willing to take my chances.

Saturdays are a busy time for restaurants, especially during the summer, and getting reservations, particularly at a place that was as exclusive as "The Captain's Table", proved to be a Herculean task. The Captain's Table was a very posh restaurant in Cohassett harbor. Built on the thick pilings of an old wooden pier, you had to walk across a long trestle-like bridge to get from the parking lot to the entrance. The inside was a maze of dark little alcoves, many of which had large windows that looked out over the harbor. The place was decorated with nets and lobster buoys, and other fishy things. And the dim lanterns on the walls and the candles on the tables made it the perfect place to pop the question. With carefully worded explanations, a little begging and the promise of a generous tip, I managed to get us in. An extra twenty dollars bought me a table next to a window. I was hopeful that the water and the boats swinging lazily at their moorings would add just the right touch.

Now for the most important element in this noble scheme: I needed to buy a ring. It had to be something breathtaking and yet not so ostentatious that it would put me in the poorhouse. There wasn't enough time for me to travel all the way into Boston. Instead, I located a convenient jeweler's on Hancock Street in Quincy. I saw several rings that I liked, but it was difficult to determine which of them was apt to make the greatest impression. After about an hour of indecision, I finally selected a ring with a relatively small diamond that was set neatly between two emerald chips. There was a silver–plated crown surrounding the diamond that made it seem bigger. The ring was a pretty little thing, with a look of quality and elegance that far exceeded its price. Not that it wasn't costly; $325 was not much by today's standards, but it was a fortune to me at the time.

It taxed all my resources; in fact it exceeded them. I knew that I didn't have enough, but I was determined to find a way to buy it anyway. Leaving the jeweler with a deposit, I asked him to hold the ring for a couple hours while I tried to raise the money. I drove back to my local bank and cashed a personal check for fifty-three dollars which still left enough in my account to pay for our dinner and the generous gratuities that I had promised to the Maitre d'. Then I cleaned out my savings account, which wasn't a lot. Adding the two together, I still came up short. Somehow I had to find another forty-eight dollars. There wasn't any credit card to max out; the only card I owned was for Sears. And even though we had entered a new decade, most people didn't approve of personal loans. But I didn't have any other place to go. The question was, who could I find that would lend me the money? Tooey still lived in Ocean Bluff, but I hadn't seen him since I left for college. Earl had moved out-of-state. An advance on my pay was out of the question; I didn't feel that comfortable with my boss. I thought of my sister Margie, but she had recently married, and I knew that money was tight. I was too embarrassed to ask my parents. Besides, they would want to know what the money was for, and I wasn't ready yet to tell them that. So that brought me back to Margie. For better or worse, she was all I had. She could be a rough character, especially in a fight, and we still fought often, but she had a good heart. And it wouldn't be the first time that she had bailed me out of a difficult situation. If she did have the money I was pretty sure that I would be able to get it back to her in a couple of weeks.

She was living in North Quincy, so I found my car and drove over to her apartment on Granite Ave. Once she heard my story, she was more than agreeable; she even offered to give me the money as a wedding gift. But I insisted on paying her back. I told her to buy us a toaster instead. It seemed to me that a wedding gift right now might bring bad luck. After all, this wouldn't be official until it was announced in the local newspaper; and I still hadn't asked her yet.

Less than an hour after I left Margie's, I was walking out of the jeweler's holding a little black box in my hand. From there, I crossed the street to Sears, where I purchased a short-sleeve white shirt and a plain dark red tie. That credit card came in handy after all. My sister had let me borrow a plain dinner jacket that belonged to her husband and I needed a shirt and tie to go with it. The clothes that I brought along on my vacation were strictly casual. I had nothing suitable to wear to a place that was as demanding as The Captain's Table. In those days there were certain restrictions, and it was common practice for restaurants to refuse to let you in without a jacket and tie.

Arriving back at the inn about five o'clock, with no lunch and most of my day spent in my car, I was hot and a bit queasy. The roiling irritation at the base of my stomach reminded me of the stressful task that lay ahead. I had never proposed to anyone before. I suppose that when the time comes to ask that critical question, we all hope that it's something that we'll only have to do once. My father must have gone through this same ordeal, but he never told me about it. Nor do I recall that he ever shared any bits of wisdom concerning how it was to be done. Never having received any other advice, I had only the movie stereotypes to guide me. Should I actually get down on my knees, or is it only one knee? Would I have the courage to act this out in the restaurant in front of others, or should I wait till we're alone? What should I say? And even more important, what would *she* say?

I took a cooling shower and afterwards, wrapped in a towel, I sat down next to the open window and stared blankly out at the gray–green Atlantic. Not ready to dress yet, I took this opportunity to speculate about the evening that lay ahead. I tried to visualize Linda and me together in a secluded corner of the restaurant. The two of us sitting at a table lit only by flickering candlelight, the unsteady flame dancing in her eyes, and soft music playing in the background. It seemed like the perfect setting for a romantic proposal, but the setting was useless if I couldn't figure out what to say. Should I give a long speech, or should I be direct? How will I know when the time is right? Do I ask before the meal or after? When should I give her the ring? Should I just hand it to her in the box or should I take it out and put it on her finger?

Absorbed in this quandary, I completely lost track of the time. When I finally took a look at my watch, I panicked. Rushing about in frantic disorder, I nearly ripped my undershorts when I tried to pull them up after putting both my feet through the same hole. Shaving was an impossibility because my hand was shaking too much. Finally I just wiped off the soap and left the remaining stubble. With my tie slightly askew and half my shirt-tail out, I grabbed my jacket and keys and headed for the door. I would very likely be late, hopefully not more than a few minutes, but it was a bad beginning for what was supposed to be a perfect evening.

When I picked Linda up, I realized that I was already in trouble. I should have called ahead to warn her about where we were going. She had been waiting on the back steps and she climbed into my car wearing shorts and a bright colorful blouse. She looked gorgeous, but her clothes were all wrong for an evening at a formal restaurant. Looking at me with my tie and jacket, her eyes flared briefly, and I could tell that she was a little annoyed. I was prepared for a confrontation, but when she spoke her voice was calm and she expressed concern, not anger.

"Michael—a jacket and tie? Where are you taking me?"

"I'm sorry, I should have called ahead and told you I had reservations at The Captain's Table. It seems like I had a bazillion things to do today and it went a little haywire. Which is partly why I'm late. I really went all out to plan this wonderful evening, with a romantic dinner—everything was supposed to be *sooo* perfect. Instead, I've made a mess of it and put you in an awkward situation that . . ."

"Michael," she interrupted, "you don't have to impress me. I would have settled for a walk on the beach. It really doesn't matter to me where we go this evening, as long as we can spend some time together."

"I don't know how it happens, but it seems that since the first time we met you've been forgiving me for something. Trouble is, I'm not just a gawky teenager anymore, and when I screw up like this you ought to be angry, and you ought to chew me out . . ."

"Enough, there's no sense in beating a dead horse. The question is, what do we do now?"

"Well, I suppose—no," I said, feeling a little reckless, "let's forget about dinner. Instead, let's take that walk on the beach."

"But—what about all your plans?"

"Ahh, we'll make other plans . . .together," I added with a silly grin on my face.

Stepping out of the car, I loosened my tie and unbuttoned the collar, then removed my jacket and tossed it in the back seat. With the door open, I sat down on the running-board, took off my shoes and socks and rolled up my trousers. Now I was ready for that walk on the beach. Linda followed my example and removed her own shoes. Then we started off, traipsing around to the front of her house and heading for the pathway through the dunes. The walk was comfortable and familiar, and after a few minutes we reached the base of the old stairs that led to the top of the sea-wall. We both looked up and I nudged Linda with my elbow. She got the message, and with a childish giggle she leaped ahead of me and started climbing the stairs. At the top, she reached back to take my hand and pulled me precariously along the wall until we came to a convenient spot where we could sit facing the sea. How many times during that wonderful summer had we moved with careful step along this same narrow cap, and sat in like manner while the sun set slowly behind us? After all that hectic preparation, looking for the perfect time and place, I suddenly realized that I would never find any setting more ideal than this.

"Linda," I began, "after I left you last night—I came to a decision. No, actually I made this decision a *looong* time ago. Linda," I repeated, "I love you. I think I've always loved you. That summer that we spent together could've just as easily been a pleasant memory, but now that I've found you again, I want something more. Ooooh!" I moaned, "I know I'm doing a rotten job of this!"

"Why are you so determined to get everything perfect?" she asked.

"Because I'm afraid that if I don't . . .you won't say yes."

"Yes, to what?'

"Linda . . .will you marry me?" She turned to look at me and I tried to read her eyes, but I couldn't decide what I saw there.

"Michael," she said softly. "Do you remember the first time that you said that to me?"

"I do," I answered.

"I was waiting for you up there," she said, nodding her head in the direction of the Rock. "We'd had an awful breakup—and you came to me full of pathos, looking for my forgiveness. You were such a turkey."

"Hey!"

"Well, you were. Then out of nowhere you started talking about getting married!"

"Was that so awful?"

"No. But you could have knocked me over with a wet noodle! Not that I didn't like the idea, but . . . I mean, I really wanted to believe that it was possible."

"And I went on and on about how hopeless it was," I said finishing her thought.

"Yes, and that made me mad!"

"Well . . ."

"You were right, of course. It *was* hopeless. But it wasn't fair to offer to marry me and then take it away before I'd even had time to consider it. And now here we are again."

"Well," I said, pushing for her answer, but unwilling to repeat the question.

There was a long silence while I sat holding my breath, staring out at the horizon where the purple sky blended with the black sea. I refused to look at her. I was afraid—afraid of what I might see if I turned to confront her. Reaching out, she cupped her hand under my chin and pulled my face around toward hers. And when those beautiful blue eyes met mine, I was trapped. Her eyes were unbelievably clear and bright and I was sure by their penetrating intensity that she could see right through me. I felt as though she were some kind of ancient mystic or shaman who could pierce my soul and know everything about me, both good and bad. I was convinced that she could see all the joy and sorrow, the pain and confusion, the passion and heartache, as if every thought and emotion had been laid bare. If right then and there I were stripped naked, I couldn't have felt any more exposed. But I wasn't ashamed. It was an incredibly mysterious exchange, and yet nothing she had said, or might have said, could possibly have portrayed her feelings towards me more vividly than what I saw reflected in her eyes. I thought: *how can she look at me like this and not say yes?*

"Michael." Dropping her hand from my face, she laid it carefully over my wrist, and squeezed it reassuringly. "Since we parted, I haven't exactly led a cloistered life. There have been other young men—romances that for a time seemed pretty serious. I even had a proposal. But . . . then I found out he was getting it on with my roommate." She stopped again, and I wondered, is this a rejection, is she trying to tell me why we can't be married?

"In all of these relationships, I eventually reached a point where

I realized that something was missing." Here we go, now she'll tell me why this isn't right. "Though I could never figure out exactly what that something was. Not until now. It was like one of those wooden block puzzles that are so hard to solve. I just couldn't get all the pieces to fit together."

"Are you trying to tell me that we don't fit?"

"No—no—Michael, we fit perfectly. And I know it sounds incredibly corny, but I feel as though I've finally come home."

"Then you'll marry me?"

"*Yess, yessss!*" she said, softly shushing her S's.

Quickly I pulled the small black box from my pocket and opened it to reveal the ring inside. She said nothing as I lifted it from the box and slipped it on her finger. For a moment she held it up to the orange light—then, "Uuuuh, Michael," she groaned, and the sound gushed with sweet approval. Suddenly she kissed me. It was just the lightest brush of her lips against my cheek, then with a terrible intensity she hugged me tightly and I crushed her against me with equal intensity. We continued to hold onto each other for a long time before either of us would let go. At last we stood and made our way down off the wall. At the bottom of the steps Linda took both my hands, and falling back in abandon began to swing in a circle. Leaning back in counterbalance, we went round and round, scuffling the coarse sand with the pads of our feet until I lost my grip and fell in a dizzy sprawl. By now I was laughing so hard I started to choke. Dropping to her knees beside me, she said:

"Michael, let's not wait, let's do this now."

"Right now?" I asked, in amazement.

"No—no, not this minute or this night, but as soon as possible."

CHAPTER 26

SHE REALLY meant it when she said, "Let's not wait"; we were married within the month. Our wedding was a simple affair held in a charming little chapel in Cohasset, with just a few friends and relatives. After the ceremony we drove off to New Hampshire for a honeymoon in the White Mountains. We went up to the northern part of the state, driving past the Flume and past the Old Man of the Mountain until we reached a small motel in Bretton Woods. It was a lovely place, only a few miles from the Cog Railway and Mount Washington. Each room had French doors that opened onto a shielded balcony. Standing there leaning against the rail, we had a spectacular view of the Ammonoosic River and Mount Adams.

Later, when Linda stepped out of the bathroom in a girlish brushed-cotton nightie, with wide lacy straps holding it up, I was convinced that I had never seen anything more daring, or more seductive. She came to the bedside, but she didn't join me; instead she peeled back the top sheet and encouraged me to get up. Leading me to the center of the room, she stopped and turned to face me. The two of us were caught in the dusty light of the late afternoon sun as it flooded past the partially opened drapes. Without saying a word she reached down to grab the hem of her nightgown, and in one quick motion she pulled it up over her head. As her hands came down, she let go of the flimsy material and the gown drifted lightly to the floor. She stood there just as she had that summer so long ago. Only now, she was not a skinny teenage girl just developing, she was a woman, with a narrow waist, and full hips, and breasts that were heavy and round. She unbuttoned the top to my pajamas, one at a time, my heart beating harder and harder as she came down. When the last button was undone, she tucked her fingers under the collar and pushed the light material outward past my shoulders. I dropped my arms submissively, and she teased the sleeves along until they cleared my wrists and the top fell away. Next, fumbling for the drawstring, she discovered that it was tied with a bow, and wrapping her fingers around one end she gave it a quick tug. Then she took a step back and watched the bottoms tumble in a seesaw motion until they settled loosely around my ankles.

I was naked; and since Linda had worn nothing under her gown, so was she. I looked at her, saw the sunlight warming her tawny skin, the pale pattern of her bathing suit clearly visible across her breasts and hips, and though I was quietly amused, that sweet vision made my blood run hot. My heart beat nervously, my skittish stomach complained, and a needy impulse below sent up an obvious flag. With eager insistence it grew, rising steadily, until it couldn't be ignored.

"Oh—my—God!" Linda breathed softly, as she watched this amazing transformation.

"It's your fault!"

"How? I didn't even touch it!"

"You don't have to. Just seeing you like this," I said, extending my arms, "is enough."

"Are you telling me every time a man sees a naked woman, this happens?" she said, pointing at my condition.

"Well, maybe not *every* time. You know—but when you're in love—always." Even here, now, married, I was reluctant to be specific.

"Really? I mean, I've heard about this sort of thing, but—I've never actually seen it happen" she said, with a goofy smile. "And—I would never have believed that it took so little to *make* it happen."

"Well, there you go," I said looking down. Linda's eyes followed mine. Then, she reached out and took hold of me, as if she were claiming a toy that I had previously refused to share with her.

"Ouch!" I said, with a grimace, and she let go.

"I'm not hurting you, am I?" she asked, showing a little wrinkle of concern above her nose.

"Just kidding," I said, and when she saw the smile that swept from ear-to-ear, she giggled. Looking down again, her hand came forward, this time timidly, until one long finger touched the end and it sprang to life. She glanced up to see my reaction, and I deliberately raised my eyebrows and gave her a narrow smile. She returned that smile, and came back carefully to surround my erection with her fingers.

To demonstrate my approval, I covered her hand with my own, and squeezed lightly. Caught off-guard, she gave up a gleeful little squeal that made me laugh—which made her laugh—and the mellifluous mixture rose on the warm currents of air that swirled in through the open French doors.

Forgetting my pajama bottoms were wrapped around my ankles, I stepped forward to close the distance between us, and lost my balance. As I started to fall, Linda brought her hands up against my shoulders and I reached out for her waist and missed. But her effort did keep me from toppling over, and we both came to our knees on the thick carpet.

Linda laughed so hard she fell on her side, tucked in her legs, and started rolling back and forth. I sat down and swung my trapped legs out in front of me. Kicking, I managed to free one foot, but the other leg was twisted and wouldn't slide past my heel. Once Linda recovered her senses she came to my rescue. With a quick tug she untangled the troublesome garment, then held it high above her head, and let it fly.

After she watched my bottoms disappear behind the bed, she laid back, stretched herself out, and threw her arms back in wonderful abandon. It was a gesture of absolute trust, and when I looked at her long shapely form I suddenly saw the sweetness of the gift that she was offering me.

I approached Linda gently—leaning in I pressed my palm against the roundness of her shoulder, and kissed her. Bumping noses playfully, I slid to one side and crushed my cheek roughly against hers.

"Ewww—you're scratchy!" she said, wrinkling her nose and raising her upper lip in an expression that was half smile, half grimace.

"I shaved this morning," I said, dragging my palm across the prickly stubble, "but it grows back."

"Just don't rub so hard!"

"Linda, I want this to be so perfect...."

"No!" she said, pinching my lips together to stop me. "Don't! Even if we do it all wrong, it doesn't matter."

She was right of course; I was being overly sensitive. But I couldn't help asking: " Are you sure you..."

"For Heaven's sake, Michael, stop worrying! This is supposed to be fun!" she said, giving me a quick jab in the abdomen.

"Okay!" I gasped, as I sucked in my stomach. Then, I leaned in and started kissing her neck repeatedly. Little excited busses accompanied by feathery puffs of air that tickled her throat, and her giggles were thick and wet, as if she might choke on her own joy.

"Michael," she said effusively, making it sound like a supplication. She slid her long fingers between my shoulder blades and drew me down. In a moment her other hand came up, and hooking her fingers under my chin, she guided me back to her mouth, then surrounded my lips with her own. It was so easy. Whatever Linda did had an immediate and marvelous effect and I wondered if anything I offered in response could be half so powerful.

"Do you want us here—on the floor?" I asked, thinking that this was an uncomfortable setting.

"Yes," she said, "but I need some padding. Go pull off the sheet, and bring down the pillows," she suggested, looking up toward the bed.

I got to my knees, waddled to the edge of the bed, and stripped the top sheet away. I tossed this to Linda, and she flinched as the sheet billowed above her head. Coming up from under the linen folds, the first pillow caught her hard across the shoulders, and when she ducked, the second one slid off her back and landed against the pads of her feet. She scooped this pillow up and tried to send it back at me, but her aim was off, and it hit the table lamp behind. The shade flew off and the base bounced on the rug.

"Oh, shii—FUDGE!

"What did you say?"

"Never mind," she said, looking slightly abashed. "Did I break it?"

"No, it's alright," I assured her, as I put the pieces back together.

"Get the extra bedding from the closet," Linda insisted, and I saw her eyes crinkle, which made me wonder what mischief she had in mind.

Once all the sheets, and pillows, and blankets were piled around her, she arranged them into a cozy nest. Then we settled in front of the French doors where we could peek through the drapes and see the mountains in the distance. It was after six and we hadn't eaten, but I wasn't thinking of food.

We lay side by side—face to face. At first we did nothing, then Linda walked her fingers lightly down the length of my arm, and when she came to my hand, I turned the palm up, spread my fingers, and let hers slide between. This was the beginning.

With a word or a cry Linda let me know when something pleased her, and if she thought I was lost she gave me direction. Only a touch, a little pressure to the back of my hand, the curve of her foot sliding down my calf, the slightest shifting of her hips—all in an effort to get things to fit into their proper place.

I tried to come from the side, but nothing seemed to go where it should. I was all arms, and legs, and feet, and when Linda tried to help she seemed to have the same problem. When both our efforts failed she rolled away, and with one hand dragging at the back of my leg, and the other pushing against my waist, she guided me over her. With my arms stretched out for support, I hovered above her, worried that I was too heavy. But she didn't complain. Instead, looking into her face I saw an enigmatic curl to her lower lip, which for some reason suggested to me that she was ready.

I moved in slowly—gently—as if she might break. I started to speak, and she made a low shushing sound. Then I saw the tears. They welled up, spilled over and began to pool in the creases under her eyes.

"Why did you stop?" she asked.

"I'm hurting you!"

"No you're not!" she said, stretching out her words.

"But you're crying?"

"Good grief, Michael, you ought to know by now that when I'm happy I get all weepy!" she said. Then, cupping her hands over my ears, she pulled me down and gave me an eager kiss, and all my foolish fears and inhibitions evaporated. From there the intensity increased and I had this tremendous desire to rush ahead. But I fought against that urgency, sensing that if I moved too fast I would leave Linda behind. Finally there was a quickening and I seemed to fill her whole body—emptying my soul completely into hers. When it was over Linda's pupils were wide and dark, and in the dull light her wet face was all-aglow.

I felt a gushy pride, as if I had done something no one else could do. After seven years we had finally come together to finish what we had begun in Linda's darkened bedroom on that hot, rainy, summer's afternoon. What we had started so naively in that big house on the beach was consummated—a little less naively—in our bright, cozy hideaway in the mountains. This was a gift that I could only give once, and it was wonderful to know that I hadn't squandered it on someone else—Linda was the first.

I rolled away, threw my arms up in blissful surrender, and let an indulgent moan escape. Linda made a similar sound, ending in a childish tee-hee, and then there was silence. I thought of the age-old question, but didn't feel there was any need to ask.

Linda turned silly, and started to tickle me, and I tried to tickle her back. But she had the upper hand and I was forced to retreat. She chased me to the couch in the sitting area, and then into the bathroom. There, with my bare butt pressed against the edge of the cold sink, she suggested a communal shower.

"That stall is awfully small," I pointed out.

"Oh, pooh—don't think of it as small—just think of it as cozy."

Later, we climbed onto the bed, and I turned on the radio. Still wrapped in our towels, we curled up together and listened while the station played *Stardust, Body and Soul, Tenderly*. It was the sort of drippy romantic stuff that my parents liked and that I'd always complained was too old-fashioned. But right now, it fit our mood perfectly. When the station played *Someone To Watch Over Me*, we kissed and while the words from *The Man I Love*, floated in the sticky air, we came to that climatic quickening and joined soul to soul all over again.

In the end, it wasn't the warm colors of our love making, or the sharp explosions of passion, that I remember. It was what came after—after, when I had fallen limp and spent, curled up on a dark furry pillow. Lying there upon my side, overcome by the sweetest kind of exhaustion, I draped my hand loosely across Linda's breast and closed my eyes. I could feel the rise and fall of her breathing in a comforting rhythm that was remarkably soothing to my sleepy soul. Gradually her breathing slowed and I opened my eyes to see the last beam of sunlight sliding through a narrow gap between the drapes. It stretched along Linda's arm, highlighting the short downy hairs. When she turned to face me, and lifted that arm to lay it across my shoulder, a pinprick of light—a tiny golden spark—caught my attention, and I looked to see the shiny new wedding-band upon her finger. Automatically my thumb came down to press against the cool hardness of the band on my own finger, and I felt a wonderful assurance in the promise that this implied.

Life is in the details. The wedding, the drive to the mountains, the first bubbly attempts at lovemaking—these were too large, too overwhelming to hold onto, and they would soon fade into a sweet, fuzzy dream. But this single image was small enough to secrete away with dozens of others. Where one day I could pull it out, dust it off, and see it as clearly as the moment it happened.

Suddenly the blackness of the mountains swallowed the last of the sun, and I closed my eyes and drifted off to sleep.

EPILOGUE

SITTING ALONE in my office, reflecting on these singular events, I wonder about the forty years that have passed since Linda and I were married in that lovely New England seacoast town. I suppose that we did get to live the fairy tale that we had dreamed of—but not always happily ever after.

As the years have passed, it seems that the process of time has accelerated. The seasons and holidays have come and gone, and where I once interpreted their passage in days and weeks, it seems now that I recognize time and its progress in years. However it goes, that process has been filled by children, work, school projects, report cards, vacations and holidays. There has also been joy and sorrow, birth and death, wonderful moonlit nights, and lots of sunrises and sunsets that have swept by during our years together. But as I reflect back, I can honestly say that there have never been any regrets. Though our love for each other has sometimes been strained and often tested, it has never failed. A long, long time ago, when I first saw Linda, I was profoundly impressed by the soft whisperings of some ancestral ghost who told me that we were kindred spirits. My mind was enlightened and I saw a vision of a time and place far distant and infinitely more beautiful than this battered earth upon which we now live. That peculiar revelation provided me with the sure knowledge that we had always known each other. That in some mysterious spiritual realm we had been good friends and companions. I knew that somewhere in that mystical kingdom we had shared secrets and confided together often concerning our destiny. My life with Linda has been an affirmation of that unique vision. And more than that, I have come to understand that our love will endure—not just for now, but forever. I can't explain how, but I know just as surely as one day follows another that our love has an eternal nature. The skeptics will say that it's nothing more than wishful thinking—there is, after all, no proof. And that's true, I can't prove it. At least not from the world of science, which deals only with what we can measure and touch. Nevertheless, I know that it is so. Even though reason and logic might deny it, they have nothing to do with hope, and faith, and love.

The hour is late and I can hear Linda calling me from downstairs. She has rented a video and wants me to join her. We have plans for a romantic evening together, watching an old movie. When I finally come into the living room and join her on the couch, the credits of the film are already rolling down the screen. It is after ten and the room is dark and deserted. The children are grown, and those that are still living with us are not at home tonight. They are staying with their friends.

Maurice Chevalier is taking pictures of Gary Cooper through the window of the suite where he is having an affair with a married woman. The adulterous couple is dancing and shortly I hear the familiar lyric strains of "Fascination", as it is being played by the gypsy band that Cooper has hired to serenade them. The movie Linda has chosen, "Love in the Afternoon", is the one that we went to see so many years ago on our first official date.

I tell Linda that I love her and we kiss. She presses her lips to mine with the same provocative urgency that she did in our youth, and I respond with the same quick arousal that her kisses have always invoked. The magic is still there.